Redeeming
Waters

Also by Vanessa Davis Griggs

Ray of Hope

The Blessed Trinity Series

The Truth Is the Light

Goodness and Mercy

Practicing What You Preach

If Memory Serves

Strongholds

Blessed Trinity

Published by Kensington Publishing Corp.

Redeeming Waters

VANESSA DAVIS GRIGGS

Kensington Publishing Corp.
http://www.kensingtonbooks.com

DAFINA BOOKS are published by

Kensington Publishing Corp.
119 West 40th Street
New York, NY 10018

All Kensington Titles, Imprints, and Distributed Lines are available at special quantity discounts for bulk purchases for sales promotions, premiums, fund-raising, and educational or institutional use. Special book excerpts or customized printings can also be created to fit specific needs. For details, write or phone the office of the Kensington special sales manager: Kensington Publishing Corp., 119 West 40th Street, New York, NY 10018, attn: Special Sales Department, Phone: 1-800-221-2647.

Dafina and the Dafina logo Ref. U.S. Pat. & TM Off.

ISBN-13: 978-0-7582-5962-2
ISBN-10: 0-7582-5962-X

First trade paperback printing: August 2011

10   9   8   7   6   5   4   3   2   1

Printed in the United States of America

Acknowledgments

All praises to God the Father, God the Son, and God the Holy Spirit for all that I am and all that I ever hope to be. For loving me so much that You would choose me, in every sense and connotation of the word. Thank You for strength and all that you've given me along this journey we call life on earth as well as my life in Heaven to come.

I give honor to my mother and father, Josephine and James Davis Jr. I thank you for giving me life and for nurturing me throughout the years with love and belief. But I thank you most of all for introducing me to Jesus, my Lord and Savior, who loved me so much that He gave His life so that I might not just have life, but life more abundantly.

I dedicate this book to Irene Egerton Perry, a good friend, who lost her life in August 2010. She was a writer. We met at a publishers' conference in October 1999. She was full of life, with never-ending ideas, drive and dreams. Irene and I talked about the business of publishing and writing on so many levels. She had so many dreams left inside of her she didn't get to fulfill. I want to encourage all of you to please live each and every day you have on this earth to the fullest. No, things may *not* be going the way you had hoped, especially by now. But if you're still here, then you still have the opportunity to do things. Through all of the noise and disappointment, look for the good and celebrate that.

My sincere thanks to Selena James, my editor at Kensington/Dafina, and all of the hardworking, dedicated people at this publishing house for allowing me this opportunity to have yet another book that will prayerfully bless millions of people, should God see fit that we reach that many. To my husband, Jeffery; my children, Jeffery, Jeremy, and Johnathan;

my grandchildren, Asia and Ashlynn: the depth of who I am has been increased by having each of you in my life. I thank you for helping to fill that depth with love that springs up and out of me for each of you and to so many others. To Danette Dial, Terence Davis, Cameron Davis, and Arlinda Davis, who never fail to let me know that you care, and also for cheering me on as I run this race God has given me. I believe faith really can move mountains. So may the mountains in your way always recognize the power of God's spoken Word when you speak it and tell them to move, mountain, move!

To Bonita Chaney, a friend and prayer warrior: I don't know why things happen, but I know it has been a joy when you and I have gotten together and released God's Word, through prayer, into the atmosphere. I love the power of one being able to put a thousand to flight, but then two putting ten thousand to flight is something I know God has called us to do for such a time as this! Thanks to Vanessa L. Rice, Zelda Miles, Linda H. Jones, Rosetta Moore, Shirley Walker, Ella Wells, and Stephanie Perry Moore for the people you are, not only to me but to all whose lives you touch in your own special way.

I am forever grateful to all who have been in my corner for so long (some of you from the beginning), and am equally grateful for the new people just discovering my books. Thank you for one more opportunity to share with you what God has given to me. Please know that God loves you so much that He won't let me bring you anything but the best I have in me to give. I am always in absolute awe of what God is doing. And I say this with confidence: I don't know what the future holds, but I know who holds the future! Again, thank you for things done large and small to help spread the word about my novels. Thank you for choosing my books. And please know I love and appreciate you so much!

Prologue

And he shall be as the light of the morning, when the sun riseth, even a morning without clouds; as the tender grass springing out of the earth by clear shining after rain.

—2 Samuel 23:4

It was summertime, school was out, and with sky-high temperatures reaching near one hundred degrees, even the bees appeared to be chilling out from the smothering heat. Ten years old, Brianna and Alana were outside on the long, covered front porch playing a game of Monopoly—the board type, not something electronic like all the other children their age normally played. Brianna's father, Amos Wright, didn't believe children should stay cooped up in the house watching television and playing video games all day. Brianna didn't mind; she liked being outside. On the other hand, Brianna's mother, Diane, would have preferred her daughter do things inside, especially on scorching hot days like this.

Around midday, suddenly and unexpectedly, dark clouds rolled in.

"Girls, it looks like it's going to rain. You probably need to come inside now," Brianna's mother said as she stood holding the front door open.

"We're on the porch, Mother," Brianna said. "We won't get wet on the porch."

"Well, if it starts lightning, I want you to come in the house immediately. Do you two understand me?"

"Yes, ma'am," Brianna and Alana said in such perfect unison that it sounded like one voice.

"Older people sure are funny when it comes to rain," Brianna said after her mother closed the front door.

Alana loosely shook the two white dice around in her hand, then threw them on the board, rolling a double three, automatically garnering herself another turn. "I know," Alana said as she counted out loud and advanced her wheelbarrow six spaces. "Boardwalk," she said with obvious disappointment.

"Yes!" Brianna said, picking up her title deed card to that property. "Let's see now, with two houses, you owe me six hundred dollars!" Brianna held out her hand for payment.

Alana slowly counted out the money, leaving her with only a small amount of money to play with. "It's a good thing I'm close to passing go and collecting two hundred dollars," Alana said. "I just hope I don't land on any of your other properties on my next roll, or this game will pretty much be over—two hundred more dollars or not."

The rain started pouring down. And then the sun, just as quickly, came back out, brightly lighting up the sky even as the rain continued to fall.

"Look!" Brianna said. "The sun is shining while it's raining!" Brianna got up and walked over to the top step. "Wow. With the sun shining like that, all of those falling raindrops look like diamonds bouncing all over the walkway. Do you see how they're sparkling as they hit?"

Alana stood up and walked over to Brianna. "You *do* know what this means, don't you?"

"Know what *what* means?"

Alana turned and grinned at her friend. "When it's raining and the sun is shining."

"No. What?" Brianna could see that Alana was pleased, knowing something that *she* apparently didn't.

"It means that the devil is beating his wife."

"It does not," Brianna said.

"Yes, it does. If you don't believe me, then go ask your mother. She'll tell you."

"Well, I don't believe you because the devil doesn't *have* a wife."

"Apparently, he does," Alana said with a snarky shake to her head as she moved her face in toward Brianna's. "That's why the sun is shining while it's raining: to let us know that he's beating her. I feel a little sorry for her even if she *is* the devil's wife. It's got to be bad enough to be married to the devil. Then to have him beat on you like that . . . Then again, she should have known better than to hook up with a creature like him. I mean, what did she expect when she married the *devil?*"

"Well, I'm not going to let any man *ever* beat on me," Brianna said. "Not ever."

"They say if you stick a pin in the ground, you can hear her screaming when he's beating her."

Brianna frowned, then winced. "Who would want to hear anything like that?"

"Hey, let's go get a pin and see if we can hear her. That way, you'll see whether what I told you is the truth or not."

Brianna and Alana hurried into the house. "Wait right here while I find two pins." Brianna started upstairs to her room, then stopped and looked back. "Does it matter what kind of pin it is? A straight pin, a hat pin, a safety pin, or is it actually a writing pen . . . ?"

Alana shook her head. "As long as it pierces the ground, it should work."

Brianna came back quickly and handed Alana a large safety pin. They started toward the door.

"And just where do you two think you're going *now?*" Brianna's mother asked as she walked out of the kitchen into the den wiping her hands on a dish towel.

"To listen to the devil beat his wife and to see if we can hear her scream," Brianna said as easily as though she were saying that they were going to the kitchen to get a glass of water.

Brianna's mother shook her head as she smiled, but didn't protest—essentially telling Brianna that she had no objections to what they were about to do or the idea of it.

Brianna opened the large, lead-glass door and allowed Alana to go out first. Brianna grinned. She saw him before he saw her, and she ran full force, straight into his arms. "Granddad!" she said.

"Hey there," sixty-year-old Pearson Wright said as he picked her up and spun her around two full turns. He set Brianna back down. The two of them now stood close to the man who had come with him. "So where are you two going in such a hurry?" Pearson asked.

"We're going to listen to the devil as he beats his wife and to see if we can hear her screaming." Brianna held up her safety pin to prove they were serious.

"Oh, that," her grandfather said as he looked back at what he'd just come in out of. "You're talking about the rain with the sun shining. That's a beautiful sight for sure: rain and the sun shining at the same time, a phenomenon that's always fascinated folks."

The good-looking man standing next to her grandfather began to chuckle as he smiled at Brianna.

"Gracious, where are my manners," Pearson said. "This is my granddaughter"—he placed his hand on top of Brianna's head—"the lovely and talented young poet and short story writer, Miss Brianna Wright."

"And *this*"—Brianna pointed to Alana as soon as her grandfather finished introducing her—"is my best friend in the whole wide world, Alana Norwood."

"Pleased to meet you, Miss Alana Norwood. And *this* is David R. Shepherd, aka King d.Avid," Pearson said, pronouncing it "King dee-Avid." "That's a small *d,* period, capital *A,* small *v-i-d.* You're looking at the next world-renowned, recording artist."

"Are you a real king?" Brianna asked the tall man with black wavy hair and caramel-colored skin. She placed her hand in the man's waiting hand he'd presented to her to shake.

"No, not in the way you may be thinking," King d.Avid said. "But I do plan—with your grandfather advising and managing me—to rule the world of music someday."

"Sounds like a plan to me," Brianna said. "I plan on being the queen of something myself. Just not exactly sure what I intend to rule over. But I'm going to be somebody great, or at least produce something great one day, just like you. I promise you that. A lady at church spoke that Word over me last year. That's what she called it: 'A Word from God.'"

"I'm impressed," King d.Avid said, smiling at her as he continued to hold her young hand in his. "And I believe that." He gave Brianna a slight bow with his head, then let go of her hand. He reached over and held out his hand to Alana. "And you are the best friend of the queen-to-be?"

Alana walked over, shook his hand, and giggled. "Yes. Although, it's likely we'll both be queens. That's how a lot of friends roll, you know."

"Absolutely," King d.Avid said. "It's always good to be in the company of those who are going somewhere, instead of hanging around people who are going nowhere. That's precisely why I hang with Mister Wright, here, the way I do. The man is good at what he does." He glanced over at Pearson. "And I believe he's going to help get me where I'm destined to be." King d.Avid turned his attention back to Alana and gave her a slight nod.

"So, how old are you?" Alana asked.

King d.Avid laughed. "Why, I'm twenty-five."

"You're kind of old," Alana said, turning up her nose slightly. "Me and Brianna are only ten. Well, we don't mean to be rude, but we need to finish before the rain stops just as quickly as it started. Otherwise, Brianna won't believe that the devil really is beating his wife."

"Okay." King d.Avid sang the word. "But I don't *think* the

devil really is beating his wife. Because I don't *think* that the devil is married."

"That's what I told her," Brianna said triumphantly with a grin.

Alana trotted down the steps into the rain and stood in the grassy, manicured yard. She looked back up at the porch, her eyes blinking with the raindrops before she eventually shielded her eyes with her hand. "Brianna, will you come on, already!"

Brianna hurried and caught up with her friend. They unlatched their safety pins, kneeled down, stuck their pins into the ground, and placed their ears over their respective pins with the rain drenching them and all.

Pearson shook his head, laughed, then escorted King d.Avid into the house.

Chapter 1

The waters wear the stones: thou washest away the
things which grow out of the dust of the earth; and
thou destroyest the hope of man.

—Job 14:19

Brianna Bathsheba Wright Waters looked out of the window of their three-bedroom, one-and-a-half-bathroom house at the rain. A "starter home" is what her twenty-three-year-old (three years her senior) husband of eight months, Unzell Michael Waters, told her over two months ago when they bought it.

"Baby, I promise you, things are going to get better for us down the road," Unzell had said after they officially moved in. "I know this is not what either of us envisioned we'd be doing right about now. But I promise you, I'm *going* to get us into that mansion we talked about. I am."

She'd married Unzell at age nineteen, a year and a half after her high school graduation, as Unzell was finishing his final year at the University of Michigan. Unlike most women she knew, Brianna wanted to marry in December. The wintertime was her favorite time of the year. She loved everything about winter. It wasn't a dead period as far as she was concerned. To her, that was the time of rest, renewal, anticipation, and miracles taking place that the eyes weren't always privy to. Winter was the time when flower bulbs, trees, and other plants could establish themselves underground, developing better and stronger roots. Winter was the time when various pests and bugs were killed off; otherwise the world would be overrun with them. Brianna loved the rich colors she would be able to use in a winter wedding: deep reds and dark greens.

But she equally loved summertime. Summer was a reminder of life bursting forth in its fullness and full potential after all seemed dead not so long ago. Summer now reminded her of her days of playing carefree outside, *truly* without a care in the world.

So she and Unzell married the Saturday before Christmas. It was a beautiful ceremony; her parents had spared no expense. After all, this would be the only time they would be the parents of the bride. Her older brother, Mack, might settle down someday. But even if he did, they would merely be the parents of the groom, which was a totally different expense, experience, and responsibility.

Unzell Waters was already pretty famous, so everybody and his brother wanted to be invited to the wedding ceremony. Unzell was the star football player at the University of Michigan and a shoo-in for the NFL. As a running back, he'd broken all kinds of records, and the only question most had was whether he would be the number-one or number-two pick in the first round of the NFL draft the last Saturday in April. Unzell was on track to make millions—more millions than either he or Brianna could fathom *ever* being able to spend in *several* lifetimes.

Still Brianna's best friend, Alana Norwood had been her maid of honor. Alana had grown wilder than Brianna, but Brianna understood Alana . . . and Alana understood her.

"Girlfriend, I'm glad you're settling down so early, if that's what you want," Alana had said when Brianna first told her she and Unzell were getting married in a year. "But I plan on seeing *all* that the world has to offer me before my life becomes dedicated to any one person like that."

Of course, when Alana learned *just* how famous Unzell was even *before* he was to go pro, then heard about the millions of dollars sports commentators were predicting he'd likely get when he signed—no matter which team he signed with—she said to Brianna, "God really *does* look after you! Of course, He's always looked after you. People on TV are talking eighty-six million dollars, over five years, just for one man to play . . . one man, to *play*. And you're going to be his wife? I know you used to say all the time that you were God's favorite. Well, I'm starting to believe maybe you really are."

"Alana, now you know I used to just *say* things like that. I don't *really* believe God has favorites," Brianna said. "The Bible tells us that God is no respecter of persons. We're all equal in His sight."

"Well, we may have the *opportunity* to be equal, but it's obvious that not all of us are walking in our opportunities. Not the way you do, anyway. So you're definitely ahead of a lot of us, not equal by any means. All I know is that you spoke that Word of Favor with a capital *F* over your life, and look what's happening with you so far."

The wedding was absolutely beautiful, every single detail and moment of it. But with the championship game being played the first week in January, Brianna and Unzell were only able to spend one day of a honeymoon before Unzell was off again to practice.

Michigan's team was the team to beat with number twenty-two, Unzell Waters, being one of the main obstacles standing against the other team having even a *semblance* of a chance. Brianna was at the game in Miami watching it along with her family. With two minutes remaining in the fourth quarter, Michigan was already a comfortable three touchdowns ahead. In Brianna's opinion, there really was no reason for Unzell to even be on the field. She, her grandfather Pearson Wright, and father Amos Wright were saying as much when that play happened—the play that would alter Unzell's career and life.

One of the other team's players grabbed Unzell by the leg as he ran full speed and yanked him down, pulling his leg totally out of joint. With him being down, everybody on the other team piled on him. Unzell was badly hurt. Instantly, his prospective stock for the NFL plummeted. Then came the doctor's prognosis. Even with the two necessary surgeries, Unzell would never be able to play football at that level again.

Brianna assured him things would be all right. "God still has you, Unzell."

"Yeah, but if God had me in the first place, then why would He allow something like this to happen to me . . . happen to us?" Unzell said as he lay in that hospital bed. "God knows both of us. He knows us, Brianna. He knows our hearts. God knows we would have done right when it came to me being in the NFL. So why? Why did this happen? And if God is a healer, then why can't He heal my leg completely? Why can't He make me whole again?"

"I believe that God *can* heal your leg, Unzell," Brianna said. "But right now we have to deal with reality. And from all that the doctors are saying, football is out for you, at least for now. So you and I need a new direction, that's all. We're going to be all right though." She lovingly took hold of his hand, then squeezed it. "We are." She smiled.

"So, you're not going to leave me?"

Brianna frowned as she first jerked her head back, then primped her lips before forcing a smile. "Leave *you?* Where did *that* come from?"

"Face it; I'm not going to be making millions now. In fact, I'll be doing well just to find a job, any job at all, in this economy."

"First of all, *Mister* Waters, I did not marry you for your money or your potential money. I've known you since we were in high school. You were in the twelfth grade; I was in the ninth. You didn't have any money then and I fell in love with you. So if you think I married you for your money, then maybe I *should* leave you." Brianna put her hand on her hip.

"I know, Bree-Bath-she," he said, calling her by the pet name he sometimes called her. "But do you know how many women wanted me because they saw dollar signs?"

"Yeah, I know. I'm not stupid. I even think you thought about getting with a few of them. In fact, who knows, maybe you did. But still, I married you for you. And I married you for better or worse; for richer or poorer."

"Come on, Brianna. Nobody really means that part when they say it. Who truly wants to be with someone poor? Sure, we may feel that's where we are at the time, but all of us believe our lives are going to get to the better and the richer at some point—sooner rather than later—not worse or poorer."

"Well, if me staying with you now after you've lost millions of dollars—that if I'm not mistaken, you never really had anyway—means I meant what I was vowing when I said those words, then please know: I meant them when I said them. Okay, so those in the know were saying you'd likely get a contract worth eighty-six million dollars over five years with a guaranteed fifty million and now it looks like you won't. So be it. I'm just glad you're okay. You could have been paralyzed on that play. You and I will do what we need, to be all right. Besides, you're graduating in May. You'll get your Electrical Computer Engineering degree. Do like most folks and either get a job or start your own business. Regardless, Unzell, I'm here to stay. So deal with it." Brianna flicked her hand.

Unzell smiled, then looked down at his hand. "God has certainly blessed me richly." He looked up. "God gave me you."

"Oh," Brianna said, all mushy as she kissed him. "That was *so* sweet."

Brianna couldn't help but think about how far she and Unzell had come since that fateful day. Following Unzell's two surgeries and the rehabilitation period, she'd suspended attending college and gotten a job as a secretary, living with her parents while he finished his final months of college in Ann Arbor. After Unzell graduated, he moved back to Montgomery, Alabama. He was relentless about getting a job, even when it felt like no one was hiring. He was diligent, beating the pavement and searching the Internet. In four weeks, he landed a job as an assistant stage manager setting up stages for music concerts, but was told if he wanted to excel in this business, he needed to be in Atlanta.

So that's what he and Brianna did: moved to Georgia.

It didn't hurt when Alana told Brianna that she was also moving to Atlanta to pursue her dream of becoming a video girl. At least now, Brianna and Alana would each have a friend in their new city. Brianna especially needed someone after quickly learning that in his position, Unzell could be gone for weeks, sometimes even months at a time.

Brianna continued to stare out of the window. She suddenly began to smile.

"And what are *you* smiling about?" Unzell said, jarring her back to the present.

Spinning around, she kissed him when he came near. "I didn't hear you come in."

He embraced her. "You were gazing out of the window. It looked like you were in deep thought; I didn't want to disturb you. Then you broke into that incredibly enchanting smile of yours, and I couldn't hold myself back any longer. Did you just think of a joke or something that made you happy?"

"Look," she said, pointing outside.

He looked out of the window and shrugged. "And what exactly am I looking for? All I see is rain, the sun shining, and trees and other things getting drenched."

"Don't you know what that's supposed to mean? Rain while the sun is shining."

He laughed. "Here we go again. Another something you learned when you were growing up? Like not stepping on a crack so you won't break your mother's back. Not walking under a ladder or splitting a pole because it will bring bad luck. Not sweeping someone's feet or you'll sweep them or someone else out of your life."

"No. Not exactly like *those* things, which are merely superstitions. This is different. I'm not saying that I believe it, but they say that when it's raining and the sun is shining, the devil is beating his wife."

"Yeah, right." Unzell smirked. "Actually, the scientific term for it is 'sunshower.' "

"Scientific term, huh? Well, people also say that if you stick a pin in the ground and listen, you can hear her screams."

"Oh. So do you want to go outside and do that so we can put that old wives' tale to the test?" Unzell's eyes danced as he spoke. "I'm game to play in the rain if you are."

"Nope. Alana and I tested it out when we were younger."

He laughed. "And the verdict was?"

"I didn't hear a thing. Of course, Alana claimed that she did. She said the scream was faint. But honestly? I think she heard something because she wanted to believe it was true. Then she said we'd used the wrong kind of pin and that's why it didn't work right."

"Alana is something else, that's for sure. So how is she these days?"

"Still trying to get a contract as a video girl or video whatever they're called."

"I wouldn't ever count Alana out. Before you know it, she'll be over here forcing us to watch her DVD, showing how she was 'doing her thing.' " He made a quick pumping dance move followed by the long-outdated Cabbage Patch.

Unzell wrapped his arms around Brianna. She fully submitted, lying back into him, then rubbing one of his hard, muscular arms that gently engulfed her.

"The devil beating his wife," he said with a sinister giggle as they both looked out of the window. "Well, now, I think I've heard just about everything."

Brianna broke away from his embrace and turned to face him, playfully hitting his arm. "Just don't *you* ever try that devil move on *me*."

He grabbed her and lovingly locked her again into his arms, gazing deeply into her brown eyes as they faced each other. "Never. I promise you I will *leave* before I *ever* raise a hand to you." He hugged her. "I would never abuse a blessing of God; I'm too afraid of what God would do to me if I did."

He gently pushed her slightly away from him to look into her eyes again. "Besides, I love you too much. We're one body now. So whatever I do to you, I'll be doing to myself. And I would *never* lay a negative hand or word, for that matter, on myself. Therefore, I won't ever do anything like that to you."

"See, that's why I love you so much." She cocked her head to one side. "You really get this whole concept of loving your wife the way Christ loves the church."

"I wouldn't want our life together to be any other way. Not any other way." He pulled her to him and squeezed her as he locked her in his arms, causing her to giggle out loud. He stopped, cupped her face, and kissed her with an overflow of passion.

Chapter 2

*Blessed is the man that walketh not in the counsel
of the ungodly, nor standeth in the way of sinners,
nor sitteth in the seat of the scornful.*

—Psalm 1:1

Alana stomped into Brianna's house as soon as the door opened. "Man, it's a jungle out there!" Alana said as she went straight to the den, then flopped down on Brianna's floral couch.

Brianna came and sat down beside her, shaking her head. "Well, a good day to you, too."

"I'm sorry," Alana said, leaning over and giving Brianna a quick hug. "Hi. How are you? What's going on with you?"

"Well, I'm—"

"I am so sick of getting nothing but runarounds," Alana said without allowing Brianna to finish. "Why can't people just say what they mean and mean what they say?" Alana placed her feet up on the coffee table.

Brianna's eyes immediately zeroed in on Alana's red stiletto shoes on the table.

Alana followed where Brianna's eyes rested and quickly removed her feet from the table. "Sorry. I always forget."

"Nice shoes though," Brianna said.

"You want to try them on and see how they look on you? You and I still wear the same size." Alana reached down and began to unfasten one of them.

"Oh, no," Brianna said. "Those are a bit too high for me."

"You know, Bathsheba," Alana said, calling Brianna by her barely known middle name. Bathsheba was the name Alana called Brianna whenever she wanted to pick on her or point out that Brianna was either acting uppity or a little too queenly for her taste. "Since you married Unzell, you've become a real fuddy-duddy."

"I have not. I've *always* been a fuddy-duddy." Brianna laughed. "So"—she turned squarely to her friend—"do you want to talk about what's wrong with you or not?"

"You mean what's wrong now or merely life in general?"

"Now will do."

"It's the same ole, same ole. Here it is October, and I've been in Atlanta for what? Three months now? And so far I've only gotten a few auditions and asked to be in only one video. And it was a little, *minute* part with somebody nobody has ever heard of. I'm not even sure they were a legitimate group. I think they might have been just tricking us into doing stuff so they could film us and sell the tape for something entirely different than a music video. That's what I'm beginning to believe."

"I just hope and pray you haven't done anything you're going to regret later," Brianna said. "I've told you, Alana. You know how women can become desperate and mess up early on trying to get their foot in the door. How they end up with something in print or recorded that comes back and bites them, just when they're on or near the top and about to finally achieve their dreams. Vanessa Williams, the first black Miss America, comes to mind."

"Oh, you're so sweet!" Alana leaned over and hugged Brianna. "You really believe I'm going to make it to the top one day, don't you? As for Vanessa Williams: look where she is now. I loved her in *Ugly Betty*. Now she's on *Desperate Housewives*." Alana leaned forward and started browsing through a stack of music CDs on the table.

"Of course I believe you're going to make it to the top someday, Alana."

"Yeah," Alana said. "Between us, you *were* and still *are* forever the optimist." She stopped at one CD. "Hey! You have the latest CD by King d.Avid!" She pronounced the world-renowned psalmist's name, King dee-Avid, with adoration and pizzazz.

Brianna smiled. "Yeah. I *love* his music. And he *is* one of the hottest recording artists out there whether in gospel, contemporary gospel, contemporary, R&B, pop, or otherwise. King d.Avid's music has crossed borders and barriers."

"I know. I'd love to be in one of his cross-over songs' videos. Not the gospel; I'm talking about one of his songs slated for channels like VH1, BET, and MTV—whenever MTV plays music, that is. I remember when the M in MTV stood for music. Maybe they should change their name to RTV for Reality TV," Alana said. "Can you believe you and I actually met King d.Avid when we were just ten? He was cute and all. But who had a clue he would ever become mega? I mean, he's all over the world, topping charts, selling out arenas *every*where. And you and I knew him before any of this."

"I wouldn't say we actually *knew* him," Brianna said.

"He came to your house with your grandfather. Even bowed to you; only gave me a little twerpy nod. Oh, I remember." Alana flipped the CD over to the back. "Do you think your grandfather could put in a good word for me and get me in one of King d.Avid's videos? Or better yet, I'd love to travel with him and be a part of his concert entertainment entourage."

"I doubt it," Brianna said. "He and my grandfather parted ways some years back. In fact, you remember when I turned sixteen, I was a huge King d.Avid fan. My grandfather knew this. So as a surprise, he wanted to get me a backstage pass to one of his concerts. King d.Avid's people wouldn't even put my grandfather through to talk to him. As much as Granddad

did to help King d.Avid get to where he was, and he couldn't
even garner a mere courtesy return phone call. At least, that's
what I overheard my father tell my mother."

"What happened that caused them to part ways?"

"The usual, from all I've heard and read. You have the people who get you in; then when you get big, other people
swoop in and convince the 'rising star' that the person who
brought them to the dance, so to speak, can't quickstep them
to where they are desiring to be. It's all about money and
power. Always has been, always will be."

Alana opened the CD case. "So King d.Avid got rid of your
grandfather after all he'd done to help get him to the top?
That's jacked up."

"I'm not long on details, but it sounds like my grandfather
was sort of forced out by others around King d.Avid. The new
people who had come in conspired against my grandfather so
much that Granddad had to tell King d.Avid it was either him
or them. After Granddad saw how the decision was weighing
on King d.Avid, he decided to make it easy on him and just
bow out completely. But it must have been okay with King
d.Avid because he didn't come after my grandfather and try
to convince him to stay. At least, that's what my father concluded. But my info is both secondhand and from eavesdrop-
ping."

Brianna reached over and took the CD. "It's fine though.
Granddad was getting to the age where he said he didn't need
to be wearing himself out being bothered with all the junk
that comes with the recording business anyway. He's enjoying
himself relaxing, which is what a seventy-one-year-old *should*
be doing, in my opinion."

Brianna went over to the stereo, put in the CD, and pressed
PLAY. The music started.

"Oh, snap!" Alana said. "I love that beat!" She started bob-
bing her head. "That's the one that was just released. What's it
called?"

"'Firmly I Stand,'" Brianna said. "It's the words found in Psalms, chapter one."

The words to the song began.

Verse 1
Blessed is the man that walketh not
In the counsel of the ungodly,
Nor standeth in the way of sinners,
Nor sitteth in the seat of the scornful.
But his delight is in the law of the Lord;
And in His law does he meditate day and night.
Chorus (full choir):
And he
Shall be
Like a tree
Planted by the rivers of water,
That bringeth forth his fruit in his season;
His leaf also shall not wither;
And whatsoever he doeth
Shall prosper.
Verse 2
The ungodly are not so:
But are like the chaff
Which the wind
Driveth away.
I said like the chaff
Which the wind
Blows away.
The chorus played again, then verse 3.
Therefore the ungodly shall not stand
In the judgment,
Nor sinners
In the congregation
Of the righteous.

For the Lord knoweth the way
Of the righteous (Full choir) Yes, He does
But the way
Of the ungodly
Shall perish.
I said, the way
Of the ungodly
Shall perish.

"Wow, I love that!" Alana said, having risen to her feet when the chorus began.

"I know," Brianna said. "It's so good! He has a lot of great cuts on this CD."

"You need to burn me a copy," Alana said. "That CD is *slamming!*"

Brianna turned down the volume and cocked her head to the side. "I will *not.*"

"See, you're always so self-righteous. Nobody's going to care if you burn me a copy."

"Oh, yes, somebody *will* care. Me. The Bible tells us that a laborer is worthy of his hire. In other words, if someone works, they should be paid for their labor. If I burn you a copy of a CD, then that's money we're taking out of the pocket of the ones who did the work. And that's not right."

Alana waved off Brianna. "Girl, please. What's King d.Avid or any of them going to actually miss if I don't buy it? Fifty-four cents . . . a dollar? I don't believe even losing a dollar will break anyone. But my having to pay twelve to eighteen dollars for a CD will *seriously* hurt me *and* my pocketbook, especially now. This whole video thing is just *not* working out the way I had hoped. And waiting tables just to pay rent on that sorry dump where I live is getting real old, real fast. I'm all for sacrificing for your dreams, but this dream is fast becoming a nightmare. Here's my take on things going on in my life these days. All of this has me by the neck and it's *sucking* the bloody life right out of me!"

"Okay, before we address 'poor you' and how terribly wrong things are going for you as a wannabe video vixen, let's go back to your question about what an artist will miss should I do something like burn a copy of a CD, and give it to you," Brianna said.

Alana flopped back down on the couch and picked up a small throw pillow. "Oh, come on. Please! Please! Let's not have an ethics lecture. Not today. Please! Didn't you catch when I came in that I'm experiencing a small bout of depression?"

"You were the one who brought it up, so we're going there," Brianna said, turning the music down even lower. She sat down beside Alana. "Okay, let's say the artist is only *personally* getting a dollar for each sold CD, which I believe is a high number compared to the actual truth. Let's say *I* or *someone else* burns a copy of the CD and gives it away. Let's say a mere ten thousand people do this. How much money has that artist lost?"

Alana took the pillow and covered her face. "I don't want to think today."

"I made it easy for you," Brianna said. "One dollar with ten thousand people." She grabbed the pillow and pulled it away from Alana's face. "One times ten thousand."

Alana looked at her, then squinted her eyes. "Ten thousand dollars."

"So, would you care about losing ten thousand dollars?" Brianna asked.

"Of course, I'd care! I'm *broke!* Listen, I get mad when cheap people come in the restaurant and don't tip me or leave some wimpy little tip. Like they can't spare ten to twenty percent of twenty dollars," Alana said. "Two to four measly more dollars. Ugh!"

"Now do you understand?" Brianna said.

"I understand that I'm not rich. I also understand that King d.Avid is mega rich. He should consider you, or anyone else, burning a copy for people like me as part of his program for giving back to the poor." Alana again fell back, limp, against the couch.

"Okay," Brianna said. "I'm going to give this one more stab, and then I'm through."

"Thank you," Alana said, quickly sitting back up.

Brianna laughed. "You're so crazy. All right. Let's say you, Alana Gail Norwood, happen to really enjoy the work of someone: a recording artist, someone's book, someone's movie. But you're managing to always get it in a nefarious way."

"Please, no big words today," Alana said, rolling her eyes.

"Okay, you're getting it illegally or free. And I'm not talking about checking it out of the library, which is totally fine and legal *and* shows support. I'm talking about—"

"I know what you're talking about. So, please get on with it and finish already."

"What do you think happens when the record company or the book publisher or the movie executives start looking at sales numbers? If it doesn't look like what was produced is selling well, do you honestly believe anyone wants to get behind or stay behind something like that? Do you think the company still wants to put out that type of product, at least by that artist, if it looks like the project isn't faring well financially?"

"Yeah, but a whole lot of people *are* interested because they're bootlegging it, buying bootleg copies, burning it, passing it on, or lending it out when they're finished."

"But it's all about the colors *red* and *black,* and the final numbers. And it doesn't matter about the underground distribution if those in charge can't see that it's making any money. Then those artists are cut from the company and you can't get their products. How will you feel? How will you then be blessed by their gifts and talents?"

Alana threw up her hands. "Okay, okay, okay! So *don't* burn me a copy then!"

Brianna also threw up her hands, but in triumph. "Finally!" she said.

"Hey, can you let me borrow it? I'll give it right back, after I put it on my iPod."

Brianna started laughing. "Okay, I give up. You're hopeless. *Hope*-less!"

Alana tilted her head sideways. "What? *What?*" She started laughing as well.

Chapter 3

He divided the sea, and caused them to pass through; and he made the waters to stand as a heap.

—Psalm 78:13

Brianna could hardly wait for Unzell to get home. She continued to look out of the window for the first sign of his car pulling up in the driveway. As soon as he drove up, she ran out of the house and straight into his arms. "I'm so glad you're home!" she said, then kissed him several times.

Unzell smiled. "I've missed you, too. But you shouldn't have waited up for me like this. It's past midnight."

"I know. But you've been gone for three weeks now. Besides, I couldn't have fallen asleep anyway knowing you were coming home tonight. I knew you would try not to wake me when you came in. Somehow, you always manage to slip into bed without waking me."

He released her from his arms, then popped open the trunk with the keyless remote.

"Why don't you just leave your things until the morning," she said. "You can take them out then."

Unzell continued walking toward the trunk. "You know me; I like to handle things in the now instead of putting them off until later."

Brianna smiled. "I know. But I've missed you." Her voice was purring . . . flirty.

He lifted the large suitcase out of the trunk, then closed it back. "We have a whole three days to catch up and spend together," Unzell said. "Just the two of us."

"So you're only going to be home for three days?"

He put his arm around her as he carried the suitcase in his other hand. "Yeah."

They walked into the house. He set the suitcase down. "Why so quiet all of a sudden?" he asked.

"Oh, nothing."

"See, I knew you were tired. Why don't you go on to bed, and after I get a quick shower, I'll be right in."

"I'm not tired. I told you; I've missed you." She stood on her tippy-toes and gave him a peck on his lips.

He instantly began to yawn. "Well, you may not be tired, but I am *beat.*" He began to grin. "But I do have some good news."

Brianna grinned back. "What? Tell me." She bounced a few times.

"I just got promoted from assistant stage manager to stage manager."

"Oh, Unzell, that's wonderful! You've only been with them for four months and you're already moving up the ladder. That's my baby! I knew you would."

He yawned again. "Yeah. Management says they're impressed with my work as well as my work ethic. In fact, Jock Adamson—that's the guy over the whole operation—says at the rate I'm learning and doing all of this, he can see me stepping into being production manager quicker than anyone he's ever worked with. But you know how to land the job you want, don't you?"

"And how is that, my fantastically brilliant hunk of a husband?"

"By doing the work of the job you desire to have. When people in position see you doing the work before you get there, they'll be able to see that you can do it. I'm learning and doing as much as I can about production managing. And you just watch. I'll be a production manager before you know it."

Brianna smiled.

"What are you smiling about?" Unzell asked.

She entwined her fingers with his. "I missed you. I'm just glad that you're home."

"Well, you go on and get in the bed, *Mrs.* Waters. And I'll be in there, right next to you, before you even have time to miss me again. I promise." He raised their entwined hands up to his lips and softly kissed hers. He then turned her toward their bedroom.

"Okay," Brianna said. "But make it snappy! I'm starting to miss you already."

He laughed. "No doubt." He scanned her body with longing eyes. "No definite doubt."

The next morning was Saturday. Brianna woke up around nine and made Unzell breakfast in bed. She placed one purple pansy in a small vase on the tray. Although she tried, nothing she did would fully awaken him. She put his plate in the refrigerator.

No longer enrolled in college and still in search of a job, Brianna logged onto the Internet and put in a few applications to places she'd learned last night were possibly hiring. Like most companies, these companies no longer accepted applications in person.

Around noon, she heard Unzell moving around. By the time she reached the bedroom, he was stumbling back into the bed. "Baby, I'm sorry I'm so tired," he said, fluffing his pillow, then lying back down. "This job can be *rough.* And my bum leg bothers me from time to time. Still, I keep on pushing. For us, I keep on pushing."

"I understand," she said, snuggling up next to him. But that conversation was promptly cut short by the sound of snoring; just that fast, he was back out like a light.

Brianna decided to go to the grocery store and buy some things to fix some of his favorite dishes. She'd originally hoped they'd go out later. But she knew, just from these last hours, he was not likely going to want to go anywhere. Not on *this* day anyway.

Back from the store, she began preparing the meal. Besides her being smart, Unzell had told her that was another thing she was: a terrific cook. Unzell loved to eat out, from Thai to Mexican to Italian to Greek to Japanese to Chinese foods. But he always bragged that there was "nothing like a good ole home-cooked, Southern meal where the alchemist creating the meal" (usually a woman but not mandatory) "threw down," essentially "putting her or his foot in it." A meal so good it made you "want to slap somebody."

Of course, Brianna already knew that whether she decided on fried chicken, fried pork chops, or her mother's tried-and-true meatloaf, along with fresh vegetables—not the canned or frozen kind, unless it was canned or frozen by the hands of someone personally known—this meal *had* to include fresh, hot-out-of-the-oven cornbread with melting butter smashed and lathered in between, and perfectly brewed, perfectly sweetened, sweet tea. And anyone who *really* knew Unzell, knew that his favorite cake was German chocolate.

Brianna decided to go with her special herbs and spices fried pork chops, turnip greens, mashed potatoes sprinkled with cheese, creamed corn, freshly sliced Big Boy tomatoes and red onions for the greens, a seven-layer salad, and sweet potato mallow. And for dessert: made-from-scratch German chocolate cake. She kept everything warm that should be, until she knew for sure Unzell was up. That's when she popped the pan of cornbread into the bottom oven to ensure it would be piping hot when he sat down to eat.

"My goodness," Unzell said when he walked into the dining area of the kitchen and saw how beautifully Brianna had set the table. "What is all of this for?"

Brianna smiled as she sauntered over to him. "Welcome home, husband." She stood on her tippy-toes and pecked him on his lips.

He leaned down and gave her a real kiss, complete with passion, and beamed. "You did all of this for me? Just for me?"

"Yes." She pulled away and went to the oven to check on the cornbread. It was a perfect golden brown. "The bread is ready. Sit, so you can eat while everything is hot."

He rubbed his hands together and grinned as she placed the food in bowls and plates and set them on the table. "I'm so hungry! All of this looks *so* great!" Before he sat down at the table, he went into the den, picked up the remote control off the coffee table, and turned on the television. "There should be a football game on somewhere."

"But it's Saturday," Brianna said.

"I know. You know colleges play their games on Saturday. One should still be on. And if not, I'm sure there's a replay of one of the games I missed earlier today." He sat and began to fix his plate, glancing at the TV as he scooped various items onto his plate.

"Would you prefer eating in the den so you can see the television better?" Brianna asked, hoping he would see how rude what he was doing really was.

He smiled. "You don't mind?" He began putting the food on the plate even faster. "Baby, you're the best!" He went into the den with a full plate and a tall glass of tea and sat down. Saying a quick prayer, he glanced back at Brianna and said, "*The* best!"

Brianna came in with her plate and sat down next to him. She forced a smile and hoped he didn't sense her disappointment. "Thanks," she said.

On Sunday, Brianna and Unzell went to church. Brianna was hoping they might go out to dinner and a movie after the service was over.

"With all that food we have left at the house?" Unzell said. "There's not a restaurant around that can throw down like you did yesterday. I was looking forward to finishing off the leftovers today."

"Are you sure?" Brianna asked.

"Oh, yeah. When you're gone from home all the time the way I'm gone these days, you find yourself just like Dorothy in *The Wizard of Oz:* 'There's no place like home,' " Unzell said as he headed home. "Besides, there are all of these games coming on today, one right after the other. Now what could be better than eating the best food in town in front of some of the best games in town along with the best wife in town?"

"Maybe watching a movie with your wife," Brianna said, almost mumbling it.

He glanced over at her and smiled. "Oh, you want to watch a movie together?"

Brianna's face lit up. She blushed a little. "Yes."

"Okay, okay. I'll tell you what. After the games are over tonight, we'll pop in a nice little movie. Or better yet, we can order a video on demand so we can catch a new release. We can watch a movie in bed. How about that? You certainly can't go to a movie theater and get your romance on the way we'll be able to get ours on in our own house."

"Unzell, I was hoping that we could do some things when you came home." Brianna looked at him, then felt bad for what she'd just said. She never wanted to become one of those whining, nagging wives. "I suppose you *are* tired of going all the time though. We can spend some time at home if that's what you'd rather do. As long as we're together, that's all that really matters. Right?"

He smiled. "I love you so much. I hope you know that."

"I do," Brianna said. "I really do." She smiled at him, then turned and gazed out of the window, watching the changing scenes, almost like a blur, zip by.

Chapter 4

And the king said, is there not yet any of the house of Saul, that I may shew the kindness of God unto him? And Ziba said unto the king, Jonathan hath yet a son, which is lame on his feet.

—2 Samuel 9:3

Brianna had looked forward to Thanksgiving. She was hoping Unzell at least would be off from work and home on Thanksgiving Day. Originally, he was supposed to be. But when he was promoted to stage manager, he went to a new assignment. It really was a fantastic assignment. He would be setting up the concert stages for none other than King d.Avid, who was starting up a new leg of his "Destroying the Yoke" concert tour.

Brianna had already invited her parents; her brother, Mack; and her grandfather Pearson to her house for Thanksgiving dinner. Her folks hadn't visited her in Atlanta since right after she and Unzell moved there in July. Mack had yet to visit her new home. And once again, he had things going on, so he called and said he wouldn't be able to come this time around, either. But her parents and grandfather came.

Dinner included the traditional turkey and dressing along with gravy, yams, and cranberry sauce. Brianna cooked everything, so her mother got a true break for a change. Usually, her mother did all of the holiday and Sunday cooking. But Brianna told her this was her day off this time around. And on *this* day, she was to do nothing but rest and enjoy. Diane didn't argue with her about that *at all.*

Dinner was fabulous. Brianna's parents went into their bedroom to lie down after stuffing themselves. Brianna and her grandfather sat in the den watching television.

"That was some kind of a dinner you cooked there, little lady," Pearson said.

"Thanks, Granddad. I'm just glad you were able to be here."

"I wouldn't have missed it for the world." He patted her leg. "It's not often I get to see you these days. And I'm sure it was a little hard not having your husband home for your first official Thanksgiving as a married couple."

Brianna smiled. "I should have been prepared for this. If Unzell had been playing professional football like we'd thought, it's possible his team would have been playing on television today and he wouldn't have been home."

"Yeah, well, I'm sure you weren't expecting that, especially now that he's not playing in the pros," Pearson said.

"I'm just glad he's found something he seems to love. And he's obviously good at it; he was promoted in less than six months, which was ahead of his goal. They're talking about him moving up to a production manager, possibly in as little as a year's time."

Pearson leaned forward, tapping the matching fingers of each hand against the other. "That really *is* an accomplishment. But Unzell is a smart young man; a quick study. He's more than just muscles, that's for sure. The man has brains . . . and drive."

"I told you whose concert stages he's setting up."

Pearson nodded. "Yeah. My former client, David R. Shepherd, now aka world-renowned, famous recording artist King d.Avid. I came up with that stage name, you know."

"No, I didn't know that. But King d.Avid is *mega* these days," Brianna said.

"'Mega' is not even the word. Although if I know him, I'm sure King d.Avid is working on inventing a new word to describe what he has become."

Brianna turned to her grandfather, smiled quickly, then

dropped it just as quickly. "Granddad, what happened between you and King d.Avid? I remember meeting him when I
was ten. You brought him over to the house. He wasn't mega
back then. In fact, no one had even heard of him—at least, as
far as I knew."

Pearson leaned back on the couch. "It's the usual things
that happen in business-related matters. People start out with
good intentions. But somehow, problems always seem to
come back to money. At first, money is tight, and it's hard to
get the things done that you need to. But you persevere . . .
you find ways to make it work. Then, if you stick with it and
continue to sharpen your skills and your mission plan, and
things start to work in your favor, you get in. And when things
are truly flowing, you end up getting where you once only
dreamed of. Then money becomes an issue again, only it's due
to a profusion of it."

"So you and King d.Avid fell out because of an abundance
of money?"

"No, I wouldn't say *that*. King d.Avid is really a great guy. At
least, he was back when I had dealings with him. I can honestly say he was a man after God's own heart. That's rare to
find these days. I see that in you; you're a woman after God's
own heart. Like most of us, King d.Avid had a few friends that
truly stuck by him along the way. King d.Avid didn't have a lot
growing up. But if he was your friend, and he made you a
promise, you could rest assured he would do all he could to
keep that promise. When he came into money and power, he
tried to help those who'd been with him from the start." Pearson looked toward the kitchen. "Could I trouble you for a
glass of sweet tea, please?"

Brianna hurried and got the tea. She handed him the glass.

He took a swallow. "Ah, that's good." He shook his head.
"You have the art of making tea down to a science. Your
mother taught you well."

"Yeah," Brianna said. "It really *is* an art of science. It's all in
the brewing time—no less than three, no more than five min-

utes—that's what keeps it from having a bitter taste. And of course, the right amount of sugar: not too much, not too little—"

"But *just* right!" Pearson laughed as he took another swallow, releasing yet another "ah" of sheer satisfaction. "Sounds like Goldilocks."

"Yeah, that did, didn't it?"

"It's good to have passion. That's what makes successful people. Whatever you do, do it with passion. That's what your husband does; that's what your brother is doing."

"How did you know I was thinking about Mack?" Brianna asked, sitting back.

"I know you were disappointed that Mack didn't end up making it today."

"I just don't get him. He's taken in a child who has trouble getting around, and he's not even blood to him. I learned he was doing this earlier this year. I don't get it."

"Just like you, Mack is a good-hearted person. Melvin Samuelson—that's the child Mack's been looking after these past years and who has become a part of his family as a foster child, for now, with permanent hopes later—is the son of Jonathan Samuelson."

Brianna shrugged. "Jonathan Samuelson. Who's Jonathan Samuelson?"

Pearson took another swallow of tea. "Jonathan Samuelson was a true and dedicated friend of David's before there ever was a King d.Avid. In fact, Jonathan is credited with saving David's life when they were mere teens."

"You sure know a lot about King d.Avid, don't you? You should write a book."

"I know enough. Anyway, what he did wasn't anything heroic like diving in a pool to save him from drowning or stepping in front of a bullet. Nothing like that. But the word was that Jonathan's father was out to get David. Of course, Jonathan didn't believe that was truly the case, but he decided to find out for sure. You see, Jonathan and David were in this singing group. David was a better singer than Jonathan, but Jonathan's father had gotten behind them, putting up his finances and resources to front them."

"So naturally, Jonathan's father thought his son should be the star of the group," Brianna said.

"You got it," Pearson said. "But Jonathan was a true friend. He knew David was destined to take the group where it was going. Most times, he deferred to David, which only made his father that much madder. So the father tried to expel David from the band using some trumped-up reason. Jonathan told his father if David wasn't in it, he wouldn't be in it. So Jonathan's father tried to set David up to go to jail. Some say he was really trying to get David killed, but I don't want to believe an adult would even *think* that way about another adult, let alone a sixteen-year-old kid." Pearson shook his head, then picked up the glass of tea and drank some more.

"Anyway, to make a long story short: Jonathan told David he would find out for sure whether or not his father really was trying to harm him. He set up a little test to see if his father was truthfully trying to get David mixed up in some kind of gang rivalry where David would either have to get in a gang to be protected or possibly be accused of a crime he didn't do. Jonathan and David were supposed to be meeting up at a gig where they were scheduled to perform. Jonathan told David to lay low in the venue. The two friends set up a coded message. If Jonathan discovered that his father, in fact, was trying to set David up, he would say one thing. If things were fine, Jonathan would say another. Turns out, Jonathan's father *was* trying to set up his best friend, that very night."

"Whoa. That had to be hard on Jonathan."

Pearson nodded. "I'm sure it was. But Jonathan loved David. They were more like brothers, more than mere friends. David left the group, graduated high school, then began his own thing. Getting nowhere, he was told to seek me out, which he did. I knew about the music business from my brief recording days. He told me he felt I could help him get where he was trying to go. With his talent, I agreed. The rest, they say, is history."

"But I don't understand what Mack has to do with Jonathan's son."

"After I took on King d.Avid as a client and he started to get bigger, Mack became interested in getting into the business. He hung around me as much as he could so he could learn the operation. I think Mack was preparing to take over once I retired."

"I was ten when you came to our house with King d.Avid. Mack would have been thirteen," Brianna said.

"Oh, this was some years later. Mack was just about to graduate from high school. He was seventeen, and honestly, good at managing. But as I said, he'd been hanging around me, soaking in as much as he could prior to then. He met Jonathan. Shortly afterward, King d.Avid and I parted ways. Jonathan was killed in a home robbery. The only one to survive that horrendous day was Jonathan's son, Melvin, who ended up lame from the incident. I believe Melvin was five when those hoodlums broke in, threatening to kill all of them if they didn't cooperate. They say Melvin's mother grabbed him and started running. She was shot in the back at the top of the stairs. She dropped Melvin, he was propelled and tumbled. She rolled down just as fast and hard, landing on him. They say that's really what ended up saving that little boy's life; he was protected under his mother's body."

"Wow," Brianna said. "But I still don't understand how Mack got involved in all of this."

"Mack had met Jonathan a few years earlier when King d.Avid was trying to get Jonathan to come work for him. King d.Avid was really taking off, and like I said, he wanted to bless those who had been there for him early on. Mack and Jon hit it off."

"Okay," Brianna said. "Mack meets King d.Avid's friend, Jonathan. The two of them click. I'm sorry, I still don't get what would make *my* brother go this far."

"Melvin had no one left who would take him in. There was an aunt, Jonathan's half sister Michaela, born to a woman Jonathan's father had an affair with. Ironically, Michaela and King d.Avid married when he was nineteen, she seventeen. Of course, Jonathan's father still despised him, so he had her annul the marriage. Michaela's father claimed he had someone else he wanted her to marry. When all was said and done, she didn't end up with anybody. After the shooting incident, the word was that she didn't want to be burdened with taking care of her half brother's son for the rest of his life. So being his mother's child, a few years ago, Mack stepped in. It's been a hard fight, but he was officially awarded guardianship this year. Now Melvin lives in Mack's home."

"What about Jonathan's family? His parents? Surely, there *has to* be someone."

"As I said: there really is no one. Jonathan's parents both died from various illnesses within three months of each other right after the shooting incident happened. And none of the extended family members wanted to be 'saddled with a cripple'—their words, not mine. Especially learning there wasn't any real money to speak of in it for them. A woman who used to babysit Melvin took custody of him as a foster parent after everything happened and no one else would step up. But she was old, too old for what was needed. Mack helped. I believe she took sick and died a few years after getting him."

"Why didn't King d.Avid step in to help out?"

"I guess he didn't know. You see, this happened around the same time as when those other jokers came in trying to take over King d.Avid's operation. I'd been pretty effectively cut out of the loop by then. It had gotten to where I couldn't even see him or get a call through or a call back. When we *did* finally talk, I told him it was either them or me and that he knew who had his best interests at heart. It was on that day that we both learned he hadn't gotten any of my messages regarding Jonathan's death or his funeral."

"And still, it looks like he chose them instead of you."

"Maybe, maybe not. After a few weeks of nothing being re-solved, I made it easy."

"You stepped aside. But he didn't try to talk you out of leaving," Brianna said.

"From all of his success now, it looks like he made the right call." Pearson stood up. "I don't begrudge him at all. I always wanted the best for him. I'm so proud of him, and I keep him covered in prayer daily. It's hard out there; you don't know who to trust. We who love the Lord, and know that our fellow yoke men are doing what they can for the Kingdom of God, must lay aside egos and do whatever we can for one another.

"King d.Avid is getting the Word of God out in a big way. Lots of folks won't step foot in a church building, don't care to read a Bible or a Christian book, can't sit too long with their eyes open for a sermon, but they'll sit up, even get up, when music starts. And King d.Avid's work has crossed over. They're playing his songs on R&B stations all across this country. King d.Avid is spreading the Gospel of Jesus, reaching a *lot* of souls. A lot! I can't be mad at him for that. God is sovereign; God knows what He's doing."

"Well, I definitely love King d.Avid's music. He has truly blessed my life. I just wish things had turned out differently between you two. If it hadn't been for you—"

"Then God would have used someone else. God is not limited to getting what He wants done, how He wants it done, when He wants it done. He's not." Pearson beckoned for Brianna to stand up. He hugged her, rocking her as he spoke. "So don't you worry your pretty little head about any of this. I'm good, King d.Avid's good, and it looks like your husband is moving on up now in King d.Avid's concert troop, and that's good."

Brianna pulled back from her grandfather's embrace. "Hey! Did you happen to have something to do with Unzell getting this job with King d.Avid's outfit?"

"Who, me?" Pearson shook his head. "Nah. When I tell you I'm on the outside still, believe me, I'm on the *out*side. I couldn't even manage to give you that little special surprise for your sixteenth birthday. You remember how much you wanted to meet King d.Avid? Well, I tried to get you a back-stage pass. I couldn't even get through to him to get *that*. Now, I'd love to talk with King d.Avid someday, you'd better believe that. If nothing else than to just let him know how proud I am of him. But the people standing between him and the rest of the world don't intend on letting anyone, especially anyone who truly cares about him, to ever get that close to him. Not if they can possibly help it."

"Well, Granddad . . . you never know. We know that God can do the impossible. He can make the crooked places straight. He can do *what* He wants, *when* He wants."

"Listen to you; standing here preaching the words back to the one who usually preaches these same words to you." Pearson beamed as he lovingly shook his head at her.

Brianna also beamed. "You know . . . I love you, Grand-dad." She squeezed him.

He returned the hug with a manly grunt. "Love you, too, baby. I love you, too."

Chapter 5

And the king said unto him, Where is he? And Ziba said unto the king, Behold, he is in the house of Machir, the son of Ammiel, in Lo-debar.
—2 Samuel 9:4

King d.Avid read the piece in the December edition of the magazine. He couldn't believe how much this seven-hundred-word article was affecting him. It was talking about promises and those who've truly touched our lives, whether large or small. King d.Avid instantly thought about Jonathan Samuelson.

He and Jonathan had started out as friends, then formed a singing group. There had been three of them in the group, but it was Jonathan who had encouraged him the most and told him he was definitely going to be big someday, sooner than most folks knew. Sadly, Jonathan didn't live long enough to see just how great he'd become.

Jonathan was the one who had insisted on stepping back and allowing him to be the lead singer, even though it was Jonathan's father who put his time and money into support-ing their little group. Jonathan was the one who always had his back, even when it eventually came down to him having to go against his own father. King d.Avid couldn't help but think about how Jonathan should be here, right now, enjoying some of the fruits that God had blessed him with.

But Jonathan wasn't.

Instead, he'd been killed in a senseless robbery. King

d.Avid hadn't even been told about the death until weeks after the funeral. He'd been furious with those around him for not informing him. Their defense was that they didn't know it had been important for him to know. King d.Avid felt partly responsible for that; he'd allowed the ones who knew him best to be pushed from his life without a real fight from him. Like his advisor and manager, Pearson Wright, who had given him that ultimatum: *"It's either them or me."*

King d.Avid had never considered he couldn't have both: those who believed he could go much farther in his career if he had new blood with new (sometimes polar opposite) ideas, and those who were grounded and seasoned and had been with him practically from the start, and who actually knew him and his calling best.

But Pearson had decided to make it easy on him and just quit. King d.Avid had considered going after him to convince him to stay. But Vincent Powers, the man who would become his top manager, argued against the weakness he'd be demonstrating in allowing *anyone* to have that kind of power over him to the point where someone could control him in that way. Still, when King d.Avid allowed Pearson to leave, it seemed everyone he had trusted, and in his inner circle (which was less than a handful of folks), went as well.

Later on, King d.Avid would have his new assistant (who replaced Sandy) to put in a call to one of them, but no one ever bothered to call him back. "We haven't heard from him yet?" "She hasn't returned my call?" King d.Avid would ask repeatedly, having waited a few weeks for, say, Pearson or his former assistant to call back or come by.

"I hate to say it, but if you ask me, I'd say that Pearson was never really there for you. Especially not if he could just leave you like he did without ever even trying to check on you," Vincent said. "But it's okay. I'm here. Kendall is here," he said, referring to Kendall McNair, the assistant he'd brought in when he took over completely and cleared out all the remnants of King d.Avid's past associates. "Neither of us have any plans on going anywhere anytime soon, either. And you can *bank* on that."

So King d.Avid stopped trying and decided when they wanted him, they knew where and how to find him. His door, as well as access to him, would always be open for people such as Pearson, his trusted former assistant Sandy, ex-bodyguard Jake, Pearson's grandson Mack, and a few other people he'd instructed his staff to always put through or let in no matter what, when, or where, should they ever reach out to him.

But after four years, no one had tried. Not one. And Jonathan was dead.

He and Jonathan had promised they would always be there for each other. It had been hard, especially when Jonathan's father turned so viciously against David. And shortly after David became King d.Avid the solo artist, Jonathan's father fed the tabloids (and any news outlets that would listen) all kinds of information (lots of things flat-out lies) about him. Jonathan's father wanted to kill David's career before it could take off good. Not wanting to hurt his friend or his career, Jonathan had thought it best that they distance themselves, at least until he could ensure that his father had calmed down. The last time the two friends actually spoke in depth was right before Jonathan married.

King d.Avid chucked the magazine onto the coffee table. He decided it was time he took matters into his *own* hands. He may have missed out on doing what he could for Jonathan while he was alive, but there had to be something *now* that he could do to keep his promise to his friend. Something. King d.Avid called in Chad Holston, the head of his security, and asked him to find out whether Jonathan had any children left—legitimate or otherwise.

"Oh, and Chad, don't let anyone know I asked you to do this," King d.Avid said. "And whatever you find out, bring that information directly to me and me only."

"But, sir, Vincent has given us strict instructions that we let him know of anything you need or have requested of us. He

said that as your manager, he always needs to be in the know,"
Chad said.

King d.Avid nodded. "Chad, who signs your paycheck?"

Chad smiled. "Yes, sir. I'll get right on this and do *just* as
you've requested, sir."

"Thank you. I appreciate that."

Within hours, Chad had come back with information that
he read from a printout. "Jonathan Samuelson was killed during a robbery invasion in his home. His wife of six years was
shot, apparently while trying to flee from the robbers in an attempt to save their five-year-old son's life. When she was shot,
she dropped him, then must have tumbled down after him,
landing on top of him, which, as stated in the police report, is
probably what ended up saving the child's life. Both of his
legs were badly crushed from the traumatic fall. Nine years
old now, his legs have never fully recovered."

King d.Avid looked up toward the ceiling. "And where is
he? Who has him?"

Chad looked back at the printed paper. "After his parents
were killed, there was no one to take care of him. Grand-
parents were gravely ill, then both died from their illness
within months of each other. An elderly woman named Stella
Reid, who had been his babysitter since he was an infant,
quickly stepped in and became his foster mother."

"He has an aunt—Jonathan's half sister. Her name is Michaela."

"There's nothing listed on this report about a Michaela.
But two years after the elderly woman took custody, she fell ill
and died. The state was about to take the child and put him
through the system when a man named Mack Wright stepped
in and petitioned to take him in."

"Mack Wright? I remember Mack," King d.Avid said with a
puzzled look. "He was Pearson's grandson. Pearson is the
man who got my name on the map. Mack used to shadow his
grandfather whenever he could, trying to learn the business. I

suspect he was planning on taking over for his grandfather when his grandfather retired. I remember the day he and Jonathan met that first time. Jonathan never met a stranger. But I never knew they were close enough for Mack to do something like take in his son."

"According to this"—Chad shook the paper—"that's exactly what he did. He'd been the only other constant in the child's life, other than Stella. After the father was killed, Mack became something of a father figure to him. I suppose the courts felt it was fitting to allow him to have custody, even though he was a single man, especially when no other family member contested or appeared to want him. They moved from Montgomery and now live in Tuscaloosa, Alabama, where Mack is presently employed."

King d.Avid shook his head as he frowned. "I hate hearing something like this. My best friend's child left with almost no one wanting him? That's just wrong, so wrong, on so many levels." His body shuddered. "Chad, I'd like for you to arrange for him to be brought here to my house to see me."

"Sir?"

"I'd like for you to bring him . . . what's the child's name?"

Chad looked down at the paper again. "Melvin Samuelson."

"I'd like for you to bring Melvin here to visit with me," King d.Avid said.

"But sir. I can't just show up and make someone just come with me. His guardian is not going to let me just take him and bring him here merely on your orders," Chad said. "Even if that someone *is* King d.Avid. And you also know you can't trust letting everybody in here. Too many people want a piece of you these days. You *know* this."

"Give me that, please," King d.Avid said, holding out his hand for the paper Chad held.

"Sir, I'm not saying I *can't* do it. I'm just saying you have to think this through. What if he and his guardian come here and start trying to plot ways to get money out of you. It's my job to protect you. And I must say that I'm paid handsomely to do just that."

"And you do an outstanding job." King d.Avid flicked his hand out again, letting Chad know he still wanted the paper he held.

Chad handed him the paper. "Listen, King, sir. Let me do a deeper background check on them both first to make sure things are safe before you proceed."

King d.Avid took out his cell phone and began to press the corresponding phone number on the paper that was listed as being Mack's.

"Sir, you shouldn't be calling someone like him from your private cell phone number." Chad reached over and respectfully took the phone away. Chad then pulled his phone from its holder. "Here." He handed King d.Avid his phone. "At least use mine. That way if there's a problem down the road, they'll be phoning me and not you."

"You worry too much," King d.Avid said with a slight chuckle.

"No, sir. It's my job to ensure your protection, and that's what I intend to do."

King d.Avid pressed the numbers, using Chad's phone. He spoke with Mack, who confessed he was more than surprised to hear from him.

"I know Christmas is next week," King d.Avid said to Mack after they'd put to rest most of the suspicions either may have had about the other. "But if you don't mind and you feel it's okay, I'd love to have Melvin come here to my home in Atlanta and spend a day or two with me. I'm available this weekend if that would work for the two of you. I can fly you in or send my limo for you, whichever you feel would work best for you."

When Mack didn't readily agree, King d.Avid added, "I owe his father at least *this* much. Come on, Mack. Please. I'd love to see and visit with Jonathan's son."

Mack took a little more time, asking more questions before he finally agreed.

An hour hadn't even passed before Vincent stormed in to King d.Avid's all-white living room where he sat. "If you're going to do something charitable like this, then you should consider using it and getting all you can out of it," Vincent said. "Do you know what kind of publicity you can receive bringing a crippled child into your home for a day of Christmas cheer, no less? It's a brilliant PR move! Golden! I don't know why I didn't think of it. And why didn't you tell me that you were thinking about doing something like this? Instead, I had to find out from Kendall, who by the way, is an excellent shopper. So asking her to go Christmas shopping for this nine-year-old child was absolutely right up her alley."

"We're not using this as a publicity stunt," King d.Avid said solemnly and matter-of-factly.

"What?" Vincent came closer and stood over King d.Avid as he sat there on the glaringly white couch with his legs crossed. "What do you mean we're not using this for publicity?"

"Just what I said. I'm not doing this to further my career or to make people think I'm some great, charitable person. I'm doing this because of a promise I made to a dear friend a long time ago. A friend I didn't even get to talk with much before he died. A friend, in fact, that I didn't even know had died until weeks after his funeral."

Vincent sat down in the white wingback chair across from King d.Avid. "I told you I was sorry about that. I didn't know he was *that* important to you. Had I known, I promise I would have made sure his calls got through. And I definitely would have made sure you got the message that he'd been killed. But then again, you were dealing with that PR nightmare of a divorce from your third wife, much like now with your current wife. Man, that one *still* gives me chills thinking about it. We were *all* in a tizzy back then."

"But I told you who all were important to me, Vincent. I

told you. It's hard for me to believe you merely made a mistake when it came to my friend Jonathan. Well, there's nothing either of us can do to change that now. My friend may be gone, but there is something that I can do for his son. And I'm planning on doing that without fanfare from your end or any ulterior motives. Period. End of discussion. Whatever I do for him is coming completely from my heart. Understood?"

"Of course," Vincent said with a smile and a nod. "But you know I can't control what other people do. Who's to say that this Mack fellow won't leak it to the media?"

"Who said anything about Mack?"

"Excuse me?" Vincent said with a slightly nervous frown.

"I never mentioned Mack or Jonathan's name. All I told Kendall is that I needed her to buy things for a nine-year-old boy. I informed her he was crippled because I wanted to be sure that whatever she bought was appropriate, considering his condition. But I never told her his, my late friend Jonathan's, or his guardian's name." King d.Avid uncrossed his leg and leaned forward. "So how would you happen to know this?"

"Listen, I know you might not understand this fully, but I've worked very hard to get you where you are today."

"Oh, *you've* worked very hard? So I suppose the Lord and I had nothing to do with my ultimate success."

"King d.Avid, you know what I mean. And I'm not going to let up on doing my job and allow you to do something that will undermine *all* of our works: mine, yours, or the Lord's. So I keep my finger on the pulse of everything that goes on around here. That's my job. After I found out that Kendall was about to go shopping on your behalf, I questioned Chad."

King d.Avid began to nod slowly. "Oh, yeah. And Chad *sang* like a bird."

"Actually, he didn't. It took a bit of doing, but I finally got it out of him. Chad's loyal to you, you can believe that. And as long as he's a good and loyal team member, I will agree that he should remain as head of security."

"Hmmm. I see. So I guess *you* make all of these types of decisions on my behalf?"

"In accordance *with* you," Vincent said with a grin and another nod. "King, what's getting into you? You've never acted this way before. You know I'm your ace; you know I'm here for you and only you. There's still more for us to conquer; more listening hearts, more fans waiting to be possessed. And between the two of us, we're going to get all we can. You always told me you didn't like 'yes' people in your life. Well"—Vincent leaned forward—"I'm the one who will stand up for you and *to* you, even if it means having to fight *you*, in order to do it."

"Right," King d.Avid said, biting down on his bottom lip. "Well, you just make sure that my visit this weekend with Melvin doesn't end up leaving these walls. And I'm not worried about Mack putting it out there. So if it does just *happen* to leak out, believe me, I'll be looking uncompromisingly in your direction. And trust me, Vincent: things won't be pretty. Understand?"

Vincent smiled curtly. "Absolutely." He stood up. "Don't bother getting up. I'll let myself out, the same way I let myself in."

King d.Avid sat back against the couch and closed his eyes. He began to pray and to thank God for all of his blessings.

Chapter 6

*Then king David sent, and fetched him out of the
house of Machir, the son of Ammiel, from Lo-debar.*
—2 Samuel 9:5

Brianna looked out of the window. For some reason, there was a white, stretch limousine in her driveway. She didn't have a clue who it could be. The front passenger-side limo door opened and a big bulked, light-skinned man, with a perfectly clean-shaven head, stepped out. He walked to the driver's side back door and opened it. She saw the tall, lean, and handsome dark-skinned man step out and stand up, adjusting his stylish, long black suit coat, his signature apparel.

She opened her door and ran outside, straight into his arms. "Mack!" Brianna said, as the two of them hugged.

"Little sister," Mack said. "Look at you." He stepped back and scanned her from head to toe. "Marriage looks like it's *definitely* agreeing with you."

"Yeah, well." She hugged him again. "What are you doing here? Why didn't you call and let me know you were coming? I would have cooked already."

"Well, I can't stay but a few minutes. I'm here visiting with someone else, but you know I couldn't dare come to Atlanta and not stop by and say hello to my beautiful little sister." Mack glanced at the house. "So this is where you live?"

"Yeah. It's not much, but it's a start."

"It's more than a lot of people have, so don't knock it," Mack said.

"Oh, I wasn't knocking it. I would never do that. I'm thankful for what we have," Brianna said. "But you still haven't answered my question. What are you doing here?" She looked inside of the limo and saw the young boy.

Mack smiled. "As I said, I'm here visiting with someone, but I wanted to swing by and see you first . . . see where you live and all. I also wanted to introduce you to Melvin." He nodded toward the nine-year-old in the limousine. "He's part of our family now. After two years, it's finally official. The adoption was *just* finalized."

Brianna smiled as she stuck her head inside of the limo. "Hi there, Melvin. I'm Brianna. It's nice to meet you." She presented her hand to him to shake.

"Hi, Auntie Brianna. Daddy Mack has told me all about you. He even showed me pictures of you when you were a little girl. I'm pleased to finally meet you," a bubbly Melvin said, giving her hand a quick and deliberate pump.

"Oh," she said, placing her hand over her heart. "You called me Auntie Brianna." She touched his other hand that rested on one of his legs. It was then that she really gave notice to the braces on his legs. Standing back up straight, she looked at Mack and said, "You're not going to come inside at all? Not even for a few minutes?"

"No. We have to be somewhere." Mack discreetly used his head to point at Melvin to indicate it was for him.

Brianna lowered her voice, almost to a whisper. "So . . . where are you going?"

The man who had opened the door for Mack suddenly rocked his otherwise stilled, at-attention stand, a few times. Mack didn't even glance his way.

"Brianna, I'm going to have to come up another time, and you and I will spend some real quality time together." Mack hugged her. "But we do have to run. I love you."

"Oh, I get it. Nona," Brianna said, nodding her head as she grinned.

Mack grinned back, then let out a quick, short laugh. "Nona. Well, I must say, I haven't heard or said that one in a long while. 'What are you doing?' Nona. 'Where are you going?' Nona. 'What's nona?' None of your business."

Brianna smiled. "So you don't have to say it, big brother. I get it. It's nona—none of my business. But, I *am* glad you came by. I absolutely would have been upset with you had I found out you were here in the city and you didn't even have the decency to come by. Especially since you didn't make it to my Thanksgiving dinner, which, incidentally, was fabulous. And you haven't been here to see us since we moved to Atlanta."

"That's precisely why I came by. It's just been a lot going on lately. You know. It's been really hard." Mack put his arm around her shoulders, squeezing her against him.

Brianna broke away from her brother's grip after a few more squeezes, bent down, and smiled once again at Melvin. "I'm looking forward to you coming back soon and *really* getting to visit with me. You hear? I know my husband would love to meet you. So you can't be a stranger any longer. I want to spend time with you. I mean it."

"Okay, Auntie Brianna," Melvin said. "I'm sure Daddy Mack and I will be back." He leaned toward her. "If Daddy Mack says it, he's going to keep his word. You can count on it, no matter *what* the devil may do to try and stop things. Right, Daddy Mack?"

"Right," Mack said, winking Melvin's way, then sticking his hand inside of the limo where Melvin promptly slapped it, effectively giving him five.

"Okay," Brianna said. "I'm going to hold the *both* of you to that."

Mack got back into the limo. The bulked, light-skinned, shaved-head man closed the door, then gave Brianna a polite smile and a quick nod as he walked decisively back around to the front passenger side, never saying one word.

Brianna stood and waved as she watched the limo back out of her driveway. She was glad to see her brother after almost a year now. But she couldn't help but wonder where the two of them were going, and why Mack felt he couldn't trust her enough to tell her.

But then, Mack was strange like that. He'd kept Melvin away from them through this whole process of getting, then adopting him. But he had told her that things had been hard. Maybe that's why he'd done things in this way—keeping all of them from meeting and spending time together until the papers were officially approved. It was his way of protecting all concerned. Why have all of them end up bonding, just to have their hearts wrenched apart later, if there was even a remote possibility Melvin might not get to stay with him?

That would have been hard on everybody. But especially difficult on someone who'd been through so much in his short little life already. And Melvin had indeed endured a lot—too much for Mack to be responsible, in any way, for any more pain and heartache, if it was at all possible not to do so.

So when she really thought about it, Brianna understood her brother's possible motive and reasoning behind some of his actions better now. Much better now.

Chapter 7

He made darkness his secret place; his pavilion
round about him were dark waters and thick clouds
of the skies.

—Psalm 18:11

"Girl, I'm telling you," Alana said. "That preacher stood right there on that pulpit, preaching his heart out, and he said, 'Shadrach, Meshach, and a billy goat.' "

"Girl, no," Brianna said as she cracked up laughing. "Maybe he was only trying to make a cute little joke."

"That's exactly what I thought at first: he's just joking. Because you know when we were little girls, children used to get it wrong and say stuff like that all the time. But all throughout this man's sermon, and I mean he thought he was preaching up a storm, too, he said, 'Shadrach, Meshach, and a billy goat did this,' and 'Shadrach, Meshach, and a billy goat did that.' " Alana fell back against the couch, her right hand pressed against her chest as she snickered.

"I hope you didn't laugh out loud like you're doing now."

Alana continued laughing. "I promise you, I tried not to laugh when he first said it. But when he kept on saying 'And a billy goat,' I thought, This man doesn't have a clue that's not his name. I wanted to yell out, 'It's Abednego! A-bed-ne-go! Not a bil-ly goat!' But I confess, Brianna, I was laughing so hard, I started falling all over the person sitting next to me. Of course, anyone there who knew he didn't know what he was talking about couldn't hold their laughs in, either. So we were letting loose all over that place. And do you know what the people without a clue said when service dismissed?"

Brianna shook her head. "I'm almost afraid to ask."

"They said, 'The Holy Ghost sure did move today. The Spirit of Laughter was jumping all over folks in church. That was some powerful message that Pastor preached, wasn't it?' " Alana fanned herself in an attempt to calm her laugh and her giggles. She wiped at her eyes to rid herself of the tears that had now come from laughing so hard. "I looked at those folks and burst out laughing right in their faces when they said that to me. I keep telling you, Brianna. You need to come visit this church with me one Sunday."

"For what? All you do is talk about the silly stuff that goes on there. I don't want to go to church and when I get home I can't tell anybody anything the pastor said—"

"I just told you what the pastor said," Alana said, chuckling some more. "Shadrach, Meshach—"

"I mean anything that really matters."

"I can't help it if those people are funny." Alana took in a deep breath and began to snicker again. She fanned herself some more, then burst into a belly laugh once again.

Brianna glanced over at Alana and shook her head. "I think the only reason you even go there is so you can get your comic relief."

Alana continued to fan her face, trying to dry up her laughing tears before they emerged. "Hey, it's certainly cheaper than the comedy club. It's not my fault they don't know that they're funny. To them, they're just 'having church.' Can I get an Amen?"

"I'm not going to play with you," Brianna said. "Last week, you talked about a lady who was up fussing while testifying. What you said was like texting while driving."

Alana started laughing again. "Brianna, please, don't get me going again. That lady got up and started talking. She started telling folks' business by way of calling out the folks who needed to get their lives together and repent for sins that '*everybody* in the church knows' they're doing. Everybody, apparently, except *me*." Alana paused. "Hey, wait a minute, unless she was talking about me." Alana smiled. "Anyway, she was giving little shouts in between her testimony. But as she was talking, her false teeth kept slipping out. I think they're supposed to glue false teeth in or something like that; I'm pretty sure that's what they're supposed to do. Because I've seen people with false teeth before, and they don't normally have to keep pushing them back into their mouths when they talk."

"Stop, Alana," Brianna said, doing her best to hold back a laugh that was on the verge of bursting forth. "You're not going to get me to laugh again about this. It's wrong, and God is going to get us both for this. I'm telling you. God is going to get you."

Alana kept on, laughing and occasionally nudging Brianna as she spoke. "That woman must have gotten tired of pushing her dentures back in while she was talking, so she just reached up, yanked them bad boys out of her mouth, stuck those teeth in the pocket of her fancy silk dress, and kept right on talking like nothing ever happened."

Brianna was laughing and shaking her head at this point. "You're wrong for that, Alana. You're wrong. You keep on, and you're going to Hell with gasoline drawers on. And if you do, don't say I didn't warn you."

"Well, you're laughing. So I suspect if you'd been there, you would have been falling out with me. And FYI: I don't *wear* drawers *or* granny panties, I'm just saying."

Brianna sat up straight and pulled herself together. "Okay, no more. That's why I won't visit that church with you. I'm looking for a church that's preaching the Word. And if I was there with you, you'd have us both cutting up most likely. You need to find a church where you can be fed."

Alana frowned and held her head to one side. "I'm being

fed. I'm just getting the best of both worlds. I get to go to church while at the same time getting my comedy relief on. Think of it as a two-for-one special. For instance, I learned today that Shadrach, Meshach, and a billy goat were bound with their coats, their leggings, and their hats and other garments and thrown into that fiery furnace. Coats, leggings, *and* a hat in a hot, fiery furnace . . . *that's* sizzling hot there! And when Nebuchadnezzar looked in, he saw the three were loose, walking in the midst of the fire, without a hurt on them. And there was a fourth man in there with them who Nebuchadnezzar declared was like the Son of God."

"Well, that was good," Brianna said.

"Yeah. You and I have heard this story many times before. Anyway, then Nebuchadnezzar called out, 'Shadrach, Meshach, and a billy goat, you servants of the most high God, come forth, and come hither!' And Shadrach, Meshach, and a billy goat came forth out of the midst of the fire." Alana smiled and moved her head in rhythm to an unheard, but lively beat. "See, now that's the Word right there. Go in the fire looking good; and come out looking just as good. What a mighty God we serve!"

"So, did you ever tell the preacher that the name is Abednego and not a billy goat?"

Alana pulled back and looked Brianna up and down two times. "Who, me?" She placed her hand on her chest. "Try and tell a preacher something he's doing is *wrong?*" Alana huffed. "Oh, I think not." Alana then turned more squarely toward Brianna and composed herself. "Okay, enough of the silly stuff. So . . . how is married life?"

Brianna was glad she'd gotten to spend her anniversary with Unzell. They had planned on going on a real honeymoon on their one-year anniversary, but that wasn't possible this year. Again, Unzell only had a few days home and he had to work hard just to get those. For the Christmas holiday, he was off for three days, then back to work. King d.Avid's troop was scheduled to be gone for two more weeks, having already been gone the whole week during New Year's. Brianna put on her best face for her friend.

"It's great," Brianna said cheerily. "Unzell will be gone another two weeks. King d.Avid and his troop have a pretty heavy concert schedule. But Unzell always comes home whenever he can."

"They sure do work a lot, even around the holidays. I would think someone in King d.Avid's position or any of these big entertainers would make sure they were off for a long time during Christmas and New Year's."

"Well, you know how it is," Brianna said. "Most folks like having something special to do around the holidays. So, that's when people in the entertainment field find themselves working the most. Like that party you attended on New Year's Day: people had to work so you all could celebrate and enjoy yourselves the way you did."

"And girl, I'm telling you: I brought the New Year in *right*, do you hear me? But you're right. You're right. There was a smashing band playing, so that meant they had to work. The hotel staff folks had to work; the people who prepared all of that food and kept the champagne flowing, they were working their tails off. I guess we don't think about the folks who clock in on those types of days so that the rest of us can enjoy ourselves partying. It's almost like we believe little work fairies come in and get things done."

Brianna nodded. "So, have you found another job yet?"

"I knew that's where you were going to end up. Just as soon as we started talking about people working to ensure that other folks are able to enjoy their special days, I knew the conversation was going to somehow pivot to me," Alana said. "But I'm telling you: those people should have let me off like I asked them to. I don't want to work like a Hebrew slave every single weekend. Who does? I realize that's their busy time, but I'd like to be able to get busy myself and have some fun. How else is a girl or guy going to meet Mister or Miss Right?"

Brianna held up both hands in surrender. "I didn't say a

word about that. I just asked if you'd found another job yet. That's all."

"No . . . I haven't. And honestly, I think all of this turned out for the best." Alana smirked a bit.

"Okay, spill it," Brianna said.

"What?"

"Don't *what* me. Who is he? What's his name? Give me the lowdown."

Alana broke into a full grin and again turned back squarely to Brianna. She became all giddy. "His name is Vincent Powers. And from all I can tell, he's doing quite well for himself. He does something or other in the music industry."

"Is he a singer? Anyone we've ever heard of?"

"No, he's not talented in that way. I think he does something behind the scenes."

Brianna frowned. "So how long have you known him?"

"I met him a month ago at a club. I was dancing and stuff, you know me. He came over, started talking, asked me to dance, then asked for my digits. Later, he said he was in the music industry and was always looking for new talent in all fields of the spectrum."

Brianna started laughing. "And you believed that weak pickup line?" She shook her head.

"I thought that's what it was at first, too," Alana said. "But he really does have some kind of job associated with the industry. He gave me a business card and everything."

"Do you have any idea how easy it is to create a business card with anything you want on it?"

"Well, I've been to his house. And if he's not doing something to pull in big money, then I don't know how he's paying for that lap of luxury."

"Have you ever heard of illegal drugs?" Brianna said. "The sex industry—"

"He's not into drugs or sex stuff. He's a very respectable man. Very intelligent. Highly controlled."

"But you didn't ask him specifically what he does and or for whom?" Brianna asked. "You do know that stuff can be verified, say, by going to Google, Yahoo . . . Bing?"

"No, I didn't push him further about his job. He told me what he wanted me to know . . . for now. I'll learn more as time progresses," Alana said. "I'll make sure he's on the up-and-up before I get knee deep into something I can't step out of."

"So the two of you are getting a little more serious? I thought this was about your dancing career."

"Yes, and yes," Alana said. "We *are* getting a bit more serious. We've gone out. I've been to his house—"

"Please tell me you didn't spend the night with him? Please tell me you didn't."

"Fine. I won't tell you then," Alana said, sitting up and staring forward with a straight face.

"Okay, so is he looking to do something for you in the line of your dancing?"

Alana turned back to look at Brianna. She smiled. "He is. But I don't think he's all that interested in really getting me a job. I think he and I might be moving toward something a little deeper."

Brianna began to shake her head.

"What?" Alana said. "See, that's why I didn't want to tell you anything just yet. I knew this is how you'd respond."

"You think he's interested in marrying you? After meeting him a month ago, then going out with him one time—"

"Two," Alana corrected.

"Okay, two times. And it looks like you've apparently spent the night with him. And now you actually believe he's interested in pursuing something more with you?"

"Why not, Brianna? Why can't someone meet me, spend some time with me, and be interested in me, enough to at least look at me as possible long-term material?"

Brianna took Alana's hand. "I didn't say that can't happen. It's just: you know more about these playas than even *I* do.

You know how playas are. You know how they run their mouths. And let's not even *begin* to talk about the sin you're stepping all in—"

"So now I'm supposed to be some kind of a playa expert?"

Brianna threw up her hands and released a sound of exasperation. "Alana, if anyone believes in you, you know that I do. I know what a great person you are. I'm not saying things to try and put you down or to take anything away from you. But you keep doing the same thing over and over again and expecting different results. The names change, but you're singing the same old song."

"Why can't you just trust me the way I trust you, and be happy for me the way I'm always happy for you?"

Brianna looked at Alana. She saw the watery pleading begin to pool in her friend's eyes. "Okay. Okay. You're the one with this guy. You certainly know more about him than I do. I've not met him in person, so what do I know? As long as he's not a drug user, drug dealer, a drug kingpin, a pimp, a porn director, or something that could land him behind bars, I'm okay with you seeing him."

"Oh, so now you get to sign off on the men that I'm allowed to date?" Alana said, smiling.

"Somebody has to look after you," Brianna said. "Now, back to the original topic: jobwise, what are your plans?"

Alana shrugged. "I just know I'm not planning on serving tables again. I know that much. I'm not waitress material. Waitresses should get congressional medals."

"In other words, you're going to put yourself into the hands of this new man you really know nothing about, and hope for the best."

Alana stood up. "For now, I'm just going to see where things lead. Not everybody can be like you. You don't have to get a job if you don't want to. But Vincent knows people in the industry. He knows I'm interested in dancing in videos. Who knows, maybe . . . just maybe, he'll come through for me. And if things happen to continue heating up between the two of us and continue to move forward, who can say. Maybe I won't need to worry about working outside of the home unless I want to, just like you."

Brianna forced a smile, but it was hard to keep the corners of her mouth from betraying her true feelings. "Sounds good to me."

Alana cocked her head to one side. "Do you mean that, or are you just trying to keep from arguing with me?"

Brianna stood up. "I mean it." She hugged Alana. "I mean it." She let go and looked at Alana. "Oh, and since I've not been able to find a job, I'm planning on doing something different the next few months. I've signed up to take a college course."

"You're going back to college?" Alana sounded excited.

"Not full time. I've always wanted to take some courses on religion, so I thought I'd do that now. You know . . . get back in the swing of things, especially with Unzell being gone so much these days."

"Well, I think it's great. You adored college back when you were there that time."

"Yeah, I did. It was Unzell's idea. I was looking for a job and you, of all people, know how slim the pickings are, especially now and particularly in the secretarial field. So Unzell suggested I go back to college and pursue my dreams. Maybe you should think about going to college as well. We could do this together. It would be fun. Just like in the old days—me and you, tackling school, doing homework together and stuff."

"I'm not interested in going to college. Nope. It's just not something I care about. So we can drop *that*," Alana said. "But your husband really is a great guy. He really is."

Brianna smiled. "He is. He's just *gone* so much. I only wish we got to spend more time together. And then when he *is* home, he's tired. And all he really wants is to chill out around the house and watch sports. Of course, there's always a game on. From August until the first week in February, it's generally football with sprinkles of basketball when basketball season begins. After football, he's usually full-blown into basketball. Unzell is really not all that crazy about baseball, not until it's playoff time, anyway. But he *does* love himself some sports—that's for sure."

"Well, that's what happens when you marry a jock. And not one merely in heart alone, but one who dreamed about being out there on a professional basis," Alana said.

"I know. But he's such a good man. He works, and pretty much puts every single dime that he makes into our joint account. He comes home every break he gets . . ."

"And still, I detect a twinge of unhappiness lurking there," Alana said.

"Not unhappiness. I just thought being married would be different. You know, you have these dreams of what married life will be like. At least, I did. The love you had when you were dating, you're looking for it to become even more intense, to move to an even higher . . . greater level. You know what I mean?" Brianna said.

"I know. Those fairy tales really kick our reality tails, don't they? The handsome prince riding in on a white horse to take us away to 'happily ever after' land," Alana said.

"I don't think we look for a prince on a white horse. At least, I never did."

"Oh, we do. We don't want to admit that we do, but we do. We want this man to come into our lives and treat us like a princess . . . a queen. We want to be the center of his world. We want to feel like we're loved, and that no one or nothing else trumps that love for us." Alana chuckled. "Then reality sets in. And it's back to the real world with real problems and real issues with real consequences." Alana reached over and hugged Brianna. "And on *that* note, I think I'll make my way out of your door. I have to figure out how I'm going to pay my rent for two months, or get an extension. Otherwise, I'll be looking for *my* prince to come riding in on his white horse or black horse . . . his donkey; I don't care what it is. It can be a mule . . . a bicycle . . . a tricycle . . . electric scooter. I'll be looking for someone."

Brianna shook her head. "I *do* hope you're joking."

Alana hugged Brianna again as she opened the door to leave. "I wish." She waved good-bye, then smiled. "I wish."

Chapter 8

He bindeth up the waters in his thick clouds; and
the cloud is not rent under them.

—Job 26:8

Brianna stepped into the house and out of the pouring rain, putting her wet umbrella inside the umbrella holder near the door. She quickly looked around the room as Alana stood there wearing shades. It had been more than a month since they'd seen each other. Brianna immediately let out a short laugh. "What's up with the shades in the house?" Brianna asked her.

Alana touched the arm of the shades. "I had misplaced them and found them when you called and said you were on your way over. I just put them on," Alana said.

"Well, they're real cute on you, but you need to take them off in the house." Brianna looked around the dark room. "It sure is dark in here. You don't seem to get a lot of daylight, that's for certain. Maybe you should open up the blinds or something."

"I was cooking when you called. I need to finish before Dre arrives." Alana led Brianna to the kitchen, her shades still intact. "He likes for his food to be ready when he gets home from work."

Brianna touched Alana on the arm. Alana immediately jerked back as though Brianna's touch had burned her. "What's going on with you?" Brianna asked.

"Nothing."

"You moved in with this guy last month and I don't ever see or hear from you," Brianna said. "Something's up?"

Alana opened the refrigerator and took out two thick, grade-A cut steaks. She rinsed the cuts in the sink. Putting them on a board, she began to beat them with a steel mallet. "I told you: nothing's up. I've just been really busy, that's all. You're in college doing religious studies. You should appreciate busy." Alana didn't look up as she spoke.

"Can you put that down for a minute and look at me?"

Alana glanced up. "I need to finish. Dre will be home pretty soon. I'm glad you stopped by. You're right. It's been too long since we've had a good chat. I need to do better, and I promise that I will." She returned to beating the steaks.

Brianna walked closer to Alana so she could hear through all of the pounding. "You need to tell me what's going on. And I'm not going anywhere until you do."

Alana began to pound the steaks harder. "How is school?" she asked.

"School is fine. I'm taking this course on Jewish culture and religion. You know, I told you I wanted to learn more about their traditions since, in truth: Jesus was Jewish before Christianity took hold. I want a deeper understanding of the story behind the story. I want to know the basis of some of the things we as Christians practice."

Alana stopped beating the steaks and seasoned them. "Yeah, I remember. You were talking about things like sacrifices from the Old Testament and how they apply to things we see in the New Testament. What was it you called it?" She flipped each steak.

"Types and shadows," Brianna said, sitting on a barstool. "It's when things in the Old Testament point toward the fulfillment of things in the New Testament. You know, like the sacrifices for sin being certain animals in accordance to the sin. The sacrifice of a lamb without a spot or wrinkle and the blood of the lamb found in the Old Testament as atonement for sin, being a type and shadow of Jesus—the ultimate Lamb without a spot or wrinkle given by God, the ultimate sacrifice with the ultimate atonement for our sins."

"Yeah, that's real interesting. I'm glad you're enjoying the class. You seem to be learning a lot." Alana put the meat on a pan and in the bottom oven. She digitally keyed in four hundred fifty degrees. "I need to keep a good watch on this. Dre doesn't like for his steaks to be overcooked. He hates for his meat to be dry."

"Alana, I understand why you decided to move in with this guy. I do. But then, I don't. I mean, I offered one of our spare rooms to you until you got back on your feet."

Alana put the towel down, having rinsed and dried her hands. She hugged herself as she spoke. "I told you back then, when you suggested it, that I wasn't going to impose on you and Unzell. This is fine. It works."

"I don't think so," Brianna said. "Something is off with you. The last time you and I *really* talked was around the end of January."

"Yeah. That's about when I got kicked out of my apartment. I can't believe that man wouldn't give me just a little more time to come up with my rent. That was just wrong." Alana sat down on a barstool at the counter next to Brianna.

"How was he wrong? He'd already given you extra time," Brianna said. "Twice."

"Yeah, I know. But I thought things were going to go differently with Vincent. Then I wouldn't have needed to pay at all. That went south quicker than I saw it coming."

"Well, I kind of told you—"

"I know, Brianna. You told me he was a playa. You told me he wasn't really that into me. I know."

"I never said he was a playa. And I never said he wasn't into you. I've never even met the guy. When I mentioned playas, I was speaking in general."

"Well, you were right. He didn't do anything to help me get a video dancing job. And after that last time I stayed the night over at his house, he conveniently became unavailable. Lame excuses about him being out of the state or out of the country for a week, which is the reason he gave for not getting back to me, as though cell phones don't work in other states or countries. He was probably lying anyway about being some big shot. He was most likely house-sitting that house he claimed was his. You know, if I really cared, I'd go over there and watch the house, just to see who comes and goes in and out of it." Alana began to play tiddlywinks with her fingers.

"Please don't do that, Alana. Please don't stalk this guy the way you did that other one."

"Oh, I'm not. I've moved on. And I'm not a stalker. But Dre came along at the right time. He said I was welcome to stay here. We're doing all right. But I definitely wasn't going to stay at your house, imposing on you and Unzell during this time of your marriage. Now, if the two of you were old married coots or at least had a few years of wedding bliss under your belts, I might have taken you up on your offer," Alana said. "But nope, not this early in the game. And on top of that, you say the two of you don't get to spend that much time together as it is." Alana shook her head. "No way am I going to add to the problem. This is fine. Things seems to be working out okay for everybody."

"I keep telling you that because of his job, Unzell is hardly ever home. And when he comes home, he mostly sits in front of the television. If you had come and stayed with us for a while, at least I would have had some company, *somebody* to talk to."

Alana got up and turned the meat over. "You're just saying that to try and make me feel like it would have been okay if I had come and stayed with you."

"I mean it. I'm worried about you." Brianna stood up.

Alana closed the oven door and stood back straight. "Well, don't be. I'm here with Dre. He likes me being here and being like the little wifey."

"But you're *not* his wife." Brianna snapped a little.

"I know *that*," Alana said with just as quick of a snap back, but harder.

"Well, you don't have to bite my head off about it."

Alana released a smile, albeit forced. "Sorry. I'm sorry. I guess I'm a little touchy about the subject. I never thought I would actually stoop to living with a man I wasn't married to. Remember when we were young and we used to say, 'No ring, no thing.'" Alana began to snicker. "Well, I needed a place to lay my head, and Dre stepped in and gave me a bed." Alana grinned. "Get it? My own little rhyme . . . lay my head, gave me a bed. Look. I can't be mad at a man for caring enough to do that."

"Alana, why don't you take off those shades? Here it is raining outside, and you're parading around the house sporting shades."

"Excuse me, but these happen to be Dolce & Gabbana, thank you very much. And why does it bother you what I do in my own house?" Alana stepped back from Brianna, effectively putting more than an arm's length between the two of them.

Brianna walked back toward her. "Why won't you take them off? You're in the house no less, in March, cooking with shades on, albeit Dolce & Gabbana. I'd like to know why."

"I don't mean to be rude, but Dre will be home any minute now, and I'd rather you not be here when he arrives. So if you don't mind . . ." Alana walked toward the door, handed Brianna her now-dry umbrella, then put her hand on the knob to turn it.

Brianna quickly put her hand on top of Alana's and stopped her. "Take off the shades and I'll go."

"Brianna, leave it alone, okay?"

"No. I want you to take off those shades, look me in my eyes, and tell me you're really okay."

Alana tried to smile. "I'm okay. I'm okay."

"Then take off your shades and say it as you gaze into my eyes."

Alana slowly took off the shades. She began to chuckle a little. "I know you're not going to believe this. But I was getting something out of the cabinet yesterday, and this bottle fell down out of nowhere and pow . . . right dead in my eye."

Brianna touched Alana gently on her chin as she turned her face to get a better look. "That's *really* black and blue."

"Yeah, I know. And it hurt like all get out, too, when it happened."

"And you *claim* it was a bottle that fell out of the cabinet is what hit you?"

Alana moved her face out of Brianna's hand. "I don't *claim* anything. I told you what happened. That's why I put on these shades. I knew if you saw me, you would immediately jump to the wrong conclusion. That's what people like you do."

"Well, you have to admit, it's mighty suspicious. You have a black eye that was conveniently put there from a fallen bottle," Brianna said. "What kind of bottle was it again?"

"Look, Brianna. I don't have to lie. You of all people know that if a man had done this to me, I would have beat the crap out of him. I then would have called and told you that I did it, and why."

"Yeah, the Alana I used to know would have done that. But you're not the Alana I used to know. You're changing."

Alana sighed. "We're both changing. It's called life, Brianna. Life. We evolve. We change. Things change. Situations change. But I can promise you, if Dre, or anybody else, had been responsible for this"—she pointed at her black eye—"you would know it."

Brianna nodded. "Okay. I just hope you know that I'm here for you. And I hope you also know that you don't ever have to put up with a man, any man, hitting or mistreating you. Not when you have folks like me in your corner. And, Alana . . . with me newly married or not, if you need to come and stay with me and Unzell while you get it together, our door is open." She touched Alana's hand.

Alana hugged Brianna like she didn't want to ever let go. "Thank you for that."

Just then the door opened, almost hitting Brianna and Alana. Alana immediately stiffened up, eyes widened. "Oh, my goodness! The meat!" Alana sprinted to the kitchen.

The man who had opened the door closed it, then reared back as he began to scan Brianna from her head to her toe with a deep slow sweeping of his eyes. "Hi there. I'm Draper Simpson." He presented his hand to her. "But everybody calls me Dre."

"I'm Brianna Waters, Alana's best friend." Brianna half-heartedly shook his hand.

"Yeah, she's mentioned your name several times," Dre said. "I'm glad after all of this time, I finally get to meet Alana's friend *Bri*anna." He looked around the room. "So, where did Alana go?"

Brianna looked toward the kitchen. "Into the kitchen. She was cooking. I sort of interrupted her when I stopped by unannounced. In fact, she was seeing me out, and—"

"Hi, baby," Alana said, walking toward Dre. "How was your day?"

He looked at her as though he didn't know how to respond. "It was good." He swiftly looked back to Brianna. "Did Alana tell you what happened to her eye?"

"Yeah, baby," Alana said. "I told her what a huge klutz I am."

"Yep," Dre said. "She's always falling or running into a door. I'm starting to think I need to child-proof this place or something."

"Except this time, it really wasn't my fault. That bottle just seemed to come out of nowhere and bam!" Alana chuckled. "Right in my eye."

"Oh, yeah . . . the bottle," Dre said.

"Listen," Brianna said to Alana, "I'm going to go. I hope I didn't cause you to overcook your steaks." Brianna turned toward Dre. "If the steaks are overdone, it was all my fault. Alana was walking me to the door, kicking me to the curb, and you know how it is with best friends."

"Oh, yeah. No problem. If it's overcooked, I'll just tough it out, or she can cook another one." He put his arm around Alana. Brianna saw Alana cringe when he grabbed her, although she tried her best to play it off, flicking her hair off her forehead.

"Well, it was nice meeting you," Brianna said to Dre. "I'll call and talk to you later," she said to Alana.

Alana smiled. "It was good seeing you. Thanks for stopping by." She opened the door. "Oh, look. The sun is shining while it's raining."

Brianna nodded without comment, then left. She stood outside the door for a minute. "The devil is beating his wife," she whispered as she opened her umbrella.

Just as she was about to walk away, she heard Dre say, "What was *she* doing here?"

"She's my friend. That's what friends do."

"Well, from now on if the two of you want to visit, you need to go somewhere else. She was just over here being nosy. That's all that was about. And why were you walking around with that shiner showing like that?"

"What am I supposed to do? Walk around the house with shades on?" Alana said.

"Oh, I *know* you're not getting smart with me," Dre said. "I know you're not. I have told you about your big mouth. Because you know that you're more than welcome to get your stuff and get to stepping. You got me?"

"Dre, stop being such a drama queen." There were a few seconds, then Alana said, "Let go! You're hurting me."

Brianna started to knock on the door to interrupt, but she stopped her fist in midair. She knew Alana wouldn't appreciate her doing something like this. She and Alana would talk later.

Oh, they would *definitely* talk later.

Chapter 9

And it came to pass, after the year was expired, at the time when kings go forth to battle, that David sent Joab, and his servants with him, and all Israel; and they destroyed the children of Ammon, and besieged Rabbah. But David tarried still at Jerusalem.

—2 Samuel 11:1

It was the end of April. Brianna was still disturbed about Alana, but Alana insisted, first of all, that she was not being abused—physically or otherwise; and second, that Brianna needed to stay out of her business. So Brianna tried to oblige.

Brianna called Alana on her cell phone. "Alana, in class, we've been learning about a mikvah. I'd like to visit a real one in person. Why don't you come go with me?"

"Not that I'm interested in going, but what is a mikvah?"

"It's associated with a Jewish ritual dealing with water," Brianna said. "Okay, a mikvah is a pool-like place used when there's a need or desire for purity, repentance, or in removing the impurity of sin." Brianna said it as though she were taking a test. She then stopped. "Are you really interested in knowing this, or are you just humoring me?"

"I'm interested. I love it when you learn stuff and then share it with me. It definitely keeps me in the know. And you always break the hard stuff down and make it so easy that anybody can understand it," Alana said. "So, please; continue to school me."

Brianna smiled. She loved having someone to share with. The last time Unzell had been home was about four weeks ago. King d.Avid was performing in cities across the United

States, one city right after another. Unzell and the rest of the crew had to arrive before King d.Avid to have everything set up for the stage. Then after the concert was over, they had to break everything down. The set, the lighting, the sound, everything that made King d.Avid's concerts the talk of the town they had become, his stage crew was responsible for it.

Now that Unzell was part of the crew, Brianna had been hoping he could get her in to at least *speak* to King d.Avid. And even though it was known that King d.Avid had a lavish mansion in Atlanta where he generally returned after being on the road, Unzell didn't think it was appropriate to impose.

"Maybe later," Unzell had said. "I just don't want to appear like I'm using my position in the wrong way. Let me get better established first. I've never truthfully spoken to King d.Avid on a personal basis. He sends his messages and requests through Jock."

"It's fine. I just wanted you to know I'd love to meet him again. I told you he and I met when I was ten. But that was before he was *the* King d.Avid he's now become."

Unzell laughed. "Well, you know it is said that there are six degrees of separation between us and people we want to meet, no matter how famous the person might be. I suppose maybe it's true. There was a time, not so long ago, when you were six degrees between me and King d.Avid. Now it looks like I'm six degrees between you and him."

Brianna knew Unzell was referring to her grandfather having known King d.Avid at one time. Still, it didn't appear she'd be saying hello to the King himself, not anytime soon—six degrees or not. And now, because of King d.Avid's unrelenting and extensive tour schedule, there seemed to be six degrees separating her from her husband.

"Earth to Brianna!" Alana continued to repeat over the phone. "Earth to Brianna!"

Brianna snapped back to the present. "I'm sorry. Were you saying something?"

"Yeah. I asked if *any* pool would work for a mikvah?"

"I apologize. My mind wandered there for a minute. I was thinking about Unzell and how much I miss him. He's been gone for four weeks now and not due home for eight or so more weeks, if what he says still stands. That's a long time to be away."

"Do you think he needs to find another job then?" Alana said.

"Oh, no. This is sort of how things would have been had he been playing in the NFL. He would have been gone a lot. But with the NFL, he would have been home for a few days, or I could have flown to where he was, and we could have seen each other a bit more regularly. Here, it's not the case. Unzell compares what he's doing now somewhat to military duty. Not putting his life on the line the way deployed soldiers do, but having to be away from family and friends and sacrificing time with them for a greater good."

"I can see that analogy. King. d.Avid will tell you in a heart-beat that there's a war going on, and we're soldiers on the battlefield for our Lord," Alana said. "Charge!"

"Oh, girl. I love that song! 'On the Battlefield.' Yes!" Brianna cheered. "Yes! King d.Avid takes being in the army of the Lord seriously. According to Unzell, King d.Avid thinks of his concert tours as a way of conquering the world, as a tool to win souls to the Lord. He's tearing down strongholds, destroying yokes, and building up the people of God. Some who are in the fight *for* their lives; some in the fight *of* their lives. He says that the devil doesn't take time off and neither should we. Except to recharge. King d.Avid is serious about his calling. Unzell loves what he's doing; he won't find another job. He feels like he's part of a ministry, and his assignment is to ensure the atmosphere is properly set for those who are to receive what God is doing through King d.Avid onstage. Besides, they're getting a two-month break at the end of June. It'll be all right."

"Okay, so finish telling me about this mikvah."

"Yeah. I'll try to condense this down as much as possible.

Whenever you hear me say the word *mikvah* or anything that
has to do with God and water, I'd like for you to think of redeeming waters."

"Redeeming waters?" Alana said. "Well, okay."

"Yeah. You see: water is an important factor when you think
of God. What I mean by that is: in Genesis we find in the first
chapter the mention of waters. In verse two, 'the earth was
without form, and void; and darkness was upon the face of the
deep. And the Spirit of God moved upon the face of the waters.' "

"I need to be there with you while you do this. I can see this
is going to be good."

"Come on over then. I'll fix us something to eat," Brianna
said. "It's been a long time since we've sat and broken bread
together."

"Oh, I don't want you to work. I'll stop and pick up something, and you can just reimburse me when I get there in, say . . .
forty minutes," Alana said with a laugh.

"Aren't you generous with *my* money? All right. Pick up
something, my treat."

"Okay, since you insist," Alana said. "I'll be there in a few!"

Alana showed up two hours later with Chinese food. "Sorry
I'm so late. But Dre came home tripping, asking me what I
cooked. I told him I hadn't cooked anything. And that I wasn't
going to cook anything. Not today. I told him he could do
whatever he did *before* I moved in."

"Are you sure he's going to be all right?" Brianna asked. "I
don't want him going off on you because of me. And I sure
don't want any more 'accidents' taking place."

Alana waved Brianna off. "I'm not worried about him. He
was gone for two days, and then comes home talking about
'What did you cook?' He can go back wherever he was those
two days and eat there. I ain't no fool now." Alana sat down in
the den and took the food out of the bag. "I got our favorites.
It really *has* been a long time since you and I have had a good

visit like this." Alana bowed her head and said a quick, silent grace, then began eating. "I am *starving!*"

Brianna laughed. "I see. I was going to go get us a plate to eat on."

"We don't need any plates. This is fine just like it is," Alana said, chewing and eating out of the box. "Now, finish telling me about mikvah and the waters and whatever else you want to talk about. Tonight is girls' night out."

Brianna sat back as she ate and talked. "Let's see, where was I?"

"Genesis. Talking about how the Spirit of God *moved* upon the face of the waters. I wonder why it said the waters had a face? Like that means something or something."

"You know . . . I hadn't thought about that," Brianna said.

"Well, you're the thinker. Anyway, go on." Alana picked up some rice on her fork and hurriedly placed it in her mouth. "I just *love* how you put things together."

"Yes. Okay, so around the sixth verse, it says that God made the firmament. Firmament is—"

"See how you know me," Alana said. "I was just going to ask you about that."

"Yes, I know you well. Anyway, firmament is like an expanse between the waters. God had the waters supernaturally suspended, probably in vapor form. You know, half the waters on the earth, half suspended in the air, causing a greenhouse-like effect. This is likely where all of those flood waters suddenly came from—"

"You're talking about Noah and the flood? Because it had never rained before then. Redeeming waters!" Alana grinned. "A washing . . . a re-cleaning of the earth."

"Yeah. I just wanted to point out how water fit in early on. Then you think about when we were in our mother's womb. And where do we spend those nine months? What makes up over fifty percent of our bodies? And what must we drink in order to live?"

"*In* water, water, and we have to *drink* water to live," Alana said, smiling. "Oh, my goodness! This is *awesome!* We're in water for nine months, and then we come out and instantly learn to breathe air out here. Then we have to learn how to breathe and swim in water all over again. Our bodies are made up of water. And we need to drink water in order to live. That's really something when you actually think about it."

"Okay, now back to mikvah. This pool of water would be called 'mayim chayim,' which is living, nonstagnant waters. The Jewish have special pools just for mikvah, so you can't go get in any pool and think that will do. The word *mikvah* is based on the root 'hope.' If you can't get to a special pool for this ritual, then the ocean, a river, a well, or a flowing lake will work. In fact, that's what people used in the old days. That's the primal form of a mikvah. Going into a mikvah is like 're-turning to the womb' and being reborn."

"You must have a test coming up on this or something," Alana said, taking a sip of her soda. "You sound just like you're rehearsing for a test."

Brianna quickly chewed the food she had just placed in her mouth, then just as quickly swallowed. "I do, but I just love learning and then sharing what I've learned. Plus, I guess it *does* help when I say all of this out loud to see how much I really have retained. But I think this is *so* fascinating, especially when you consider our relationship to water. That we bathe to get the dirt off of us, we're baptized to outwardly show that we have repented of our dirt-laden sins. But I see a lot of Christian ideals that correspond to practices that originated or are rooted in the Jewish culture and religious traditions. Now, back to mikvah. Okay, there are times when married couples are not allowed to engage in sexual relations. That's called 'niddah.' When a married woman is on her menstrual cycle, Jewish Law calls for a time of separation from her husband . . . that means no sex."

"I'm not Jewish, but I'm down with that one," Alana said.

"That's in Leviticus 18:19, where it states that the husband shouldn't come to a woman to uncover her nakedness—in other words have sexual relations, as long as she is put apart for uncleanness or in her customary impurity. That's talking about her menstrual cycle. Then she should have seven days of what they call 'clean days,' which is when her cycle is over. She then immerses herself in a mikvah, and after that, she and her husband are to come together again."

"Whoa," Alana said. "Five days of unclean, then seven more days of clean, before you can get it on with your spouse? Whoa, Nellie! Hold your horses!"

"Stop that," Brianna said, laughing. "You are so silly sometimes."

"I can see why that would keep the homes fires burning." Alana started dancing in her seat. "That man will *really* want his wife by then. Twelve days? Twelve whole days!"

Brianna scowled at Alana, then laughed again. "I suppose that's right though. Twelve days of being apart in that area. Now, those seven extra days were added by a rabbinic proclamation. So if you go strictly by what the Bible says, it would only be while the woman is on her cycle, and that's usually about five days. Anyway, the woman then takes the ritual cleansing of mikvah, which signals she is now spiritually cleansed. And then, it is her *duty* to have relations with her husband at that point."

"Duty for real. I'd say she'd better. You know a man is quick to go somewhere else if he's not getting what he needs at home. Twelve days and you're married, too," Alana said. "What a time, what a time."

Brianna shook her head. "Mikvah is also used by both men and women when they have been involved in sin. In marriage, the wife's immersion in a mikvah is essential. It purifies her and makes it okay to now touch that which was unclean. In repentance, it serves as washing away that which is unclean and making it clean again."

"This is *really* interesting," Alana said. "So you wanted to go check out a place where you can go to or do a mikvah?"

"I would. I'd like to see it. I just don't want to go by myself.

I thought it would be nice if I had a friend who would go with me," Brianna said.

"Okay, okay. I'll go with you. But we're just going to see it, right? We're not going to convert to Judaism or anything like that, right? Because you know I'm strictly Christian, and I like the place where I worship now."

"All I want to do is see what a mikvah looks like. Maybe get a little more information."

"Well, according to you, if you can't find one, you can go to the ocean or a lake."

"The water just can't be stagnant," Brianna said. "That's the required criteria. You can't have on clothes or anything to obstruct the waters from reaching the body."

"Well, since you have to be naked, then I guess the ocean and the lake is out."

Brianna shook her head. "You do know you're crazy, right?"

Alana finished off the last of her egg roll. "I do know that you love me."

"Like a sister," Brianna said. "Like my very own sister."

Chapter 10

Nevertheless a fountain or pit, wherein there is plenty of water, shall be clean: but that which toucheth their carcase shall be unclean.

—Leviticus 11:36

Brianna waited on Alana as long as she could. She'd called several times in the past hour, but each time, it had gone straight to Alana's voice mail. She'd left her several messages, but hadn't heard back yet. Her appointment to meet with the rabbi's wife at the synagogue about the mikvah had been firm, and it was stressed to her that she be there on time. So Brianna left to ensure she made her appointment.

Ruth Bernstein, the rabbi's wife, was most helpful when it came to Brianna's many questions about mikvah and the Jewish life. Brianna had learned a lot in class, but there was something special about talking to Ruth and seeing many of the things discussed in class in person.

"I hope you will forgive me for not being able to allow you to take part in mikvah," Ruth said. "But I'm sure your professor must have told you that married, Jewish women are allowed to come to mikvah. Not single women, even if they are in sexual relationships. Not divorced women. And not those married women who are not of our faith. Now, should one convert to Judaism, then the mikvah is open to both the man and the woman who have converted."

Brianna smiled. "Actually, my professor didn't express that point. I suppose he was only teaching us the fundamentals and didn't consider that one of us might actually attempt to come and try out a mikvah."

Ruth returned the smile. "Well, I'm more than happy to show you around. It's an honor to be able to share what we do and believe with others. Most people aren't interested in even *hearing* what other people believe, let alone why they believe it."

"Well, to be honest with you, I'm a born-again Christian. But I recognize that Jesus was an orthodox Jew who practiced the Jewish faith. I also know that there were many things Jesus rebelled against during His time on earth. He really let a lot of those Pharisees and Sadducees have it, that's obvious from the scriptures. And it was Jesus who started that whole 'He that is without sin among you, let him first cast a stone' revolution. People are still using that one, and I mean a *lot* these days. But I merely wanted to see how some things you believe apply to what I, as a Christian, believe."

Ruth nodded. "I will admit: we don't get many like you in here. But as I said over the phone, I am happy to show you around and answer any questions you may have."

Ruth proceeded to lead Brianna toward an area. "Our facilities are more modern than some." She stopped. "And *this* is the mikvah you inquired about." She pointed at a small pool-looking, concrete hole in the ground, large enough for one person to walk down the stairs and fully immerse. "Mikvahs are built to certain specifications, into the ground, in accordance with Halakah, which means Jewish Law."

Brianna nodded. "Yeah, my professor did mention a little about that, the specification part, that is. He said a bathtub, whirlpool, Jacuzzi, or a regular pool cannot be and does not make a mikvah."

"That's correct," Ruth said. "The mikvah pool has to contain at least two hundred gallons of rainwater gathered, tapped into, transported, and handled according to specific regulations. Now, the rainwater can be mixed with tap water. Different from the old days of mikvahs, our pools have filtration and water purification systems." She looked at Brianna. "We must still be health conscious in our dealings with one another."

Brianna smiled and nodded. She loved the way the mikvah reflected a dark blue from its painted bottom and walls.

"When one steps in," Ruth said, "they'll find the mikvah waters to commonly reach the chest and the temperature to be quite comfortable. As for those with an infirmity or who are handicapped, we have lifts to get them in and out."

"That's great," Brianna said.

"Through that door"—Ruth pointed—"is where those who are about to enter the mikvah go to prepare. It's equipped with baths and showers, soap, shampoo, and any other cleaning aids needed to ensure cleanliness. Contrary to what some may think who are not familiar with our law, when it comes to the mikvah, one must be meticulously clean before entering a mikvah. Cleanliness is next to Godliness."

Brianna laughed at the cleverness of Ruth's words. She pointed at the door to the bath, then the mikvah. "Cleanliness is *next* to Godliness. Yes, the fact that you have to be clean before you get in a mikvah was something most in our class were surprised to learn. Many were under the impression that a mikvah was a type of bathing place."

Ruth shook her head. "No. There is a different purpose behind the mikvah. Even if you prepare yourself at home, when you get here, you still must rinse your hair, wash your feet and other areas again. And because the point of mikvah is for the water to reach every area of your body, anything that is false— jewelry, hair extensions, fake nails, piercings, artificial limbs if that applies, false eyelashes, contact lens; anything that is not one-hundred percent you—must be removed."

"Okay," Brianna said, nodding. "Now *that* . . . we weren't told, either."

"When you are clean, you wrap yourself with a towel or a robe. A woman, we call a *balanit,* will assist you, including holding your towel or robe as you step into the mikvah. She is the only one who will see you naked, but she is absolutely a professional. And believe me," Ruth said with a smile, "a balanit has seen all shapes and sizes, so nothing moves her. We take modesty and respect very seriously when it comes to this, so no one has to feel embarrassed or ashamed during this sacred time."

"I'm sure that's comforting to know. For those who happen to do this, I mean."

"It is. The balanit checks you before you go into the mikvah waters to ensure that the feet, under the nails, and all areas in between have been cleaned, including your hair. She ensures that no makeup has been missed. She also inquires to confirm that you have come during the right time of the month."

"Oh, I have that part, I believe," Brianna said. "Seven days clean after your cycle has ended. For most people with a cycle of five days, that's twelve days total."

Ruth nodded and smiled. "I'm impressed. Now, one may say a prayer before one enters, but it is not a forced requirement. When you enter the mikvah, you put the right foot in first as the balanit holds your towel or robe. Once in the water, you submerge several times. Some do it three times; some seven. You may also say a blessing in Hebrew while you're in there after your first dip . . . again, this is entirely up to you. The balanit watches to make sure you don't touch any walls or ball up your fist when you immerse. The idea is for the water to have maximum contact with every part of you. You keep your fingers spread, your arms out in front of you, and there will be the time when you must lift your feet off the floor as well. Again, this is to ensure that the water reaches every part of you."

"There is definitely a lot more to this than we were taught in class," Brianna said.

"I know. If you don't have to do this and stick to certain rules, most people don't concern themselves. For instance, if you should say a Hebrew blessing while in the water, the balanit will hold your towel or some type of covering over your head to ensure that your head is covered, as our custom demands. Once you've completed the mikvah blessings and the number of submersions required, you take the steps up and out of the mikvah, and you're what we call kosher for another two weeks or so until the cycle begins again."

"And when you get home, you get a really happy husband," Brianna said.

"Oh, if you're married to the right man, believe me, it's not just the husband who is excited after this," Ruth said. "It's like having a honeymoon over and over again every single month. You know what they say about absence making the heart grow fonder. Also, there's something exciting about the forbidden. You know, when you're told you can't do something, for some reason, humans are wired in such a way it makes us want to do it that much more."

Brianna smiled. "Yeah, Adam and Eve proved that much in the Garden of Eden. They had access to every tree in the garden except the one in the midst. And which one got attention? The one they were told *not* to touch."

"Absolutely," Ruth said. "The good thing about what we do in our culture, those who actually practice it—I hope you know that not everyone who is Jewish does this, and not everyone who does, does it on a monthly basis—"

"Yeah, we learned that as well," Brianna said.

"The good thing about what we do in doing this, is the mandate of no sexual relations happens to be from the one you are *one* with. So it's fine to have the hots for your own spouse. In fact, it's a *very* good thing," Ruth said. "I, for one, can vouch for this." She laughed a little.

"You know, you're okay," Brianna said.

"Thank you." Ruth began to walk out of the area. Brianna followed, walking alongside her. "The thing that's important for you to know about mikvah is that mostly women do this, but it's not restricted to just the women. Men come before their weddings. Some people bring their pots, dishes, and utensils prior to using them to ensure that they're 'clean' or I suppose the more appropriate term would be 'purified.' Mikvah is used to take that which was unclean and make it clean, that which was impure and make it pure. It's a way of taking that which was considered dead, but now is in a place of the possibility of new life. As is found in the case with a woman's menstrual cycle that has signaled there will be no new life inside at that time, to afterward, now the prospect and preparation of life is once again possible."

"Do you know what I think is interesting when it comes to the timing of mikvah with women? Especially with that rabbinic-mandated seven days that were added, to what could essentially be called a sex moratorium," Brianna said.

"What's that?"

"That it's generally twelve days. And according to what I have heard and read about when a woman ovulates, ovulation is said to be around the fourteenth day. So the timing appears to be absolutely perfect for conceiving a baby . . . a new life."

Ruth tilted her head to the side, then nodded with a smile. "You know, I've never thought of that. Perhaps that's why there was so much being fruitful and multiplying in the old days, before birth control took such a prominent place in our world."

"Maybe. I'm just amazed at how God gives us the answers, and then scientists later prove what God said really is true," Brianna said. "I mean, think about it. Thousands of years before anyone figured out ovulation, God had already instructed his people on mikvah and timing sex at just the time of ovulation when one is *most* likely to conceive. But I will say this much: most of the people I know couldn't be Jewish. There's no way they could wait that long to make love. Nope. No way. Well, maybe some of the women would be okay with it. But the men? Not too many I know. Nope."

Ruth laughed. "Oh, I understand." Ruth stopped at the glass front door. "I hope I was able to help you with the questions you may have had."

Brianna shook Ruth's hand. "Oh, you did. I just appreciate

you for opening your heart and your doors and allowing me this opportunity. I only wish I'd been able to actually get into the mikvah. I would love to experience what that's like. But I understand there are rules. And even though I'm a married woman, I'm definitely not Jewish."

"Well, you are always welcome to convert," Ruth said with a bit of a smile.

"No disrespect to what you believe. But I believe in Jesus Christ. I believe He is the Son of God. That He died on the cross and that God raised Him from the dead. I believe that Jesus ascended into Heaven. He is my High Priest, and He is sitting on the right hand of the Father making intercessions for me. And I believe that He's coming back again. I believe all of this without apology or disrespect to what others believe."

"And I respect that," Ruth said. "I have many friends who believe as you do as well. And there are those called Messianic Jews who believe the Messiah has come in the person of Jesus. For the orthodox Jews, we still wait. But you know, before there were mikvahs inside of buildings like this, there were the natural bodies of water that were our mikvahs. Those natural bodies still exist: the ocean, rivers, wells supplied by underground springs, and spring-fed lakes—Jehovah God's naturally provided mikvahs."

Brianna laughed. "Yeah, but if I'm to adhere to *all* the rules you just told me are necessary in mikvah, I might be arrested for indecent exposure if caught in public naked."

"Yeah," Ruth said, smiling and nodding. "But should you go to a natural mikvah after the sun is down, or late at night, in a big old ocean with no one around . . ."

"Ruth!" Brianna said, then laughed as she covered her mouth.

"IJS—I'm just saying."

"And to think I thought you were going to be a real prude," Brianna said.

"I know, right?" Ruth said. "Well, it was truly a pleasure

meeting you, Mrs. Brianna Waters. And I hope you have much success in class and whatever you do in life."

Brianna leaned over and hugged her. "Thank you. I really enjoyed this. You have no idea how much. You made everything come alive for me. I honestly have a better appreciation for mikvah and the concept behind it. And even though I was not allowed to get in the waters today, what you have done has been the next best thing to being there."

Ruth squeezed Brianna's hand. "Perhaps our paths will cross again. Shalom."

"Shalom . . . peace." Brianna gave a slight nod of her head. "Perhaps so." She left.

Chapter 11

Though the waters thereof roar and be troubled, though the mountains shake with the swelling there-of. Selah.

—Psalm 46:3

"**B**rianna, I'm sorry," Alana said, standing at Brianna's front door. "I'm so sorry."

Brianna pulled the door all the way open without saying one word. Alana stepped inside. Brianna then closed the door and headed toward the den.

"Listen," Alana said, trailing behind Brianna. "I know you're upset with me. I told you I was going to go do that mikvah thing with you, and I didn't."

Brianna sat down on the couch and folded her arms. She still didn't say anything.

"I had every intention to go, but—" She stopped, allowing seconds to pass without speaking.

"But what, Alana?" Brianna said to get Alana going again.

Alana eased down next to Brianna. "Look, I'm not going to even try to make up an excuse. There's nothing excusable about what I did." Alana began to chew on her bottom lip. "I left Dre."

Brianna turned totally to face her friend. "You did? You finally left him?"

"Yeah. He was always fighting me. And frankly, I got tired of being his punching bag. Although I still kind of gave as much as I got. But having a place to lay your head is not worth all of that. I need some peace."

"I knew he was hitting on you. But you kept insisting that he wasn't." Brianna hugged Alana. "I don't understand you. How could someone as strong as I know you to be allow someone to mistreat you like that?"

Alana pulled away from Brianna's embrace. "Oh, yeah, it's easy to judge when it's not you. Take it from me: it's easier than you think to allow yourself to be abused."

Brianna let out a sigh. "I'm not judging you, Alana."

"Yes, you are. You're asking, how could I think so little of myself that I would sell out for a cheap roof over my head? But you know what, Brianna? Married people around this world are doing it every single day. They claim to stay together because they love each other, because they made a vow to stick it out for better or worse, for the children. But the truth is: a lot of them stay together because it's cheaper or easier to stay than it is to live on their own or worse: have to start all over."

"Number one, you weren't married to Dre, that's number uno." Brianna held up a finger. "In fact, you were *actually* living in sin."

Alana raised up her hand. "Please, don't go there. Are you seriously trying to tell me that all of those hot and heavy years you and Unzell dated, that before you and him were married and said, 'I do,' you kept yourself from 'I did'?"

"I don't see what me and Unzell have to do with *this* conversation we're having about *you*," Brianna said, pointing at Alana.

"I'll take that as a 'no' then."

"Can we just stick to you for now? Can we do that?"

"Why? I just told you I left Dre. Me and you talking about what he was doing to me isn't going to make my having left him any more *gone* than I'm already gone. I've left him already. I'm out of that situation. I've moved on." Alana fell back hard against the couch. She picked up her favorite throw pillow and began to hug it. "It's done."

"We need to talk about it because you need to figure out why you got into this situation in the first place so that we can make sure you don't get into it again," Brianna said.

"Oh, so what are you? My shrink now?"

"No." Brianna grabbed the pillow out of Alana's clutches. "I'm your best friend. I'm someone who cares about you. I'm the one who had to look into your black-and-blue eye and pretend like I believed that lie about some bottle falling and hitting you in it. I'm the one who touched your arm and watched you flinch from pain—on more than one occasion, I might add. I'm the one who wasn't able to put my full weight on you about it because it caused you to run away when you didn't need to be running away from me. Not then, not when you really needed someone in your corner."

Tears began to roll down Alana's face. "You're a good friend," Alana said. She wiped her face, but the tears kept coming. "And I know I deserve better. But I also know that I get lonely, and I get tired of being rejected. Everywhere I turn, it seems like I'm being rejected, that I'm being told no. No, I'm not a good enough dancer to be in that video. No, I'm not a good enough date to be asked out again. No, I'm not good enough for anyone to ever want me enough to marry me. Brianna, I'm *tired* of being made to feel like I really don't matter. That my being on this earth really doesn't mean anything."

Brianna hugged Alana as Alana released a floodgate of tears. When Alana began to calm down, Brianna said, "Okay, so you left *Dra*per. Where are you staying?"

Alana started laughing. "I don't know if I want to tell you."

"Why not?"

"Because you're just going to tell me what a bad idea you think it is."

Brianna let go of Alana and looked at her. "I will not. Tell me: are you going back to Montgomery to stay with your folks for a little while until you get back on your feet?"

"No," Alana said with a slight force behind the word. "Please. I'm not *even* trying to go backward. Not at this point in the game."

"So where are you staying? Do you need to come here for a little while?"

"Double no. I told you I'm not going to do that, and I meant it."

"Alana, will you just tell me where you're staying? Are you at the Y? A women's shelter? I'm not going to judge you, I promise. Will you just *tell* me already!"

Alana smiled. "I'm sort of house-sitting . . . for kind of a friend."

"You're house-sitting?"

"Yeah," Alana said. "You see, it really works out for both of us. I need somewhere to stay, and he needs someone to watch his house for a month or two while he's overseas and out of town working or something or other."

"And who is this 'kind of' a friend?"

"I'm going to say his name, and I don't want you having anything negative to say about it."

"Who . . . is . . . *the* . . . friend?"

"Vincent. You remember Vincent? He's the guy I told you I met, back in January."

"Yes. I remember Vincent," Brianna said. "He's the guy you thought was going to help you get a video gig. Oh, no . . . wait! He's the guy you were planning to marry. No, wait. He's the guy you were just going to live with, then maybe someday you two would get married."

"See, you're making fun of me." Alana stood up.

Brianna laughed, grabbed Alana by her hand and pulled her back down. "Sit down. You know you're not going anywhere. Okay, so spill it. All of it."

Alana giggled. "I hate you. You know me all too well." Alana turned her body totally toward Brianna. Kicking off her shoes, she put her left foot on the couch; her right leg on top of it, in effect, sitting on her foot. "Okay, I was at the club the other week when I ran into Vincent again. He said he'd meant to call me, so this had to be some kind of divine intervention or something—"

"Of course," Brianna said.

Alana looked at Brianna crossly. "You're being funny. Do you want to hear this or not?"

Brianna waved at her. "Please. Do continue."

Alana grinned. "Okay. Anyway, we talked. He got my phone number *again*. He called. We were in this deep conversation, okay? He was telling me that he had to be out of the country for about a month. He was thinking about hiring someone to house-sit his vacation house, in particular. That one, he said, was too easy for folks to get into and become like squatters. Later, Dre came home and started clowning about his food not being ready. He started talking about me like I was a dog, like he had lost his doggone mind. We got into a fight, as usual. He said I could get my stuff and get to stepping anytime I felt like disrespecting him. So I got my stuff and I got to stepping. In the meantime, I was supposed to be meeting you to go to that mikvah thing. You were calling. I was boo-hooing. I didn't want you to know what had happened, so I decided not to answer your calls, hoping you would go on without me."

"Okay, so that's why you didn't answer your phone or call me back," Brianna said.

"Yeah. I knew you'd somehow be able to tell I'd been crying and that I was upset. I didn't want to mess up your plans. I called Vincent, told him I would really be interested in house-sitting for him."

"So, you're going to get paid to stay at his house?" Brianna said. "I mean, he was going to hire someone else to do it."

Alana frowned. "No. I'm not going to charge him to house-sit. I'm home*less*."

"Of course not. Besides the fact that you think it would be in bad taste to charge someone for a place you hope to live in, with him, after he gets back from his month- or two-long excursion out of town." Brianna shook her head in utter disgust.

Alana rapidly tapped Brianna on her arm. "You'd better be glad that I love you and that you're my girl. Because if I didn't, I would get my purse and walk right out of your door, right this minute."

"Yeah . . . right," Brianna said with a short, fake laugh.

"I'm not going to charge him because I need a place to stay. And this house he wants me to sit for is on the beach . . . in Georgia, of all places. Right here in Georgia!" Alana said. "I'm thinking you and I can have a really nice time over there, relaxing, taking dips in the water, when the water is warm enough, that is. See, Brianna, I was thinking about you, too, even during all of my mayhem. Unzell has been gone for over a month now. What else do you have to do with your life and free time? Huh?"

"Okay. I have to admit. It does sound like something that will work. This man needed a house-sitter; you needed a place to stay. It's a win-win for both of you. And Unzell will be gone for at least another eight weeks. I'll be finished with my class next week. Honestly, I can't find anything wrong with any of this. I really can't."

Alana burst into a full grin and started to bounce up and down. She put her foot back on the floor. "Now you're getting it! I know you've been really praying for me. That's why things are falling into place like they are lately. I know that's why. Anyway, I went to Vincent's beach house earlier today so he could show me all the things I need to know. I moved my clothes and a few other little things in just to give the place a feel of home for me. You know how I do. But it's fully furnished. Vincent leaves in two days going overseas. At least, that's what he said he was doing. But who cares whether he is or isn't. I have a place on the beach for weeks to come. And as far as I'm concerned right this minute, everything is *right* with the world!"

Chapter 12

*He maketh me to lie down in green pastures: he
leadeth me beside the still waters.*

—Psalm 23:2

A week later, Brianna met Alana and followed her to Vincent's house. On Tybee Island, the house was a little more than a two-and-a-half-hour drive. *Not too bad.* Driving instead of choosing to let Alana come and get her as Alana had suggested meant Brianna could go home when she was ready. She knew Alana; Alana would have her over there for the entire time, sipping Long Island teas or something.

Brianna stepped out of her car, set her overnight bag down at the back door of the house, and hurried around to the front. "This is nice," she said. "The view is stunning. The waters are so calm . . . tranquil . . . still. I've never been to a house on a beach before."

"Isn't it nice?" Alana said. "This is Vincent's beach home. It's not as large as his regular house or that huge four-story house right there." Alana pointed at a light yellow house— with separate white painted railed porches in its front, that looked to be about twelve feet deep, and was as wide as the house, and with what appeared to be an observation / sunning deck on the roof also enclosed with intricate white railings— three houses down. "But it's *really* nice. I can see why Vincent was worried about it sitting here without any activity for an extended period of time while he's out of town. This is the time when most people start coming or, at least, start thinking about coming to the beach."

"Or he just did this to set you up." Brianna went back and retrieved her red overnight bag from the back area. "Maybe he knew you were in a desperate place in your life and this was his way of making sure you had somewhere to stay without you realizing what he was doing. Maybe he's really a nice guy after all. Then again . . ."

"Is that all you brought, Bathsheba?" Alana asked, looking down at the red bag.

"Yeah. I told you I wasn't planning on staying but a day or two. I just wanted to see where you were. You never know when I might need to have this information."

Alana shook her head, then slid a sandal across some stray sands on a rock, causing a sanding sound. "That is so sad. You'd rather sit at home all alone for weeks on end than to spend it out here with me on this heaven of a beach."

Brianna waited as Alana unlocked the back door. "It's tempting, that's for sure."

They settled in for the rest of the day. The next morning, Brianna got up early from the baby blue–painted guest room and strolled outside. She immediately took off her flip-flops and let the sand slip and glide between her toes. She'd brought a few books with her as well as her notebook, just in case she felt inspired to write a poem or two. Around 10 A.M., she went back into the house. Alana was up now, sitting in the bright yellow kitchen, with its white cabinets, at the round, oak dining table that seated six.

"I wondered if you were up yet," Brianna said.

Alana sipped her coffee. "Yeah. But you can't help but sleep like a baby out here."

"Yeah, I know. However, it's so wonderful outside that you, or at least *I*, don't want to miss one moment sleeping it away. I had to get out there. The waters and the beach were calling my name. Brianna. Brianna."

Alana set the cup of black coffee back in its saucer. "It looks like you're loving this place even more than I am. At least, you're appreciating it the way it should be appreciated." Alana yawned. "I suppose I'm so worn out from fighting for the last three months, I just want to sleep in peace."

"Well, you'll have lots of opportunity later to enjoy this place and all of its benefits. You'll be here for several more weeks to come."

"So, you never told me: how did you do in your religion class?"

Brianna broke into a grin. "I received a 4.2. I aced my test and even got bonus points for that impromptu visit I made to that mikvah. My professor was impressed."

"Yay! Great!" Alana picked up her cup of coffee and took a sip. "So, are you going to sign up for more classes now that you're back in the swing of things?"

"I think so, starting in the fall. But I'd like to take a heavier class load, maybe three classes this time around. I'll wait until Unzell gets home and see what he thinks."

"You don't have to ask Unzell if you can take a heavier class load," Alana said.

"I know. But I'm not certain of his schedule for later this year. It's possible he may be home a lot more since King d.Avid's concert tour will officially be over. The last thing I want to do is to be out of pocket because of some college schedule, while Unzell's in town," Brianna said. "I've told you we haven't gotten to spend much time together as husband and wife. First, there was his injury, surgeries, and recovery. He then finished college in Ann Arbor—again, away from me. He got this job that's both rewarding and exciting. But as I've said, it can be quite taxing, to say the least, on a relationship."

"Well, I say sign up. It wouldn't be any different than if you were working full time," Alana said. "Go for it. The way you talk, Unzell doesn't do much with you when he's home anyway. This way, at least you'll have something to keep you busy instead of you watching him watch TV, then him glancing at your patient self and saying, 'Baby, you the *best!*' " Alana mocked, using a man's voice when she pretended to be Unzell.

"Listen to you." Brianna laughed.

"What?"

"And what are you doing besides sleeping all day?"

Alana stood up. "Ten o'clock is not *all day*. Besides, I'm planning a wonderful little dinner for us this evening and that's going to be work."

Brianna stood up. "Well, I'm going back outside. Maybe I'll sit on the porch until later in the day. I might even decide to take a little dip in the waters, stick my toes in."

"There's a hot-water shower outside if you decide you want to use it," Alana said. "It's that little outhouse-looking shed right next to the house."

"I suppose that's a good thing to have around. Especially if one is inclined to have guests over. That way you don't have to worry about people tracking sand in and out of your house, traipsing from the outside into the house and back, to shower," Brianna said.

"Yeah, I guess." Alana set her cup in the sink, then scratched her uncombed head.

"Call me when you're ready to cook and I'll come in and help you."

"Nope. You're my guest, and I'm going to take care of *you* for a change."

Brianna lowered her head and tilted it toward Alana. "Seriously. You're going to cook for *me*? And you don't want my help? Not at all? Not in the least?"

"Seriously. I've become quite the little chef over the past few months, thanks to Dre. I guess that's one good thing that came from me having lived essentially with Dr. Jekyll and Mr. Hyde or who one might be inclined to call The Iron Fist Chef."

"Personally"—Brianna opened the refrigerator door and took out a bottle of water—"I find nothing good that came from you living with that jerk." She closed the refrigerator door. "If you need me, you know where *I'll* be—out enjoying the still waters." Brianna gave a little Miss America wave. "Tata," she said, then opened the screen door and sashayed out.

Chapter 13

And it came to pass in an eveningtide, that David arose from off his bed, and walked upon the roof of the king's house: and from the roof he saw a woman washing herself; and the woman was very beautiful to look upon.

—2 Samuel 11:2

The sun was setting, a beautiful humongous orange at first suspended equally between the heavens and the water, before almost sitting on and seeing its reflection on the ocean waters. King d.Avid had awakened late in the evening and walked up the short flight of stairs to the railed observation roof of his beach house.

He hadn't really been looking for a house on the beach, but his third wife had insisted that they buy it. And it had to be *this* house, because *this* one was only twenty feet from the actual beach. *This* one had full glass windows from top to bottom (on every floor) on the ocean side of the house. *This* one had three bedrooms, three-and-a-half baths, that easily accommodated a king size, queen size, four twins, and a sofa bed with a finished one-car garage on the ground floor and space for two more cars in the driveway on the backside of the house with public parking directly across the street (just in case they entertained and needed the extra parking space). And of course, there was the elevator, as small as it was, that went from the ground floor all the way to the top.

King d.Avid should have been on his plane, or at least getting ready to be on it, right about now. He had three weeks of concerts overseas, beginning next week. Then it would be right back to the states for two more weeks of concerts in four different cities, making a total of almost eight straight weeks of being on the road. Instead, he had come to his house on Tybee Island—a place he rarely visited—to get away, to hide out, to get a little peace and quiet, to regroup before his next round of concerts began again.

Vincent had gone already, excited that all of the concerts had sold out so quickly—within hours, really, of going on sale. Vincent had business he needed to take care of prior to King d.Avid's arrival in England. So naturally, King d.Avid was surprised to see someone, a woman who looked to be in her early twenties, at Vincent's beach house a few houses down from his. She stepped into the outdoor shower. The one that— when the door was closed—theoretically hid its occupant rather well from all sides, but to his discovery, not at *all* from the top. She disrobed and began to wash from her head down to her toes. Seeing this made it abundantly clear that the outdoor shower didn't keep one as private as one may have thought they were. Not if someone happened to be standing on his roof and looking down at the unroofed facility.

Normally, he would, but he didn't care that it was wrong for him to see her. For whatever reason, this woman was all that filled his thoughts now. And she *absolutely* took his breath away; she was just *that* beautiful. Long, dark-auburn hair that appeared black when wet. Flawless, light-brown skin, at least from where he stood. Petite. Curves in all the right places. Yes, he should have looked away. But for whatever reason, he didn't . . . he couldn't. He was utterly and completely, at this point, oxygen deprived and mesmerized. He then watched her do something rather interesting. She shut off the water; slipped on and tied tight a lightweight, purple robe; then trotted toward the ocean without even bothering to put on a bathing suit or anything else. She looked around as though she was searching for someone, only there was no one there except her.

She then walked straight into the ocean waters with her

robe on, until the waters reached her shoulders. Around that time, King d.Avid thought she might possibly be crazy, maybe even suicidal, and that instead of looking on, he should get down there and save her before she did something foolish. But for whatever reason that he couldn't explain, he didn't move. He merely stood there . . . watching . . . watching. And as he watched, he saw her disrobe (her body concealed by the waters), then submerge her whole self, including her head, into the waters. Her robe floated on top nearby, then once (purposely, it appeared) directly over her head. She had dipped one time, two times, three times, with no regard for her hair, which is what surprised King d.Avid the most. Every black woman he'd ever known didn't play when it came to her hair getting wet. And in unfiltered ocean waters particularly, most of them always, always protected their hair by wearing a swimming cap.

She then retrieved her robe, putting it on wet, tied the robe's belt back securely around her waist as she trudged out of the waters just as she'd gone in (albeit with a little more labor now that she bore a water-soaked robe). She slipped back inside the outdoor shower, dried herself, put on dry clothes (a white top and white Capri pants), then started toward the house that belonged to Vincent.

King d.Avid quickly pulled out his cell phone and, using its camera feature, snapped her picture just as she turned one last time to gaze out upon the ocean waters. She then bounced up the wooden steps to the house and equally into his beating heart.

Chapter 14

And David sent and inquired after the woman. And one said, Is not this Bath-sheba, the daughter of Eliam, the wife of Uriah the Hittite?

—2 Samuel 11:3

King d.Avid hurried downstairs. He summoned the head of his security. Chad was there standing before him within minutes.

"Yes, sir," Chad said.

"Not that it's really any of my business, but did you know someone was staying at Vincent's beach house? Do you know if he rented it out while he's gone?"

"Not that I know of," Chad said. "Would you like for me to check on it? Make sure someone's not there illegally?"

"I suppose I could just call Vincent and ask him," King d.Avid said.

"I wouldn't trouble him about it. I can just as easily walk over there and check things out. If whoever is there is authorized to be there, there's not a problem. If not, hey, Vincent will thank you for being a good neighbor."

King d.Avid pulled out his cell phone. He retrieved the photo he'd secretly snapped earlier. "This is the woman I just saw go in there." He showed the photo to Chad.

Chad took King d.Avid's phone and looked closely at the picture. "I know her."

King d.Avid instantly registered a puzzled look on his face.

"You know *her?*" He took his phone back. "This woman right there?" He held up his phone. "You know her?"

"Yes, sir. Her hair is different, most likely because it's dripping wet here. But that's a pretty clear picture of her face. Her name is Brianna Waters. I met her when her brother, Mack Wright, came to see you and brought Melvin around Christmastime."

King d.Avid tilted his head slightly as he took another look at the photo. "So *this* is Mack Wright's little sister? You're telling me that *this* woman *here*"—he gestured toward the phone with his head—"is Mack's little sister Brianna?"

"Yes, sir. I'm pretty certain that's her." Chad stood almost at attention, military style. "Mack asked if we could go by her house before we came to see you. So we stopped over there. He chatted with her for a few minutes. I was standing near her, so I got a good look. And from what I gathered, that was her first time meeting Melvin."

"Did Mack tell her he was on his way to my house?" King d.Avid asked.

"No. To my delight, he didn't. She asked him why he was in the city. It sounded to me like he hadn't been to visit her since she'd moved to Atlanta. Mack skillfully changed the subject. I was most impressed with him and how he handled things."

"So, you're telling me *this* woman"—he held up the phone and shook it—"is Mack's little sister, Amos Wright's baby daughter, Pearson Wright's granddaughter?" King d.Avid shook his head as he grinned. "Talk about a small world."

"It gets even smaller than that," Chad said. "Brianna Waters is also married to one of the people working in setting up the stages for your concerts. That stage manager who came on board November first of last year: Unzell Waters. Well, that's his wife."

King d.Avid looked at her picture again. "So *this* is little Brianna Wright, all grown up and now married. I met her once when she was ten. I never will forget that."

"Ten, huh? Well, she's definitely all grown up now; definitely not ten anymore."

"So why do you think she's at Vincent's place?" King d.Avid asked, not really looking for him to have an answer. "Do you think Vincent and my old manager, Pearson, have somehow become friendly, and Pearson worked out something for his granddaughter to be able to come here to his beach house? Or maybe Vincent and her husband have connected, and that's how this all came about? Although I honestly can't see Vincent getting friendly with anyone he refers to as 'the help.' Hmmm."

"Not sure. But as I said, I can go over there and check things out. This is what I do. And I know how to do it in a way where she won't have a clue that I'm gathering information," Chad said. "I'm paid to be both effective *and* discreet."

"I *would* like for you to check on her. Make sure everything is okay. You know. Especially since her husband is overseas working so hard on my behalf. They've all been away from home for so long." He shook his head.

"I'll go now." Chad turned to leave.

"Chad?"

Chad turned back around. "Yes, sir?"

"Just don't let her know I had you do this. I'd prefer she not know, at least for now, that I'm even here."

"Absolutely," Chad said. "My sentiments exactly." Chad left.

Chapter 15

The Lord is my light and my salvation; whom shall I
fear? The Lord is the strength of my life; of whom
shall I be afraid?

—Psalm 27:1

Brianna and Alana had the music up kind of loud. They were listening to King d.Avid's latest release, "The Beauty of the Lord," from Psalm 27, and singing merrily along with the chorus.

> *One thing have I desired of the Lord,*
> *And that*
> *Will I*
> *Seek after;*
> *That I*
> *May dwell*
> *In the house of the Lord*
> *All the days of my life,*
> *All the days of my life,*
> *To behold*
> *The beauty*
> *Of the Lord,*
> *To behold*
> *The beauty*
> *Of the Lord . . .*

So when the thunderous rapping came at the door, Brianna jumped to her feet and quickly turned the music down.

"I told you it was up too loud," Brianna said to Alana.

Alana waved her off. "It was *not* all that loud." She went to answer the door. "Yes?" she said, peering through the screen door. "May I help you?"

"Yes, ma'am. My name is Chad Holston and I'm down the way from you." He pointed toward the house from where he'd come.

"I *know* you're not here to complain that the music is up too loud," Alana said, putting her hand on her hip.

"No, ma'am. I just happen to know the person who owns this place, and I was wondering . . ."

Alana cocked her head to the side, her hand still on her hip as she began to rotate her neck in rhythm with her words. "Wondering what?"

"Well, I wanted to be sure that you're not in need of anything," Chad said.

"*We're* fine." She gave him a quick smile as she softened her tone. "But thanks for inquiring. Oh, and I will be certain to let Vincent know that you were kind enough to stop by and check on things in his absence."

"Oh, so Vincent knows you're here?"

Alana couldn't help but flash a big grin his way at this point. A long "Yes" was all she provided Chad.

"Great, Mrs. . . . ? Oh, I'm sorry; I didn't catch your name," Chad said.

"That's because I didn't throw it," Alana said just as quickly. "And it's Miss."

Brianna strolled over to the door and stood beside Alana. She instantly jerked her head back. "Don't I know you?" she said to Chad.

Chad smiled and nodded. "Yes, ma'am. Brianna Waters, I believe it is. Our paths have crossed once in the past."

"You were in the limousine with my brother that time. . . ."

"Correct," Chad said.

"So, are you out here accompanying someone else?"

"You might say that. The man I'm working for lives a few houses down," Chad said, directing his full attention to Brianna now. "He knows Mister Powers and just so happens to know that he's away."

"And you thought we had broken into his place," Alana said, interjecting herself back into the conversation. "And you wanted to come check us out."

Chad turned his attention back to Alana. "No, ma'am. It is quite customary, especially around here, for visitors . . . renters . . . timeshare folks to show up at various homes. So that was not my thought at all. Trust me, my goal was purely to ensure that you had everything you needed. And if there happened or happens to be something that you should need or that may require my service, then you'd know that I'm around."

"Well, we really appreciate you stopping by," Alana said. "But I think we have everything under control here. Just as long as you weren't stopping by to tell us that our music was up too loud, then I believe this should end our conversation."

"Alana," Brianna said, giving her one of her signature "tone it back a little" looks. "I think it was quite neighborly of Chad"—she nodded at him—"to come by and extend himself in this way." She turned back to Alana. "You don't find people caring enough to check on neighbors these days. Not like folks used to back in our parents' day."

"Yeah, well," Alana said, "there's a reason for that. Does the term serial killer, rapist, or robber happen to mean anything to you *these days?*"

"I assure you," Chad said, looking from Alana to Brianna, "you have nothing to fear from me in any of those areas. Believe me: I'm more of one you might call should you find yourself facing any of those situations."

"So, are you a cop? The *po*-lice," Alana said.

Chad flashed a genuine smile. "No. Just a man who considers himself to be a protector of those in need of protection." He lifted one pants leg and shook his shoe.

"Well," Alana said, scanning him from his head to his classy black A. Testoni, leather ankle boots, then back up again, resting on his dreamy brown eyes. "We'll be sure and keep that in mind." She put her left hand, vacant of a wedding band, on the screen door handle and allowed it to park there. "So if we're finished?" She said it as though it was a question, but it was, indeed, her polite way of telling him he could go now, unless there was something else he may have had of interest. She wiggled her bare ring finger.

"Oh, I'm sorry," Chad said. "Yes." He nodded at Alana, then at Brianna. "Please forgive me for interrupting. And I sincerely hope you enjoy your stay, for however long that might be."

"Well, this one *here* is going back home tomorrow," Alana said, pointing her head toward Brianna.

"Alana," Brianna said. She moved Alana's hand from the door handle, opened the screen door, then proceeded to present her hand to Chad. "We appreciate you for stopping by. It was really great seeing you again."

Chad shook her hand and smiled. "Likewise." He bowed slightly at Brianna, then turned back and nodded at Alana who now stood with folded arms. "Take care."

"You bet," Alana said, giving him a two-finger, military-type salute.

Alana and Brianna watched as he walked back toward the house Brianna had noticed when she first drove up and later admired from the beachside.

"I wonder if *he's* really the one who lives there or if he's truly working for someone who does?" Brianna said. "He was wearing a suit and ankle boots on a beach."

"Why do you care?" Alana walked away with an exaggerated swish.

"Because he was in the limo with my brother that day Mack and Melvin came by the house. In fact, had my brother not come to Atlanta for the reason he, to this day, won't disclose— to me anyway—who knows when I might have seen him?"

"Your brother *is* sort of weird," Alana said. "I've never really totally gotten him."

"He's not weird," Brianna said. "Well, okay. Maybe he is a *little* bit weird. He just likes to stay to himself. Some people are like that. And when you try to talk to him, he thinks you're merely trying to get in his business, so he erects a wall."

"So, this dude Chad . . . you say you saw him in a limo with your brother? Was he driving the limo?"

"No. He was riding in the front, on the passenger's side." Brianna walked back and flopped down on the couch.

"Well, he's *really* hot and *really* fine. So what do you think he does job wise?"

Brianna shrugged. "I'm not sure."

"Then why don't you call Mack and see if he can shed some light on who this Chad character is or at least what he does?" Alana flopped down next to Brianna. She began to fan herself with her hand. "He's a beefcake, that's for sure. *Real* easy on the eyes. Real easy. And that deep, manly, bass voice—oh, my goodness! I wonder if he's married. Some of the things he was saying when he was here, though, could have passed for a *genuine* gigolo."

"I thought you were interested in Vincent," Brianna said, looking at Alana sideways.

Alana waved her hand at Brianna. "You'll be twenty-two next month. Have you not learned *anything* in all of your years of being on this earth?"

"And what lesson am I missing that you think I *need* to learn?"

"Always . . . always keep your options open." Alana stood up. "Because you never know when you'll find yourself in need of somewhere else you may *need* to be next."

Brianna shook her head. "You know . . . you truly do *need* help. But honestly, you really need to find a job so you don't have to live your life being open to *options* that require other people's consent."

"Oh, yeah. That's right. Because I'm an independent woman.

I keep forgetting that. But I promise you," Alana said. "As soon as I see where things are going between me and Vincent this time around, I'm going to become the independent diva I was meant to be. You just watch."

Brianna leaned forward and grabbed a handful of cashew nuts. She popped one into her mouth. "Well, I'm going to get my things together so I can leave early tomorrow."

"What *things?* You didn't bring but two or three things. You didn't even pack a suitcase. And I don't understand why you won't stay longer." Alana wriggled her nose. "You have nothing and no one at home waiting for you."

"Because I could really get used to this. Then this Vincent fellow might find it hard to get rid of the both of us," Brianna teased.

"Oh, you're just like old people. They'll visit for a day or two, but for some reason, they always just *have* to get back home. Forget that there's nothing there for them to do when they get back. They just *have* to be at home."

"I have plenty to do at home, thank you very much," Brianna said with a smug, but playful look.

"What, Bathsheba? What do you have to do at home that won't or can't wait a few more days if not a few more weeks? What?"

"See, there you go. Denigrating and making fun of me again," Brianna said.

"Why? Because I called you Bathsheba? Well, it *is* your middle name, lest you keep forgetting," Alana said.

"Yes. Bathsheba is my middle name. But you only use it when you want to put me down or make a point that I'm acting uppity or something like that."

"That's not putting you down in any way. From what I've heard, the Bathsheba in the Bible was something else. Then again, they say the quiet, nice ones usually are." Alana went to the counter and pulled a banana off the bunch. She began to peel it. "And why did your folks name you Bathsheba anyway?" She bit the banana.

"I don't know," Brianna said with a twinge of exasperation. "I've never thought about it or cared enough to ask."

"Then maybe you should. It's not like there are a lot of people walking around with the name Bathsheba. Although I did see a person on Facebook with it."

"Maybe when they gave me that name, they thought it would later be popular or something. Maybe they thought when I grew up I would make the name popular. You know, the way Oprah made 'Oprah' popular. Perhaps if I trace my roots back to my great-great-great something-or-other on somebody's side, I'll find I was named after some distant relative." Brianna picked up a couple of cherries from the tray of fruit still on the table and began to eat them, holding each one in the air by its stem as she did so. "I just know, whenever you refer to me as Bathsheba, that you're making fun of me or something along that line. That much I *do* know."

"I can't help it if you're a queen, Queen Bathsheba." Alana curtsied before Brianna, and almost tipped over. She laughed as she put the banana peel into the garbage disposal.

"Yeah, well, this *queen* will be vacating these premises tomorrow," Brianna said, laughing at Alana's attempt to recover from her tip. "After I get a few more hours outside on that beautiful beach in the Vitamin D–enriching sun, that is."

"See, I keep telling you: you know you love it here. The next thing we know, you'll be getting your own beach house."

"Oh, yeah? Well, if I do, then that's a long way down the road. I can assure you of that."

"Well, now, you never know." Alana strutted over to the stereo. "Things can change in a heartbeat." She glanced over her shoulder. "If you don't know, you'd better *ask* somebody." She turned the stereo back up. King d.Avid's powerful and anointed worship song based on Psalm 91, "Abiding under God's Shadow," was just beginning.

> *He that dwelleth in the secret place of the Most High*
> *Shall abide under the shadow of the Almighty*

(Sopranos)
I will say
Of the Lord,
He is my refuge
(Altos)
And my fortress:
My God
In Him will I trust.
(Tenors)
Thou shalt not be afraid
For the terror
By night;
(Bass)
Nor for the arrow
That flieth
By day.
(Chorus: Full Choir)
A thousand
Shall fall at thy side,
And ten thousand
At thy right hand;
(King d.Avid in his tenor voice)
But it shall
Not come
Nigh thee.
No, no, no, no, no.
I said, it shall
Not come
Nigh thee!

Alana went over and hugged Brianna, as they both found the other one crying and worshipping the Lord.

"Oh, that is *such* a beautiful song!" Alana said. "That whole entire song. It always seems to take me to a special place, my secret place in the Lord."

"Yeah. I know." Brianna rubbed Alana's arm as though she were trying to warm her. "I know." She hugged Alana again and began to sing, "A thousand . . . shall fall at thy side. . . . And ten thousand . . . at thy right hand. But it shall . . . *not* come . . . nigh thee. It shall not . . . come . . . nigh thee."

Chapter 16

And David sent messengers.

—2 Samuel 11:4 (a)

"**I**'m telling you," Chad said to King d.Avid. "You don't need to go over there and speak. But I *will* say that when I walked up to the house and knocked, they were blasting your CD."

"That's a good thing," King d.Avid said with a nod. "That means they're fans, and at least they appreciate what I do."

"The one called Alana, I deduced that's the one Vincent left at his house, she's a pretty tough one . . . has a little bite to her," Chad said.

"Chad, I grew up around people who had a bite to them. And in this business, I run into those type of people all the time. I believe I can handle her. But I really would like to see Brianna again." He smiled. "I told you that I met her when she was ten. In fact, I believe she was with that very same friend—Alana, you say—back then. And do you know what the two of them were doing?"

"What?"

King d.Avid chuckled. "They were outside, about to stick safety pins into the ground so they could hear the devil beating his wife and her screaming as he did it."

"It must have been raining while the sun was shining," Chad said matter-of-factly.

King d.Avid frowned, then smiled. "Yeah. So I take it you've heard of that before?"

"Of course. And when it's thundering and lightning, it's just the angels bowling and making strikes."

"All right." King d.Avid rolled his eyes, mostly in jest.

"You never heard any of those things?" Chad asked. "We couldn't talk on the phone when it was lightning because God was also doing His business. In fact, you had to sit perfectly still, because if you didn't, well . . . let's just say lightning had a way of finding the noisy and talkative folks." Chad shook his head. "I can't believe, as a child, you never heard about the devil beating his wife."

"No, I hadn't. Not until I walked up on the Wright's porch that day. I was with Brianna's grandfather, Pearson. We'd gone over so I could meet his family before we cranked things up. Pearson wanted his son, Amos, to look over some things he wanted to do with my career. You know, get his feedback. That's when I met little Miss Brianna. She was ten, and yes, I remember because her little friend, Alana, told me how old they were as she announced that I was *old* after hearing I was a senior citizen of twenty-five."

Chad let out sporadic chuckles. "Twenty-five . . . old, huh? What I wouldn't give to be twenty-five again."

"You're only, what . . . twenty-nine?" King d.Avid said.

"Yeah." Chad smiled. "About to hit the big three-o in a couple of months."

"I still would like to go over and say hello. If it hadn't been for Brianna's grandfather, I wouldn't be standing here today as King d.Avid, the world-renowned psalmist and mega recording artist. I would be merely David Shepherd, the trying-to-be."

"I doubt *that,* not with your talent. You'd have made it regardless," Chad said.

"Yeah, maybe. Who can ever say? But there are a lot of talented, and truthfully, determined folks out there who never

achieve their dreams. We never know what one different decision might have made in our lives."

"I've always thought about that," Chad said.

"What?"

"You know: making a different decision back then. Like if
there was a way to go back in time, make a different choice,
then see where that would have led you. Take *me*, for instance.
Had I married that girl I was so in love with instead of losing
her because I wouldn't let her know how much I really wanted
her, how much different would my life be today? Had I chosen differently, what would be different about my whole life
now? Would I even be standing here talking to you right this
minute?" Chad said.

King d.Avid nodded. "Everything is connected. The good
and the bad bring us to the place where we are at the present
time. Personally, I would be afraid of going back and changing a thing. Some of what might have seemed bad at the time
may be the very thing that brought us to that which means the
most to us now. Like a person or a child in your life you love
and adore. Had you chosen something differently, would you
have been blessed with that person, that child, or whatever
means so much to you now? There are people you may have
never met, had you taken an alternate route in life. Of course,
you wouldn't know it, just like we don't know now. It's definitely something to think about. The question is: would you
want to lose something you have now for something that you
just *might* be wishing that you'd chosen differently back then,
just like now? Could a different choice have led to an alternate life that would've caused you to wish you'd made the
choice that you actually did make, this time around?" King
d.Avid frowned. "Does what I just said make any sense at all?"

Chad nodded. "Oh, I got it. I could have chosen differently.
And right now, I could be wondering how much better my life
would have been had I chosen the path that I ultimately *did*
choose: the path that has led me right where I am, at this pre-

cise moment. A different choice could have been better; or it could have been worse. Who can say?"

King d.Avid rubbed his hand over his head. "I'm pretty sure what we just said makes sense on some level. One just has to take a minute to really think about it. Our choices choose which path is taken and where we ultimately end up. Different choices; different results."

"Okay, so back to the original topic and the *choice* before you right now," Chad said. "I don't think you should go over there to speak or otherwise. First off, they'll know that you live here and, not that either might do it on purpose, that information could get out. This place is not as easy to secure as your house behind your guarded gates."

"I know. But I really would like to be able to say hello to Brianna. I'd like to find out how her grandfather is doing. How she's doing? I suppose I could wait until her husband . . . Unzell is back in town." King d.Avid shook his head. "It's something, isn't it? How things tend to happen in life. Who would have imagined that the grandfather would have helped launch me into this recording stratosphere I now find myself in, and now the husband is assisting in taking my concert tours to even higher heights. This crew this time around is awesome. Being so high up at this level . . . it almost takes my breath away."

"You know you could always invite her and her husband to your home once he returns back to the states after all of these concerts are over. But right now, you really need to be making *your* way overseas. You have quite a full schedule ahead of you."

King d.Avid nodded. "That's why I wanted to hang out here for a few days before I have to get back on the road again. I needed to restore my soul, to lie down beside the still waters."

The following morning, King d.Avid was getting ready to leave the beach house to return to his Atlanta mansion. In four days, he was scheduled to fly to London, giving him only one day to rehearse and ensure that everything was ready for his first overseas concert. Before he left, he went up on the observation roof to take in one last look of the beach and ocean, and to breathe in some untainted, ocean-fresh air.

It was then that he saw her.

The beauty he'd seen last evening. Today she sported a white floppy hat, her long hair trailing down her back. She wore a long, plain white dress that somehow—on her body—didn't look plain at all. It looked like she was leaving, saying good-bye. It definitely didn't look like she was planning on spending any more time on the beach. He took out his cell phone and snapped another photo of her as she gazed out at the ocean. And as though she'd heard what he was thinking, she lifted her hand to her mouth, blew a kiss to the ocean, gave a childlike, bending fingers–type wave to the waters, then turned around and trekked back into the house.

King d.Avid went downstairs to the den.

Chad came in fifteen minutes later. "What do you need?" he asked.

King d.Avid couldn't help but smile, mostly because he couldn't stop thinking about Brianna Wright Waters. "So what are you now? Some kind of a mind reader?"

"No. But I figured since I'm all you have here, I'd make sure you didn't need anything. Your bags are in the car. Everything is ready for you to depart whenever you are." Chad was driving King d.Avid in a Cadillac Escalade to ensure they didn't draw attention.

"I'm good," King d.Avid said.

"Okay. I'll be in the garage waiting when you're ready." Chad turned to walk out.

"Chad?"

Chad turned back around. "Yes, sir?"

"Brianna Waters."

"What about her?"

"I'd like for you to bring her to my house in Atlanta." King d.Avid's expression was unreadable. "Just her. Not her and her friend . . . just her. I'd like to talk with her before I leave for London."

"But you're leaving for London in four days. That doesn't leave much time. Are you sure about this? Especially now?"

"Yeah." King d.Avid's face was set.

"And what would you like for me to tell her is the reason for this request? Because I'm sure she's going to ask."

King d.Avid primped his lips several times before he bit down on his bottom lip twice. "Just tell her that I'd be honored if she would join me for a late lunch or early dinner."

"That's it?" Chad said.

King d.Avid looked stern. "That's it." He smiled. "I've kept my promise to do right by my friend Jonathan, although that had to be done through his heir. Now I'd like to try and make good on my promise to do something special for Pearson Wright—a bit more difficult, even if he *is* still alive. That fact became abundantly clear, rather quickly, when his grandson, Mack, brought Jonathan's son to visit me. I asked Mack to give Pearson my number and to have him call me. To this day, I've not heard from Pearson."

"Well, I just saw Brianna at her car when I was securing the premises. She was putting her overnight bag in there. I'm sure that likely means she's heading back home. I'll get right on this as soon as we return to Atlanta."

King d.Avid glanced around the room one last time, nodded his satisfaction with everything, then headed for the vehicle in the garage.

Chapter 17

And took her; and she came in unto him.
—2 Samuel 11:4 (b)

Brianna couldn't believe it. She held the phone to her ear and tried to continue to maintain her composure. Chad Holston, the guy who'd been in the limo with her brother; the guy she'd met again at the beach house, not even two days ago; the guy she was now learning worked in security for none other than King d.Avid himself—this guy was calling to invite her—of all people—to King d.Avid's house! *Lord, You are good!*

"If you don't mind," Chad continued, "King d.Avid would like to keep this invitation *strictly* confidential."

"What about my friend Alana?" Brianna asked. "Is it okay if she comes?"

"King d.Avid would really prefer it only be you at this time," Chad said. "I'm requesting that you don't even let anyone know you'll be visiting."

Brianna quickly turned somber. "Wait! Nothing's happened to my husband, has it?" Brianna unconsciously held her breath.

"Oh, no. In fact, all reports indicate that things are going magnificently on that end of the world. King d.Avid will be leaving in the next three days to connect with the rest of them," Chad said. "If anyone does, you most likely appreciate their grueling, intensely long schedule."

Brianna found herself exhaling. "I don't know if 'appreciate' is the word I'd use. My husband has already been gone and not been home in six weeks."

"Well, in another six or so, things should be winding down a bit. Come the end of June, everybody will get a nice long break," Chad said. "At least, the concert crew will. King d.Avid plans to be back in the recording studio. The man is a work-ing machine."

"Can you tell me what caused King d.Avid to want to meet me *now*? Not that I'm complaining or anything. Actually, I'm excited to meet him again. Well, sort of again. I met him when I was ten. That was almost twelve years ago, back when he and my grandfather, Pearson Wright, first began working to-gether."

"Yes, ma'am. I'm aware of the relationship between King d.Avid and Pearson Wright. But as you can imagine, I'm merely the messenger for the invitation. I'm sure King d.Avid will be happy to answer any and all of your questions regard-ing this, once you're here. But I *can* tell you that when he dis-covered you were visiting at the beach house, and that you were Pearson Wright's granddaughter . . . Mack Wright's sis-ter that he'd met when you were younger . . . he wanted to come over and say hello. I didn't think him doing something like that was wise, so I advised against it. It's my job to ensure his safety and security. I hope you can appreciate that," Chad said.

"Oh, absolutely. But I know my friend Alana would love to come to his house as well."

"This invitation is being extended to you alone . . . at least, at this time. So if you're open to the invite, I've been in-structed to personally come and pick you up—at your conve-nience, of course."

"Absolutely. I'd love to," Brianna said. "When?"

"This afternoon, if that works for you . . . between two and three P.M. As I've said, King d.Avid is scheduled to leave in three days."

"Three P.M. works for me." Brianna was jumping up and

down inside, but she remained cool. *What am I going to wear? I'm glad my hair is okay. Oh, my nails! Nails!*

"Then I will be at your house promptly at two thirty. I won't be in the limo, but a more discreet, one might say, played-down vehicle—a pearl-colored Cadillac Escalade. Not shabby by any means, but it definitely doesn't draw the attention that a limo does."

"I understand. The last thing I need is for my neighbors to see me getting into a limousine and riding off." She chuckled.

"My sentiments exactly. And it is vitally important that I protect King d.Avid. Therefore, I hope you won't be offended when I ask that you not bring a camera, any type of recording device, or your cell phone."

Brianna laughed. "Are you serious? I mean I get the camera and the recording devices. But you're saying I can't bring my cell phone with me, either?"

"Cell phones have recording devices on them," Chad said. "Cameras and such."

"Wow," Brianna said. "You guys don't play, do you?"

"Not when it comes to me doing my job. No, ma'am. We don't play."

"Well, what if I decline to leave my cell phone at home? I mean, I don't like the idea of being in a place, even if it *is* King d.Avid's, and not have a means of calling outside, should I need to."

"That's up to you. But I can tell you, as head of his security and especially at this point, that no cell phones from guests are being allowed past the gate. Now, if you'd like to bring your phone with you and leave it at the gate with the guard, that's permissible. You can then retrieve it on your way out. But taking it into the house at this point? No, ma'am."

"So this is really like a test, right? You, or should I say King d.Avid, invites me to his house. But since you don't really know me, you'd prefer I leave anything behind that I might be able to use to sell later to, say, folks like the tabloids." Brianna grinned to herself. "I guess that's fair enough. I suppose if it were me you were protecting, I'd like to know you're going to extreme measures to ensure my privacy and protection. All right. No recording devices and no cell phone past the guard's gate."

"Then I'll see you at two-thirty?" Chad said.

"I'll be ready." Brianna gave him her home address, hung up the phone, and started doing a happy dance right there in her den. "Wow," she said, looking up at the ceiling. "Hey, God! Did you just hear? I'm going to meet King d.Avid!" She set the words to a cute little tune. "I'm going to meet King d.Avid. I'm going to meet King d.Avid."

Chapter 18

*Many waters cannot quench love, neither can the
floods drown it: if a man would give all the sub-
stance of his house for love, it would utterly be con-
temned.*

—Song of Solomon 8:7

Sitting in the front passenger seat as Chad drove, Brianna
rode past the beautiful brick and iron gate and past the
guard, who merely waved Chad through. She knew without a
doubt that this place had to cost in the neighborhood of ten
million dollars just from what she could see of the outside of
the two-story European stone and stucco hard-coat mansion.
There was the luscious green lawn that looked like posh car-
pet beckoning for anyone who dared to come and roll around
in it, a circular driveway, a covered entranceway ensuring
guests would be protected from the elements. She knew the
covering was mainly for guests since this place likely had a
minimum of four garages. The gardens she saw were absolutely spectacular. And she thought for sure, as they'd driven
along the mile-long driveway, that she saw at least two separate
guesthouses.

She'd been offended at first, then impressed, when Chad
kept his word to ensure that she not bring any recording devices or her cell phone and asked permission to check her
purse. Of course she hadn't brought any of those items. She
was appreciative that, when he asked if she possibly had any of
these things hidden anywhere on her person, he hadn't done
an actual pat-down or body search when she'd said she hadn't.

Chad escorted her into an all-white living room. The baby grand piano was white. All of the furniture was white. The walls, with lots of personality and triple-crown molding, were white. And the coliseumlike column dividers were glossy white.

King d.Avid walked into the room, dressed in a casual maroon shirt and black slacks. He looked so much more handsome in person than any of his photos, even the ones that had clearly been retouched, could ever do him justice. Brianna was determined to keep any emotions she might feel, in getting to meet him at this stage in his life, completely under control. She respected him, but she was no screaming groupie.

Brianna had debated on what she should wear. But then, this wasn't a date or anything where she needed to dress to impress. Fortunately, she'd chosen to go with a white sleeveless blouse full of draping and pleats, along with a white and black cotton floral skirt—not over- or underdressed. She'd worn a pair of black shoes with the toes out and four-inch heels, only because she hated how she felt when she wanted to feel dressed up and wore flats. She made sure that her toenails were painted (a soft pink matching her pink painted fingernails) mainly because she could practically hear Alana dogging out anyone who wasn't wearing stockings and was showing unpainted toenails.

"Brianna," King d.Avid said when he walked over to greet her.

She stood and extended her hand to him. He took her hand, but for some reason, pulled her in to him and gave her a hug and a quick kiss on both cheeks. That *completely* caught her off guard.

"I hope you don't mind the hug and the friendly kiss. But I sort of feel like we're old friends," King d.Avid said. "I mean, we've met once before. And your grandfather was like family to me. How have you been? How's the family?" He held her hand as he pulled her down on the couch and sat next to her.

She was glad he released her hand after they sat. That kept her from having to figure out a way to politely slide her hand out of his. Not that she felt he was being fresh or anything like that. She just didn't care for how her body was reacting to his touch . . . not at all. In fact, she heard a voice inside of her say, "Okay, you've met him. Now get up and make your way on home." She laughed to herself.

"What's so funny?" King d.Avid said.

That was when Brianna realized that she'd actually laughed out loud. "I'm sorry. I was thinking about something. That was awfully rude of me."

He smiled. "Oh, I do that all the time. Especially when I'm bored and someone is going on and on . . ."

"Oh, you're not boring. I'm sorry if that's what you think," Brianna said.

"So how have you been all of these years?" King d.Avid asked, keeping his eyes locked on hers.

"I'm great. The family is doing well. Everything is great. Thanks for asking."

"Are you still writing poetry and short stories?" he asked.

She tilted her head slightly sideways. "How do you know about that?"

He scrunched down enough to make sure his eyes were evenly across from hers. "You told me."

"I did?"

"Yes, you did. Let me see if I get this right. You were ten. You were this cute little girl running off the porch with your friend. And the two of you were on a mission to stick a safety pin in the ground. I remember it was a safety pin because you held it up when you showed it to your grandfather."

Brianna started laughing. "It was my friend's idea. It was silly. We were trying to see if we could hear the devil beating his wife, or more to the point, her screaming when he did it." Brianna paused a second. "I can't believe you remember that." She pulled her body back a little, but kept her smile.

"You made an impression on me that day. At least you didn't knock me down by telling me that I was old at the tender age of twenty-five," King d.Avid said.

"Oh, that was *all* Alana. We're still friends. And she's still the same Alana."

"Well, if she thinks twenty-five was old, then I'm sure she thinks I'm on death's doorstep, now that I'm thirty-six. And that would make you . . ."

"I'll be twenty-two next month on June twelfth. And believe me, the older you get, the more you see that what you thought was old is really nothing like what you thought before you got there," Brianna said.

"I know. I remember when I was about to turn thirty. I held my breath thinking something huge was about to happen. That I'd be different. But to my surprise, nothing happened. I felt no different than I did the day before, at twenty-nine. Same thing when I turned thirty-five. And today, at thirty-six, I feel pretty much the same as I did the day I met you on your parents' porch." He quickly averted his eyes from her after saying that.

He stood. "Our food is ready if you'd like to go in now. I must confess beforehand: it's nothing elaborate. My regular people for everything are already in London awaiting my arrival. Everyone except for Chad, of course, and a few of the security people that are always around. So I kind of had to rent a chef for today's meal."

"Oh, so you're saying that you didn't fix the meal yourself?" As soon as the words left Brianna's mouth, she wished she could suck them right back in. That was flirtatious, even to her ears. And she certainly wasn't meaning to do anything like that.

He gave a quick smile, apparently opting not to verbally respond. She let out a slow and quiet sigh of relief, glad that he wasn't taking things the wrong way. She certainly didn't want to be sending out any mixed or wrong signals.

"My husband works for you, sort of," Brianna said. "He's

the stage manager for your concert tours. He works for the company you contracted to set up the stages."

"Yes. I'm very impressed with your husband's work. As the stage manager, he appears to be dedicated in helping to bring me the best set, the best stage, the best of everything possible. In fact, I'd look for someone like him to move up rather quickly in the organization. I know I've expressed my great pleasure in *all* of this crew's work."

"I wouldn't think people like you would even notice what people like him do?"

King d.Avid looked at her and grinned. "Why is that?" They'd finally reached the dining room. He stepped back and waved his hand to signal that she should go in first.

When she stepped into the large, mahogany wood, red and gold dining room that clearly accommodated a minimum of thirty people, her mouth visibly dropped open.

"We're going to eat in *here?*" she said, before she had time to stop herself.

"Unless you don't wish to," he said. "But I do hope you decide you'd like to. I rarely get to use this room these days. And I rather love it in here." He scanned the room as though he himself were taking it all in. "It's really a nice room. Don't you think? A little big, but when you have family and friends over, it's nice to be able to seat almost everyone at one table, whenever possible."

Brianna gave a quick laugh. "I'm sorry. I just had a flashback. You know, when we were younger, some people sat in the dining room, some at the kitchen table, and then there was—"

"The kiddies' table!" King d.Avid blurted out along with her.

"Yes!" She laughed again. "I so hated having to sit at the kiddies' table."

"What child doesn't? You feel like an outcast or something."

"Actually, it could be fun if the people you liked were at the table," Brianna said.

"Yeah, but most of the time it really was the *little* children, and you were the oldest—"

"And it was your job to take care of the little ones at the table," Brianna said.

"Absolutely. I couldn't wait to get old enough to graduate from *that* table, at least to the kitchen table. I remember some of us older children would beg to make a pallet on the floor and eat in a room with the television," King d.Avid said.

"Us, too," Brianna said.

"So, you can understand why I made *sure*, if nothing else, I had a table large enough to accommodate a lot of people, when I became able to."

"Oh, I understand perfectly. And far be it from me to be a party pooper and insist we eat at a smaller table." Brianna strolled over to the table. "That might traumatize you, and then you'd have a bad concert performance, and it would be all my fault."

He pulled out the chair for her. "Oh, I can assure you. You would never be the cause of me being traumatized. You might inspire me to put on the best concert I've ever done before. But anything negative"—he shook his head—"no way." He made sure she was comfortable, then took his seat at the head of the table, right next to her.

Brianna took the stainless-steel warming top off her plate. "This is a lot of food," Brianna said as she surveyed the food that was there.

"I wasn't sure what you might like. If you don't want something, don't feel bad about leaving it. And if there's something you want more of, just let me know, and I'll get it here in a snap."

"I could get used to this," she said, then visibly rolled her eyes at her words.

King d.Avid smiled. "I wish you'd quit doing that. Stop beating yourself up and just go on and be you. It's okay. I'm not taking anything too seriously here. Okay?"

She smiled back and nodded. "I just don't want to say something and give you the wrong impression."

"Well, you don't have to worry about that with me. I've been married four times, if you count my first marriage that was actually annulled within months of our vows. I'm almost divorced from my present wife. In fact, things should be final in the next two weeks. I've been engaged to two other women that never made it to the altar; thank God for those divine interventions. And then there's this woman now who believes we're engaged because that's her 'spiritual confession.' Forget that I've not asked and don't plan on asking. She has *decided* because we dated twice, years ago, and I'm about to be divorced, that means she and I are headed for the altar, completely her faith on this now."

"You certainly have lived, and do live, a colorful life," Brianna said.

"I have"—he looked at Brianna, then winked—"and do. May we say grace?" She nodded. He took hold of her hand and blessed the food. After releasing her hand, he pointed toward a small towel in a white bowl. "You can use that wet wash towel to wipe your hands." He picked up his towel and began wiping his hands with it.

"You know, they have sanitizers in little convenient bottles now," Brianna said.

"I know. There's a person who follows me around with one of those large bottles and squirts it in my hands after I shake folks' hands. That's my life. I have all of these people whose job it is to be sure I'm kept safe." King d.Avid poured salad dressing on his salad. He held the French dressing in the air over Brianna's salad. She nodded.

He poured until she indicated for him to stop. "Chad keeps me physically safe from those who might want to do me bodily harm. My manager keeps me financially safe from those who would try and do me harm in that arena. There's a minister who travels with me to ensure that spiritually I don't fall into harm's way. And then there's the little woman who follows me around to make sure that germs from other people don't manage to be the thing that ends up taking me out."

Brianna laughed. "You're really funny."

"I don't get a chance to show this side of me much. Most people only get to see the serious, ministerial side: the singer, the psalmist, the preacher side of me. Don't get me wrong: I love what I do. To be able to stand before so many and proclaim the Word of the Lord, whether through a song they enjoy or through the preaching I tend to do when it's called for. So many people have given their lives to the Lord because of the gift God entrusted in me and the call He has placed on my life. I don't take what I do lightly, nor do I take it for granted," King d.Avid said. "I give God all the praise."

He hurriedly put a piece of lettuce in his mouth, on purpose, Brianna believed, to give him some time to regroup and not completely break down. She had heard the tears on the cusp of his words, and she knew from him choking those tears back that they were ripe for release. His love for the Lord and his sincerity, without a doubt, touched her.

"I know how you feel," Brianna said. "That's how I feel about what you do. That's how my grandfather feels about what you do. You encourage me as I step out and do what I believe God is calling me to do. That's why I'm taking college courses dealing with theology and religion. I want to learn as much as I can about our Creator."

"Speaking of your grandfather: how is Pearson? It's been so long."

"Granddad is doing well. And just so you'll know, he is *so* proud of you."

"I doubt that," King d.Avid said. "I've attempted to reach out to him more times than I can count. But he doesn't reach back. I can't say I blame him though. I should have handled things differently. But I was young and inexperienced. And all of these people were coming at me from all sides, everybody with a thought, a deal, or an ultimatum. I just shut down. I was waiting on God to tell me what to do. But there was nothing. It was like God went silent on me. I took too long to do anything. So your grandfather walked."

"And you didn't go after him," Brianna said with resolve.

"If he wanted to leave, who was I to try and force him to do something he didn't want to do? I thought it would be arrogant of me to say that what I was doing was so important that everyone should put aside their own desires and feelings just to help make me great. I've always believed: whatever God has for me is for me. I still believe that."

"I guess I can see how you could look at it that way." Brianna nodded as she chewed, then swallowed. "But believe me: my grandfather thinks the world of you, the *world*. He lifts you up in prayer daily, at least that's what he told me when the topic of you came up."

"And I truly believe that he does. It's rough out here. Believe *me*. I thought your grandfather left in anger. When I would put in calls to him, he would never return them."

"Well, that doesn't sound at all like Granddad," Brianna said. "Even if he needs to tell you off, Granddad will stand flat footed and do just that. But he won't walk away or merely ignore you. He won't. Not unless he's told you that he's through with you. But running away and hiding? Uh-uh, that's just not Granddad's style."

"Yeah. I did find that out, although too late. The people who were supposed to be looking out for me decided not to put his calls through. And when I thought I was putting in a call to him and a few other people, or reaching out with correspondences, all of them *somehow* ended up filed in File 13," King d.Avid said, meaning they were thrown away.

Brianna shrugged. "I guess you should have kept trying yourself."

"Yeah, like I said: I've made my share of mistakes. And no matter how hard I try not to, I'll likely make more down the road. But I've also done and gotten a lot right."

"What about those people who were obviously sabotaging you? What did you do about them? Where are they now?" Brianna asked.

King d.Avid made a slow, silent chuckle. "Some are still on my payroll. I guess you can say I'm still with some of the devils that I know, rather than changing to devils that I don't know. I'm older now. I'm wiser. Not perfect by any means. But I love the Lord with all my heart, mind, soul, and strength. And as long as God will have me, and wants to use me, I'm going to do the work of Him who sent me. When I mess up, I go to God and ask for forgiveness from my heart. But I'm not going to let Satan take me out because of my foolish mistakes. That's one of his tricks. He gets us to mess up, then sit down on God because we feel we can't serve God's interest anymore. The harvest is too plentiful, and the laborers too few, for *any* of us to slack off, sit down, or quit on God."

"Amen," Brianna said. She smiled and ate her delicious smoked salmon. "Amen."

Chapter 19

He brought me to the banqueting house, and his banner over me was love.

—Song of Solomon 2:4

"Okay," King d.Avid said. "Enough about me. Tell me about you." He began to eat some of the squash casserole.

Brianna sat back against her chair. "Ooh, now you're going to make me feel bad, for real. I have nothing compared to you and your story."

King d.Avid stopped eating and looked at her. "Don't do that," he said in a warm and caring voice. "Please don't ever do that again."

"Do what?"

"Diminish your life. God has given you a beautiful smile that if you never did anything else except let it rip before the people you meet, you have blessed someone's life in ways you'll never know. Here I am with more money than I know what to do with. This big old house that cost millions, and that doesn't even count the millions I've spent to furnish it, or the money I spend every year to keep it up. I can buy any car, any vehicle I desire: a Lamborghini . . . Rolls Royce . . . Bentley. I have unrestricted access to my own private plane day or night. I pay people to keep up with my e-mails twenty-four seven due to the massive amount I receive. Same for my regular mail, which in this day and age you would think wouldn't be so much, but it is. I can sell out an arena that holds tens of thousands of fans in mere hours." He shook his head. "And your smile, oh my goodness, your smile has *made* my day. Your smile, that's pure and honest, has made me feel the truth of who I am when it comes to our Father in Heaven. From your smile, I know there is a God in Heaven, and that He loves me more than I'll ever know. So if that's all you have, if that's all you can say you've accomplished in life, then you're ahead of a lot of folks. Believe me: I know."

Brianna blushed and held her head down before looking back up, first with her eyes, then her smiling face. "Okay. Now I know *exactly* why you're the King," she said.

"See," King d.Avid said. "Now *that's* what I'm talking about! Right there." He pointed at her lips. "So pure and authentic." He began to eat again.

"So, you want to know about me. Okay, let's see. I gave my life to Christ when I was eight. I started back to college this year, taking religious studies. I met my childhood sweetheart, Unzell Waters, when I was in the ninth grade and he was in the twelfth. I was a straight-A student in school. I was the perfect daughter, who was punished minimally, mostly because I had an older brother who showed me all the things *not* to do if I didn't want to get in trouble with my parents. Unzell and I knew from the start that we would always be together. We met and became 'girlfriend and boyfriend,' so he is the only guy I've ever dated. You can say he was my first, my last, and my only. Unzell received a four-year scholarship to the University of Michigan to play football, breaking all kinds of records there. We were married in December, about a year and a half ago. He was on track to go to the pros—"

"Wait a minute. Unzell Waters? I think I remember hearing something about that," King d.Avid said. "I didn't get a chance to watch much television back then, but I certainly heard about what happened. Wasn't he playing in a championship game down in Florida when somebody tried to literally yank his leg off while he was in midstride?"

"Yes. That was my husband. And that fast track to the pros vanished right before his eyes," Brianna said. "Poof! Gone! Just like that!"

"Wow. And if I remember correctly, he was set to pull in some serious bank."

"Ye*p*," Brianna said, with a pop to her *p*. "But things changed. We adapted. He had two surgeries, went to rehab, still managed to graduate college that May. I suspended going to college and got a job as a secretary to help with the mounting bills—despite the health insurance, thank God he did have—while staying with my folks through all of that. When he graduated, he moved back to Montgomery, landed a job with a stage production company, and here we are. Unzell and I don't get to see much of each other lately—"

"Because of me," King d.Avid said. "My concert schedule has been unrelentingly *crazy*. Everybody has been gone from home for sometimes months at a time. Except I get to come home whenever I want, because I can just hop on my plane and fly in and out with no problem. They, on the other hand, are left to set up, break down, and pack up the set, while all I have to do is walk out on stage, perform, look good, and get the credit."

"Listen, I don't want you to misconstrue anything I've just said," Brianna said. "I'm thankful Unzell has this job. I'm even more thankful that he has a job he adores. And believe me: he loves what he's doing. Loves it! He respects you and what you do so much. He's often told me what an honor it is to serve you as you are serving the Lord. He looks at what you do as ministry, but he also considers what he does as ministry as well."

"'And whatsoever ye do, do it heartily, as to the Lord, and not unto men; knowing that of the Lord ye shall receive the reward of the inheritance: for ye serve the Lord Christ'— Colossians 3:23–24." King d.Avid nodded. "Your husband is absolutely right. It *is* ministry. What I do, what he does, what each of us—no matter how big or small what we feel we're doing is—do. Ultimately, it's not about us; it's about Jesus and the Kingdom of God. That's why I don't look down on any of the people who work in our troop."

"Why do you call the group . . . the crew a troop?"

"Because what we do is like being in the army. Only, we're in the army of the Lord. Have you ever heard that old song people sang back in the day, 'I'm a soldier'?"

"Yes."

"Well, I believe we're soldiers. And like soldiers, we deploy to various regions of the world. We're on the battlefield for our Lord. And sometimes, our service to God requires us to sacrifice. We may have to be away from family longer than we'd like. We have to take certain training courses so we can learn how to survive, in case we're ever under attack, or worse: captured by the enemy. Many times what we think is the devil messing with us may just be God placing us in a simulated situation in order for us to learn what we need to know. Then when the enemy *does* move against us, we'll automatically and instinctively know precisely how to respond without even having to give it a second thought." King d.Avid took a swallow of his soda that was becoming watery from the melting ice. "Our actions become second nature."

"That was deep, right there," Brianna said. "I've never thought about it like that. My husband is on deployment while in God's military operations. He sacrifices . . . we're both sacrificing; but it's all for a good cause—a cause greater than ourselves, when you actually think about it. Then, the part you said about sometimes things happening in our lives and it's for training purposes, now that's *really* something to chew on."

"We just need to know the difference between friendly training and enemy fire. It matters. Because when it's time to truly fight back, to go into combat, we'd better know it, be ready, and do it," King d.Avid said. He looked at Brianna's plate. "Would you care for any more of anything?"

Brianna glanced down at her plate. She didn't remember cleaning her plate. "Oh, no." She shook her head. "I'm good. Everything was great!"

"So . . . are you ready for dessert? We have cheesecake. And you get to choose your own topping." He smiled as he looked at her. "We can go up onto the back terrace and eat out there. It's really beautiful. I don't get to enjoy it as much as I'd like to, either." He wiped his mouth with his black linen napkin, then laid it on the table.

"It sounds to me like maybe you need to learn how to stop and smell a few roses. It's not good to work all the time and never enjoy the blessings of the Lord or some of the fruits of your labor. Even people working out in the fields get a taste, every now and then, from where they are laboring. If you ask me, not to do it is practically an insult to God."

"Ooh. Ouch!" King d.Avid said. He stood up. "The truth can hurt." He held Brianna's hand as she got up.

Brianna started to take her hand away and tell him that she was more than capable of getting up from a table on her own. *I do it all the time.* But if she was being honest, she had to admit that she enjoyed being treated the way a woman should be treated. It was refreshing to have someone pay attention to her . . . to make her feel as though she existed, at least a little bit and for a change.

They went upstairs to the second level and out onto the terrace. Brianna couldn't believe anything could be so beautiful. But it was. And it absolutely took her breath away!

King d.Avid hung up his cell phone. "The chef is bringing up our dessert."

Brianna just stood, shaking her head at the magnificence her eyes beheld. "This is the most beautiful place I've *ever* seen in my entire life! It's like I would imagine the Garden of Eden or Paradise to have looked. Yes . . . this is Paradise! The waterfall, gorgeous plants and trees in full bloom in every direction you look. Is that a reflecting pool? Yes, that *is* a reflecting pool! And those stone steps up to that peaceful-looking area with the gazebo. This is simply stunning. *Absolutely* stunning!"

King d.Avid looked around. He walked over and stood behind her, a little *too* close for her comfort. "You know; you're right," he said, nodding as he leaned forward and primped his mouth. "The view *is* stunning!" He then took her hand and led her to the patio table. Pulling out her chair for her, he looked into her eyes, and said it as though it were five words instead of two: "Ab-so-lute-ly *stunning!*"

Chapter 20

A fountain of gardens, a well of living waters, and streams from Lebanon.

—Song of Solomon 4:15

After Brianna and King d.Avid finished their dessert, they went down on the grounds and walked around. There were acres and acres of land, total and complete, with each area performing a function or a purpose. Even the natural area was natural by design. He had a tennis court, now with a possible promise from Brianna to play on it on another day, pending his return to the states. There was an outdoor basketball court and another magnificent pool area, despite having a reflecting pool right outside his backyard.

"You like water, huh?" Brianna said. "You have enough pools and fountains."

"I never have enough water. I love water," King d.Avid said. "There's just something special about water, wouldn't you agree? Water is redeeming."

Brianna didn't respond, although if she had, she would have agreed. She loved water as well. *Yes, water is redeeming.* They laughed and talked while admiring the various things in and around his home. Things that Brianna was surprised he had never paid attention to before. It was as though he resided there, but didn't really *live* there.

"Well, I thank you for the tour of this exquisite home, Brianna. You've certainly sold me. I think I'd like to own it now."

She laughed. "Oh, so are you trying to tell me that you don't own this house?"

He shrugged. "I paid for it, sure enough. But if you can show me things I should be showing you, and I can see what a great home it would be to own, then I'm not sure I truly own it. I purchased the house, but I haven't owned it. And I've definitely not made the house into a home. I guess I'll have to work a little harder on that."

"Well, I suppose I should be getting to my own house right about now," she said.

"Now?" he said in a pretend-teasing, whining voice. "You have to leave *now*? And there's so much more you need to show me about this place. Like the movie theater. I desperately need to check out the movie theater here inside the house."

"Are you serious?" Brianna asked.

"Yes, I'm serious. Do you know how long it's been since *I've* been to the movies?"

"No," Brianna said. "But I know how long it's been since I've been to one."

"I'm sure whatever number you have, I'll top it," King d.Avid said.

"Okay, if that's a real challenge, we can do this."

"Keep in mind now, you've only been married for a year and a half," King d.Avid said. "And I'm an old man who, except for work, doesn't do a whole lot of things."

"I hear you. So let's hear what you got," Brianna said, her hand on her hips.

"All right. The last time I saw a newly released adult movie was a year ago," King d.Avid said. "Mind you, the only reason I'm stating this was an adult movie is because I *did* happen to watch a movie in the theater here with little Melvin when he and your brother, Mack, came to visit me the week before Christmas. It was *The Karate Kid*, a remake of the 1984 film I happened to have seen when I was around Melvin's age."

Oh, so my brother came to Atlanta that time to see you? That's what he was doing here. Brianna didn't want to get sidetracked with her thoughts, so she didn't try to get any more information about Mack and Melvin's visit here. "Not bad," Brianna said, nodding and sticking with the subject at hand. "Well, the last time I went to the movies, adult or otherwise, was a month before my wedding. It's was a Thanksgiving release. Unzell, at the time my fiancé, took me."

"And you actually expect me to believe he hasn't taken you to a movie since that time? Honestly?"

"Honestly."

"Wow," King d.Avid said. "Well, you can't blame that one on me and my work schedule. Okay, what about going with a friend. You mean to tell me that you and Alana or some other friend have failed to go to a movie in all of this time? Tell the truth now."

"That's *exactly* what I mean to tell you. Alana goes on dates with guys, so the last thing she needs is for *me* to go to a movie with her," Brianna said.

"What about her going to see one with you?" King d.Avid said. "Aren't friendships supposed to be a two-way street?"

"Yeah. But I wouldn't do a friend like that. I wouldn't guilt her into going with me to a movie or anything else, just because I don't have anyone to go with."

"Wow, you're almost about to make me feel sorry for you," King d.Avid said.

"Well, don't. If I really wanted to see a movie, I could just go by myself."

"Pardon me for saying this, and I may be totally out of place. But you shouldn't have to either miss out *or* go alone," King d.Avid said. "But that's just me."

"So what are you trying to say?" Brianna said. "That I need to find other friends, preferably someone in as bad a shape as me when it comes to movie and dinner buddies?"

"Hmmm. That might be one thought. Another thought

would be: maybe you should tell your husband to take you to see a movie, out to dinner, or whatever your heart desires," King d.Avid said. "That's what *I* think."

Brianna squinted her eyes a little as she tightly buttoned her lips. She relaxed her stance. "Or maybe we should change the subject."

King d.Avid held up both hands in a sign of surrender. "No problem. Didn't mean to overstep boundaries. Just trying to help, that's all. But"—he began to grin—"I am serious about us trying out my movie theater. Give it a good old workout. It's state of the art with popcorn, drinks, and a completely stocked candy stand. It's the next best thing to going to the movies without being mauled and harassed for autographs and pleas to listen to 'the next smash hit' by Pookie and His Cousins."

Brianna started laughing. "Pookie and His Cousins?"

"Yeah, you know. People see you out and they want you to help launch them into stardom. Pookie is a nickname of someone who grew up in my community. I just pulled his name out of the air, purely for added effect."

Brianna nodded. "Oh, okay."

"So, is that an okay to my invitation to watch a movie? I can order up the latest thing you'll find playing in movie theaters right now. I can."

"Oh, so you have it like *that*, huh?"

"Not trying to brag or anything"—he took his fingers and did a scratching motion against his shirt as though he was sharpening his nails on sandpaper taped to his chest—"but I have it like *that*."

"So you can order up any movie I want to see? *Any* movie?"

"Pretty much."

She nodded. "Okay. Let's do it."

"You just want to see if I really can do it," King d.Avid said. "Don't you?"

She held out her hand to motion for him to pass. "Lead the way, O King."

He smiled and walked beside her as he led her to a set of eight-foot-tall, solid mahogany double doors. When he opened one of the doors, she couldn't believe just how beautiful and large a theater room in a house could be.

After excusing himself for a few minutes, as promised, he ordered up the movie she requested to see.

But what really blew her away? Really. Was that the movie she requested hadn't even been released to the public as yet, and it wasn't due to release until the following week.

Chapter 21

He opened the rock, and the waters gushed out;
they ran in the dry places like a river.

—Psalm 105:41

It was a little after 10 P.M. by the time the two-hour movie went off.

Brianna glanced down at her watch a bit surprised by how late it had gotten so quickly. "Oh, my! Look at the time. I can't believe I've imposed on you this long."

"Believe me, this has not been an imposition at all," King d.Avid said. "I've enjoyed every second, every minute, every hour of it. And trust me: I don't say that to very many people about very many things."

"Me either," Brianna said. "I've enjoyed it as well. But I really must be getting home. Chad made me leave my cell phone at the house, and if anyone has been looking for me, they've probably already sent out the cavalry to hunt me down."

King d.Avid frowned. "Chad made you leave your cell phone?"

Brianna smiled, then shrugged her shoulders. "Yeah. But it's okay. I understand where he was coming from."

"Did Chad *physically* take your phone?"

"No, he just asked me not to bring it or any other type of recording device. But I absolutely understand why he would do that," Brianna said, smiling. "It's okay. Really, it's okay." She nodded.

"I know why when it comes to people who are out to do me

harm. But not you. He shouldn't have made you leave your phone like that," King d.Avid said, visibly disturbed about this. "I'll speak with him—"

"Please don't." She touched his arm. "The truth is: I've never felt so free as I have today. I didn't have to worry about my phone ringing or having anyone asking me where I am and what I'm doing. Today was so liberating. As helpful as electronic gadgets are supposed to be in our lives, sometimes it feels like we're being imprisoned by technology. You can't go anywhere and just have some peace and quiet . . . serenity. People don't think we're entitled to be inaccessible anymore. You can't even go to the bathroom in peace. And if anyone *has* called, now they'll be expecting an explanation as to my past whereabouts, which I need to let you know right now, up-front; no one is going to get," Brianna said. "I have no intention of letting anyone know I was here. No one will know, unless it's something you or your people put out there."

"I appreciate that," King d.Avid said. "You'd be amazed at how many people want to come here just so they can broadcast that they were here. It makes it hard to be able to trust anyone or their true motives and intentions. You always feel like people don't care so much about *you,* as they do the bragging rights that make them look and feel important. I'm looking for real people in my life, especially now. And it's not easy to find them."

"Well, King d.Avid—or as my grandfather would call you, David R. Shepherd."

"No," King d.Avid said. "Your grandfather did *not* tell you my real name, did he?"

Brianna laughed. "He most certainly did. Everything except what the 'R' is for."

"I suppose he also told you that he was the one who came up with the stage name of King d.Avid?"

"Yes. He told me that as well."

"May I ask you to do something for me? And if it's something you don't care to or want to do, will you just tell me?" King d.Avid said.

"Go ahead," Brianna said.

"Would you please tell your grandfather how much I appreciate all that he did for me? And would you let him know that I was wrong. And that if I could go back and change things, I would."

"David, let me say this to you."

King d.Avid began to smile.

"Wha*t*?" Brianna said, emphasizing the *t*.

"Nothing. It's just gratifying to hear my real name being spoken so nice and respectful. I like the name King d.Avid, but you make me feel like you see *me* and not just the created persona. But I'm sorry: I rudely interrupted you. You were about to say?"

"I just want you to know that my grandfather holds nothing against you for any reason. He's proud of you. And if you ask me: I think you should call him and tell him all of the things you want him to know yourself. Stop sending messages by other folks."

"Seriously?"

"Seriously," Brianna said. "In fact"—she looked at her watch—"we're an hour ahead of him in Alabama. Why don't you call him right now? Tonight."

"I'm not very good at making things right with people I'm estranged from. If you don't believe me, ask my parents and siblings. They will tell you that we're not speaking at all. Besides, I don't have Pearson's number." He grinned and tilted his head to the side.

"Any old excuse will do. Where's your phone?" Brianna beckoned with her hand.

"I put it up. I feel the same way as you do sometimes. There are days when I don't want to be bothered, and today just happens to be one of those days. I put my phone away when we came in from outside. And I sent everybody who might even remotely attempt to interrupt or bother me home, including Chad."

"All right. I don't have my phone; yours is put up. So I suppose we need to go get your phone, so you can call my grandfather and put all of your misgivings, *and* his, to rest. Besides, if I were to tell Granddad, he'd want to know how we happened to speak."

"So you want me to go and get my phone?"

"Yes."

"Right now?"

"Yes." Brianna crossed her arms and began to tap her right foot as though she was perturbed. She knew she was unconvincing; her smile betrayed her.

King d.Avid started laughing. "You are *so* funny."

"Let's go get your phone. Now, Mister. I'm not playing with you. I know my grandfather will be thrilled to hear from you. So you're going to call him tonight before I leave this place. I'm going to teach you a thing or two on conflict resolution tonight."

King d.Avid shrugged his shoulders as he grinned. "All right. You're the boss. I'm just King d.Avid, the humble mega-super-duper-nova-star."

Brianna laughed. "Granddad said you'd do that."

"Do what?"

"Come up with a new way of describing what you are and have accomplished."

"Oh, he did, did he? I suppose he still thinks he knows me that well."

"I suppose that he does." Brianna pointed. "March," she said for him to go get his phone.

"Actually, my phone is upstairs in my bedroom," King d.Avid said.

"In your bedroom?" Brianna said, taking one step back.

"Yeah."

"And you don't have any landline phones around this monstrosity of a house?"

King d.Avid stepped back closer to her. "Oh, so now my beautiful amazing home that earlier today took your breath away is a monstrosity of a house? Is that what I'm hearing from you *now*, Mrs. Waters?"

"I asked you a question first. So answer my question. You don't have a landline phone anywhere? I mean, seriously?"

"No, I seriously don't. In this age one doesn't need a land-line. I'm hardly ever here. My cell phone is with me no matter where I am. So what's the point of having a phone that serves no purpose to anyone, except the people who dust here, and maybe the people who happily take my money at the phone company," King d.Avid said.

"Well, then, go get your cell phone and bring it down here," Brianna said. "I'll wait. Then I'll give you Granddad's phone number, and you can call him. But you need to hurry now, before it gets too late. I don't want to end up waking him."

"I tell you what. Why don't we *both* go up to my room and get my phone. That in itself will cut out a lot of wasted time. Then I can call him and tell him what's been on my heart all of these years."

Brianna shook her head. "I really don't think that's a wise idea."

"I know you're not scared of me. And you know I'm not going to do anything to you. I've been a complete gentleman since you strolled through my doors, have I not?" King d.Avid said.

"Okay. Okay. I just don't want you getting the wrong idea about me," Brianna said. "I'm married, happily married. And we're merely going to your bedroom to get your cell phone so you can call my grandfather. That's it. That, and maybe me getting to take a peek at yet another room in this palace."

"Absolutely. And for the record: I'm an almost-divorced man who has made enough mistakes not to keep repeating those same mistakes. All I want to do is get my cell phone, call your grandfather, then put the phone right *back* where I took it from," King d.Avid said. "That's it."

"And after that, you need to have me taken back to my house," Brianna said.

King d.Avid walked out of the area toward the staircase that looked more like an upscale, winding roller-coaster track with its fancy, intricate scrolls. Brianna followed him up the stairs. Walking up those steps made her feel differently . . . like royalty, even.

He opened the door to his bedroom. She let out a loud gasp, then quickly clamped both hands over her mouth and held tight. She took her hands down. "Oh, my goodness! Look at this room!" She turned to King d.Avid. "Do you not have *one* spot around this entire place that doesn't manage to somehow take my breath away? Wow. Wow. Wow, this is . . . this is . . . you know, I don't even have words for what this is."

King d.Avid walked over to his nightstand and retrieved his cell phone. Brianna noticed him as he looked down at it and frowned.

"A lot of missed calls, I take it?" she said.

He looked up. "Yeah. And they will *all* have to wait, with the exception of maybe the one from Chad. He only calls when it's important. But the rest will wait. And I'll hit Chad back as soon as I finish speaking with Pearson. Okay, so what's your grandfather's number?" King d.Avid pressed the corresponding buttons as Brianna called out her grandfather's home phone number. "It's ringing," King d.Avid said, his eyes looking up, then down, then back up again.

Brianna walked over and quietly lowered herself onto the couch in front of the white stone fireplace. She could only imagine how beautiful this room was during the days when a fire was lit and flames danced around in it. "Oh, and don't tell him I'm here," Brianna said, glancing over at King d.Avid. "Or that I was the one who gave you his—"

King d.Avid waved for her to be quiet. "Hi, Pearson? Hi. This is a blast from your past. It's David R. Shepherd. How are you?" King d.Avid paused, then chuckled. "Okay, King d.Avid. I'm great. Better than great, if I have to tell the real truth right now. I'm blessed, man . . . I'm so blessed. But listen, I just wanted to call you and let you know how much you've meant in my life, and how much you *still* mean to me, even to this day. How much I appreciate you. Because had it not been for you . . ."

King d.Avid listened, then wiped at a few tears that managed to escape from his eyes. "Thank you. Thank you so much for that. No, really. I don't know what I did to deserve someone like you in my life. Then for you to still be in my corner the way you are, still holding up the banner in spite of how things went down. . . . Well, all I can say is: God is good. And this means the world to me." King d.Avid paused again. "Say what? How did I get this number? You're asking because it's brand-new, private, *and* unpublished."

King d.Avid glanced over at Brianna. "Oh, you know what they say: The Lord will make a way somehow." King d.Avid laughed. "Yes, sir. I suppose I do have my own ways of helping the Lord out, at times. But we both know that without Him, we can do nothing. I know that much, if I don't know anything else, I *do* know that. I can *do* nothing, and I *am* nothing without the Almighty God on my side. No doubt."

King d.Avid looked at Brianna again. She was trying to keep from smiling as she tightly hugged herself. She felt like doing the waltz, one of the ballroom dances she'd learned and not done much of since she was sixteen. When he looked again at her and their eyes locked, he winked.

She quickly turned away, then bit down on her bottom lip, as she worked extremely hard to hold in a full-blown, teenage girl's giggle that was only one more look her way away.

Chapter 22

And he lay with her; for she was purified from her
uncleanness: and she returned unto her house.

—2 Samuel 11:4 (c)

Brianna awakened to a sun-filled room. It was a beautiful day. She could tell, just from the way the sun was already causing her to feel. But as she struggled to open her eyes completely, then began to look around, everything came rushing back to her. She bolted straight up in the bed.

"Oh, my Lord! What did I do?" Brianna said. A man's groan caused her to quickly close her eyes back.

"What is it?" the man said groggily as he began to stir. "What's the matter?"

Brianna opened her eyes. "Wake up." She shook him vigorously. "Wake up!"

He sat up and began to rub the sleep from his eyes, then rubbed his face with both his hands. When he turned and looked her way, he instantly broke into a huge smile and leaned over. "Morning, Bathsheba. Did you sleep well?"

Brianna pulled the covers up around the top half of herself better and clutched the bedspread comforter tightly. With her other hand, she tried to cover her face. "Please tell me this is just a dream. Please tell me we didn't do what I think we did?"

King d.Avid pushed himself to a straighter position, pressing his back against the bed's headboard. "Ah," he said, then shook his head with adoration. "Brianna."

"We did, didn't we?" Brianna took a quick peek under the covers. "We did! God, forgive me. We did. And I can't even blame this on alcohol, because I didn't have anything stronger than a cola to drink."

"Brianna, I'm sorry." King d.Avid closed his eyes for a few seconds as though he was either going back to sleep or praying.

Brianna looked upward. "God, please forgive me. Oh, God, please forgive me."

"Lord, I ask that you forgive me as well," King d.Avid said before turning back to Brianna. "Listen—"

"Why did you call me Bathsheba?" Brianna said.

"What?"

"When you were first waking up. You said, 'Morning, Bathsheba.' I want to know why you said that."

King d.Avid shook his head. "I don't know. Maybe because the last thing on my mind before I fell asleep was the name Bathsheba. So when I awakened, a bit disoriented I might add, I spoke what was last on my mind."

"Do you know anyone named Bathsheba?" Brianna asked.

King d.Avid chuckled. "Just you. Don't you remember? We were waltzing around the ballroom floor, you told me your middle name was Bathsheba. I told you the *R* in my name was for Rondell. I said it was interesting that your folks named you Bathsheba, albeit your middle name, and that my folks named me David—both biblical names."

"Well, it's neither interesting nor *cute,* right now. Not to me. Oh, my goodness. Oh, my goodness!" Brianna let her head fall back against the headboard. She gazed up at the ceiling and incessantly shook her head.

"Brianna, please calm down. It's going to be all right. I'm sorry that you're upset. But I must say that I absolutely had a beautiful time with you the entire time we spent together. Where did you learn how to do all of those ballroom dances?

The waltz, the tango, the quickstep, cha cha, rumba, and what was that other thing you showed me?"

"Viennese waltz," Brianna said, blowing a sigh of disgust with her own self.

"Look, I'm sorry you're upset. But I'm not sorry about the lovely time we had together. I'm not. And I'm not going to lie to you or God and say differently. I won't."

"Well, I *am* sorry. And I *do* regret it." Brianna got up out of the bed, dragging the comforter as she cleverly wrapped it around herself to cover her body. "I can't believe I did this. What in Heaven's name was I thinking?" She began to cry, then looked toward the ceiling again. "God, I'm sorry. I'm so sorry. I guess this proves: I *wasn't* thinking!"

"Listen, Brianna . . . Brianna, I need you to calm down. It's not as bad as it seems. No one knows you were here."

"Except for Chad, the guard at the front gate, the rent-a-chef"—she ticked off the names with her fingers—"and oh, now let's see who else? Oh, yeah, that's right—God!" She dabbed her eyes with a corner of the comforter. "God knows, David. God knows!"

"Well, Chad's not going to say anything. The rent-a-chef, as you call him, doesn't know who you are and I sent him packing after we finished our meal. And God—"

"Yeah. *And* God," Brianna said. "What do you have to say about God? You know, God who neither slumbers nor sleeps. God who promised to never leave us. God."

"We both just told Him we're sorry. We've asked Him to forgive us. That's all we can do, Brianna. We can't press the reverse button on the clock and make like it never happened."

"Yeah . . . well . . . but we can definitely make sure we're never in a position for this to ever happen again. We can do *that!* Something told me to leave. Right after dessert, I should have gotten my purse and left. For sure after that comedic, romantic, love story rolled its credits. At the very latest: when you hung up from talking with my grandfather. I should have insisted that you take me home then, Chad or no Chad. Before the dancing; before the late-night talking, whispering, laughing, and sharing. I don't care how late it was. I don't care who might have seen the car pull into my driveway at one or two o'clock in the morning. I should have stuck to my first mind and had you take me home."

"I'm sorry," King d.Avid said, adjusting the top sheet better around him. "How many times do you want me to say it? I'm sorry. I just didn't see a good reason for you to go home so late. We danced, we talked, we shared our hearts. And honestly, it was nice having someone around me where I didn't feel a need to have my guard up. I was free for a change. Free, Brianna, all thanks to you. And there was no reason for you to go home when I have six unoccupied bedrooms in this monstrosity of a house, as you call it."

"Yeah, well, I can't blame this all on you," Brianna said, retrieving various pieces of her clothing from around the room. "And I'm not. You *did* insist that I stay, then that I stay the night. But you said you had extra bedrooms that I was welcome to use. I should have gone to one of those bedrooms and locked the door behind me—"

"Whoa! Hold up. Lock the door behind you?" King d.Avid said, recoiling and registering a puzzled look on his face. "I wouldn't have tried anything while you were in another bedroom," King d.Avid said. "I don't do things like that."

"I wasn't talking about locking it so you couldn't come in. I was talking about locking it to keep me from coming out. It's obvious that I wanted you just as much as you wanted me." Brianna sat back down on the bed with the comforter still wrapped around her. "I suppose you weren't the only one who felt free yesterday. It's like the forbidden tree in the Garden of Eden all over again. You can eat from that tree, that tree, that tree, or that tree." She pointed around the room as she spoke. "But don't dare touch *that* tree over there." She pointed at King d.Avid. "And what do I go and do? I just *have* to taste the fruit from *that* tree. Yeah, God. You know, *that* tree. The one You *specifically* pointed out *not* to touch. I *had* to see for myself if the fruit from the tree I knew not to touch was any better or tasted any different from what I could freely partake of."

"Brianna, please don't do this to yourself." King d.Avid reached over to touch her arm.

She recoiled and jumped to her feet. "Please don't do that. Because I'm going to tell you, David. As upset as I am about what we did here, there is something about you that's so tender and so special, you make it hard to do what's right. You made me feel so wonderful the whole time I was with you. Maybe that's how it is. When people want something, they make the extra effort to get it. Then after they get it, that's when they slack off. I'm not blaming Unzell for what I did, because he's a truly good and hardworking man whom I believe loves me dearly. And no matter how lonely I feel or have felt, and no matter what kind of attention I craved, Unzell has done *nothing* to justify what I just did to our marriage."

"I'm going to ask one thing of you. I know you might take it the wrong way, but I have to put it out there," King d.Avid said. "Can we please keep what happened between us between you and me? Don't go running and confessing it to your husband. Don't feel a need to share what happened with your best friend or anyone else for that matter."

She let out a short, almost crazy laugh and flopped back down. "Of course not. We wouldn't want this plastered all over the tabloids or on any evening entertainment shows. And don't forget about all the Christians who would be devastated to learn you, the anointed psalmist of the Lord . . . a man after God's own heart . . . has fallen by the wayside just like the others who claim to uphold the banner of the Lord. Cue the music—another one bites the dust."

"That's not why I'm asking you this," King d.Avid said. "I'm asking this because if your husband finds out, and you love him the way you say that you do, it will most likely tear his heart and your relationship apart. And I don't think he deserves to have that done to him. You and I did this. We're responsible. It's between me and you. It wouldn't be fair to bring him into it. And honestly, if you want to make things right between you two, I don't want our night of indiscretion—bad judgment, whatever you want to call it, but definitely something you obviously hate happened—to affect what you desire in life."

Brianna stood back up. "Well, you don't have to worry about anything." She sniffled a few times. "This secret is safe with me. I'm not going to say anything to anybody. Not even Alana . . . *especially* not Alana. She thinks I'm the good, smart one."

"Okay. Then it's settled. As far as you're concerned, this was a mistake that will never repeat itself. And as soon as you're dressed, I'll personally take you home," King d.Avid said. "This way, even Chad won't have to know you stayed the night."

"He's head of your security. Somehow, I'm sure Chad probably already knows."

"I will tell him that I drove you home myself, which will be true. If he mentions that you spent the night, I'll not let on what transpired between us. And as far as all this goes, you slept in a guest bedroom, should your being here overnight ever come up."

"I'm not going to lie," Brianna said, vigorously shaking her head. "I already have one sin charged to me because of this; I'm not going to add lying on top of it. I'm not."

"And I'm not asking you to lie. All I'm asking is that you not volunteer any information," King d.Avid said. "But no one is going to bring it up, I assure you."

"Well, as soon as I get my clothes on, I'll be ready for you to take me home." She let her head drop, then lifted it back up again. "Listen, I do appreciate your lovely hospitality. Everything was *so* magnificent. So please don't think I'm ungrateful or anything like that. There was just a point we shouldn't have ever crossed, but we did. We went too far."

King d.Avid smiled. "Well, I'm glad our paths crossed again. I've always thought you were special, since that very first time

I set eyes upon you. And I believe you're *still* going to do those great things you spoke about when you were ten years old. But you're a woman now: a beautiful, intelligent, and a Godly woman, in spite of what's transpired."

"May I use your bathroom?" Brianna asked.

"Sure. And Brianna, I just want you to know: whatever I have, regardless of how things go between us from here on out, if you need it, just ask, and it's as good as yours."

"Thank you. But there is nothing between us. And all I need right now is some soap and water. I wish I had some redeeming waters, if something like that were available." She stood up, still holding on to the comforter wrapped around her, as she took the clothes she clutched in her other hand into the master bathroom with her.

Brianna stepped into the shower and let its soothing waters run down. *If only there was a way to just as easily wash away the sin I've committed against God and against my husband. If only it was this easy. . . .*

Chapter 23

*Stolen waters are sweet, and bread eaten in secret
is pleasant.*

—Proverbs 9:17

"It's a simple question," Alana said over the phone. "I
called your cell phone all yesterday and into the night.
Of course, I called your home number as well. You didn't answer either one. I finally get you this morning, and you can't
tell me where you were?"

"Alana, just let it go, okay," Brianna said, her voice weary
from crying.

"I'm just confused. I'm the closest thing you have to family
here in Atlanta, and you weren't anywhere to be found. Is that
why you were in such a hurry to leave the beach and get
home? You had another engagement, and you didn't want me
to know about it?"

"You certainly know how to blow something completely out
of proportion. Look, Alana, I turned my cell off. Besides, you
know I'm not a cell phone girl . . . not like you."

"Yeah, but you always answer your landline," Alana said.
"And I called it every single time I called your cell. In all of my
time knowing you, I don't think I've ever not known where
you were. You either tell me before you go or after you get
back."

"Well, maybe *that* ought to tell you something," Brianna
said with a little more attitude and snap than she intended.

"Excuse me?" Alana said, having picked up on Brianna's snarky tone.

"Look, I'm sorry. I didn't mean to snap at you like that. But when you ask somebody something and they don't give you the answer you're looking for, then you need to back off so they're not forced to tell you something that you might not want to hear or that *just* might hurt your feelings."

"Okay. So allow me to read what's apparently between the lines here. Since you're such a sweet person that you can't bring yourself to say it and *hurt* my feelings. It's none of my business where you *were* or *what* you were doing. And even if you *were* there, merely watching the phone every single time it rang, people don't always feel like talking. So some people just need to take a hint, get a life, and chill!" Alana said. "Now how was *that* for straight, undiluted, unadulterated truth?"

"Alana, I'm sorry, okay. It's just . . . I miss Unzell. I wish he were here. And I'm a little upset with myself because it looks like I'm not measuring up to what God is expecting from me."

"Okay, let me stop you right there. If *anybody* loves the Lord, it's you. If anyone tries to do what God is telling them to do, it's you. I think you're being a bit too hard on yourself. If anyone should be upset with her life, it ought to be me," Alana said. "I live in a *constant* state of sin, it seems. At least when *you* feel like you've messed up, you go to God and ask Him for forgiveness. Not me. I figure: if I'm not going to stop doing what I'm doing that caused me to come before Him in the first place, then I might as well not waste His time asking His forgiveness. Particularly for something I know I'll just be right back asking Him to forgive me for, most likely, a few days later."

"Alana, we have all sinned and fallen short of the glory of God. I don't care how much we try. And I'm not saying that we shouldn't try, but somehow, somewhere we mess up. Whether it's something we did that we shouldn't have; or something that we didn't do that we should have. I'm trying my best, God knows, I'm trying. But—"

"But nothing. I'm sitting over here in somebody else's house because my finances and life are so messed up that I can't get my own place. I'm hoping the man comes back and sees what a great catch I am and makes me his live-in companion permanently. And what am I willing to do to show him how great of a catch I am? Whatever I think will work, that's what. Now, if that's not premeditated sin, I don't know what is. Then there's you: Mrs. Brianna Bathsheba Wright Waters, working every day of your life, trying to do the right thing—"

"And *still*, I miss it," Brianna said. "Don't you see that? We all miss it sometimes. So can we just drop this? No, I'll tell you what: why don't you and I, right now, right this minute, confess our sins and ask God for forgiveness . . . me and you."

"Say *what?*" Alana said.

"Let's pray for forgiveness of our sins right now, while we're on the phone."

"Oh, I get it. You're ready to get off the phone now. Well, all you had to do was say so," Alana said. "You don't have to go that low to get me off the phone."

"But I'm serious, Alana. And I'm not doing this to try and make you feel or look bad. I need to ask God for forgiveness, too. I'm just saying we can go to Him together."

"I see that you are *desperately* in need of a prayer partner. And you already know that I am *not* the one. So, I'm going to get off this phone and find something constructive to do," Alana said. "Oh, Vincent called supposedly from London today. He wanted to see how things were going. I told him how Chad came by. He didn't seem too pleased about that. He wanted to know—word for word—what Chad said. Like I'm some kind of tape recorder or something. Then he wondered, out loud, what may have caused Chad to drop in like that. I guess maybe they aren't as neighborly as they'd like folks to believe."

"What did you tell him?" Brianna said.

"The truth," Alana said. "That Chad saw someone down here, and that he came by to make sure no one had broken into the place and was a squatter. Vincent seemed *really* surprised that Chad would care enough to come by, even if he did think someone had broken in and was a squatter on the place. I don't have a clue what that's all about. But I told Vincent that other than that, everything else was going along swimmingly. I didn't mention that you were here, although I doubt that he really cares."

"Well, I'm sorry you freaked out because you couldn't find me," Brianna said. "But as you can tell, I'm fine. So, I'm going to get off the phone now."

"Okay," Alana said. "I hope you feel better."

"I'm fine. I promise you, I'm fine."

Brianna hung up, sat back down, turned on the television, and began scanning through the channels. A preacher caught her attention. She stopped and began to watch.

"'The fear of the Lord is the beginning of wisdom: and the knowledge of the Holy is understanding,'" the tall, thin preacher, whose name she didn't know, said. "I'm reading from Proverbs, the ninth chapter, tenth verse; continuing with my teaching on *An Invitation to Wisdom*," he said. "In verse twelve, we find, 'If thou be wise, thou shalt be wise for thyself: but if thou scornest, thou alone shalt bear it.' Okay, did you happen to catch that? In other words: it is wise to be wise. It's smart to be smart. Wisdom is a good thing. But if you choose to do what is *not* wise, then you're going to bear the fruit of your unwise decision. It will be on you and you alone. You can't blame anyone else. Uh-uh."

The preacher took a step forward. "Now, if you keep reading, you'll find words that will encourage you to avoid foolish women. You see, a foolish woman, and I'm not just going to regulate this to a foolish woman. Because I know y'all know there are a plethora of foolish men out there as well. In fact, when you read the rest of the scriptures in this chapter, you'll see that it might be the man who is the most foolish because he *believed* the foolish woman."

Brianna was just about to change the channel when he said,

"'Stolen waters are sweet, and bread eaten in secret is pleasant.' It's right here in Proverbs 9:17. This is what the one who's trying to entice the other wants the one being *enticed* to believe. That water may be good, but *stolen* waters are sweet. However, that last verse, number eighteen, states what's *really* going on. 'But he knoweth not that the dead are there; and that her guests are in the depths of hell.' People of God, and anyone else under the sound of my voice right now," the preacher said. "There is the Wisdom of God, and then there's Folly. Wisdom invites you to her feast; and Folly, depicted in these scriptures as an adulterous woman, invites you to hers." The preacher set his Bible on the lectern.

"With Miss Wisdom you live and you gain abundant life," the preacher said. "But, should you choose to listen to Miss Folly, then you die, or in other words you miss out on the good life. *You* get to choose. So will you choose to follow Wisdom; or will you choose to listen to and follow Folly, telling you how sweet stolen waters are and how pleasant bread eaten in secret can be? It's lies, people, all lies. Stolen waters aren't the real thing. Stolen waters are full of artificial sweeteners. Stolen waters cause you to feel guilty after you finish. And bread eaten in secret? It does nothing but pack on extra weight you have to lug around later. Weight that becomes miserable to both the spirit and the body."

The preacher nodded. "There's someone out there right now listening to me who has messed up. Yes, you're saved. Yes, you love the Lord with all of your heart. But somehow Satan slipped in during the night, and before you knew anything, you found yourself out of the will of God. But glory to God, I'm here to tell you that you can go to your Father in Heaven and you can ask Him for forgiveness. Somebody needs to ask for God's forgiveness right now so you can be restored, realizing that with Jesus, you're redeemed.

"Then there's someone . . . you have asked to be forgiven already. But Satan, that sneaky little rascal, is trying to tell you that what you did was *so* bad that it doesn't matter that you've asked God for forgiveness. He's trying to convince you that you need to come back again and again and keep asking. Well, whoever you are who has asked God for forgiveness already, the Lord is telling *me*... to tell *you*... to stop asking over and over again. He forgave you the first time you asked. Now you need to pick yourself up, gird yourself, strap your armor back on, and get back out there on the field ready to stomp Satan and his imps. The game is not over yet. There's still more time left on the clock.

"And God needs you on your post. When you ask, and you keep coming back asking the same thing, it signals to God that you didn't believe it was done, even though God said it is. God needs faith in order to operate in your life. For without faith, it is impossible to please God. I say to you, son... daughter... have faith in God."

Brianna began to cry. "I'm forgiven. Thank You, Lord. I'm forgiven. Oh, Lord, You are so loving." She fell down on her knees and lifted her hands. "You are so caring. And I thank You for loving me so much that You would take the time to speak to me, little ole me... going as far as to do it through the airwaves. Thank You. Thank You."

Chapter 24

And the woman conceived, and sent and told David, and said, I am with child.

—2 Samuel 11:5

It had been five weeks since Brianna had been to the beach and then to visit with King d.Avid. She hadn't spoken with him even though he'd called her cell phone and left several messages stating that he merely wanted to check on her and be sure that she was all right. He reassured her that he was there if she ever needed anything.

Her grandfather had called her a few days after King d.Avid called him. Pearson was so excited and pleased to have heard from his old client and someone he had, at one time, considered a friend.

"God is amazing," Pearson said. "Who would have thought—just out of the blue, for no apparent reason—King d.Avid would call and say some of the most heart-touching things as what he said to me. I'm so blessed, baby girl. So blessed! Ain't God good?!"

"I'm happy for you, Granddad. You deserve every good thing that comes your way and more." And Brianna meant that.

"I don't know whether or not I deserve it, but I sure am thankful for God's mercy and His grace. You know it's the favor of God that can take us places where money and who we know can't. Now, *that* was the favor and the hand of God that had King d.Avid call me. I truly believe that from my heart. And for hi▓ ▓o have gotten my private number, not that it's hard for ▓ ▓one like him to do. But still, just the thought of him maki▓ ▓uch an effort," Pearson said. "I know he's been in contact with your brother Mack. I asked Mack if he gave him my number, and he said it wasn't him."

"Well, don't worry about how it happened," Brianna said. "I think it was wonderful of him to still be thinking of you and to have such high regard for all that you've been and done for him. I can hear the joy oozing from your voice."

"I would love for you to meet him, now that he's a big-shot artist," Pearson said. "I realize Unzell works for him, setting up his stages and things. Unzell could arrange a meeting. But since he and I have reconnected, and he wants me to come visit him when he finishes with this tour, I think it would be great if you'd come with me."

"We'll see, Granddad," Brianna said, knowing she wasn't going to. "We'll see."

Brianna was tired. She'd been stressed more than she cared to admit, which likely was contributing to her exhaustion. She also figured it was possibly stress that caused her always reliable, you-could-set-your-calendar-by-it, twenty-eight-day cycle to be a little over a week late. Reluctantly, she purchased an early pregnancy test, refusing to believe she could possibly be pregnant. But the fact was: she could. And she knew that burying her head in the sand and trying to pretend that it wasn't possible was being irresponsible and naive and, in the end, would change nothing.

She couldn't talk to Alana about this. Alana would know, just as well as she, that with Unzell having been gone for two months, it would be impossible for her to be pregnant by him. So she took a deep breath and followed the instructions for the test.

Brianna looked at the strip, fidgeting while she waited. "Pregnant," the result said.

"Pregnant? I'm *pregnant?*" she said to the stick as though

talking to it would convince it to change its mind. "This can't possibly be right."

So she took the second test, thankful two had been included in the package.

"Pregnant," it said again.

If this was correct, then she was most definitely with child.

Brianna called her doctor's office and made an appointment.

Three days later she sat in Doctor Hayward's office. "Congratulations, Mrs. Waters. You're definitely pregnant." He smiled, something Brianna had never seen him do during the entire two other times she'd been to see him.

The look on her face must have said what she verbally hadn't.

"You don't seem too happy," he said. "Is there a problem?"

Yes, there's a problem! A big problem, she thought. But she couldn't speak, for fear that she'd burst into a full-blown cry. She merely shrugged a couple of times.

"Do you want to talk about it with me? Talk with your husband first?" he asked.

Brianna shook her head fast, then bucked up. "I'm okay," she said. "How far?"

"Well, from the information you've given me, I calculated you to be around six weeks, give or take two weeks. When we do an ultrasound, we can pinpoint it more accurately."

Brianna stood up to leave.

"Here are a few prescriptions you need to have filled." He tore off the small sheets. "But Mrs. Waters, if you're not planning on carrying this baby to term—"

"Doctor, no matter what I feel right now or how I might look, I have no interest in or intention of terminating this pregnancy. I am a pro-choice person who is pro-life. I'm just a little confused right now. But one thing I'm not confused about is carrying this baby to term. I will admit that, after that, the waters get a bit murky."

Doctor Hayward nodded, then stood up. "Well, I'd like for you to make another appointment in a month. And we'll get you on a routine until delivery. Unless, of course, you talk with your husband and you change your—"

"I won't be changing my mind." Brianna walked out of his office, set up her next appointment, and drove home, pretty much all done in a daze.

As soon as she arrived home, Brianna lay across the bed, broke down, and cried. She cried for at least an hour before pulling herself together. Unzell would be home in about three weeks. They were back in the states now, but not able to come home since there was a concert scheduled in New York. She knew she would have to tell him the truth. There's no way he wouldn't figure out that this baby wasn't his. Not after almost three months—by the time he got home—of him having been away. *If he came home in a week and we were together, it wouldn't be hard for him to think this baby is his.*

"What am I doing?" she said out loud. "I can't try and pass off someone else's child as his. That's just wrong." She pressed her face down hard into her pillow.

But if I had been or could be with my husband within a reasonable time of this conception, Unzell might believe the baby is his without questioning it. And if—or better yet, when—the truth does eventually come out, since the truth always seems to, Unzell is a loving man, a forgiving man, a kind man; surely he would love this baby . . . even if the baby isn't his.

"Stop this! Stop it! What are you doing? What are you thinking?! Stop it . . ."

Brianna dragged herself up and got her cell phone. She stared at it before retrieving his number. She mustered up her courage, then pressed the call button. There was no reason to put this off any longer. It was time to face the truth.

It went to his voice mail. She wasn't going to leave a message like this. It wasn't safe. And she knew the consequences that could come if this information were to somehow fall into the wrong hands. She pressed the end button.

Not a minute later, her cell phone rang. She looked at the number. It was him; he was calling her back.

She sucked in a deep breath, then slowly exhaled. "Hello," she said.

"Hi," he said, hopefulness and joy dancing all in his voice. "Did you just call?"

"Yeah," she said, weaker than she intended. She didn't want him to hear the defeat in her voice, not before she could begin.

"Is everything all right? Is something wrong? You don't sound like yourself."

"Yeah. I guess. If 'all right' means that I'm with child," Brianna said.

"What? With child? What are you talking about? You mean you're pregnant?"

She blurted out one quick, short laugh, definitely not a laugh of joy. "That's a great way of getting right to the point," Brianna said. "Yes. I'm pregnant."

"Are you sure?"

"Yes. I'm sure."

"And the baby's father?"

"Must you ask?" Brianna said. She thought she heard him sigh, but she couldn't be sure.

"What about your husband?" King d.Avid said. "Have you—?"

"No. I haven't said anything to him as of yet," Brianna said. "I just found out for absolute certain a few hours ago. I'm still trying to process all of this. It definitely threw me for a loop. My doctor says I'm about six weeks, give or take about two weeks. Truthfully, I can do better than that; I can pinpoint the exact date that it happened and count forty weeks from there."

"Listen, don't say anything to your husband about this just yet, okay? Let me see what I may be able to do," King d.Avid said.

"I'm not getting rid of this baby," Brianna said adamantly, shaking her head as though he could see her over the phone. "I'm not."

"And I would never ask that you do anything like that. Not

to *my* child. Not my baby. I'm just asking you not to say or do anything until I tell you differently. That's all." King d.Avid paused for a few seconds, then continued. "Can you do that for me?"

"I suppose. But you know what I told you. I'm not going to lie. If my husband asks—"

"I know. Look, we're back in the states now. In fact, the stage crew, including your husband, is all up in New York. I'm here at my residence in Atlanta. All I'm asking is that you give me a few days to work on something, and I'll get back to you. All right?"

"All right."

"And I'm here if you need me now," King d.Avid said. "Okay?"

"Okay," she said. Although she said it as though she really wasn't all so sure about that.

Chapter 25

And David sent to Joab, saying, Send me Uriah the Hittite. And Joab sent Uriah to David.

—2 Samuel 11:6

King d.Avid put in an urgent call to Jock Adamson, the guy over his entire concert stage production crew. Jock returned his call quickly.

"Jock, I know we just got back to the states, and that you all are deep into getting things set up for the New York concert this Saturday. But I need for you to send Unzell Waters to my home in Atlanta," King d.Avid said, trying to push back his nervousness.

"When?" Jock asked.

"By tomorrow."

"By *tomorrow?*" Jock's voice shrieked. "You're kidding me, right? I know you're kidding. You *do* know that Unzell is the stage manager for this production, and that what he's doing and does right now is vital to the setup of your concert, right? The concert that's five days away. You *do* know all of this, right?"

"Yeah, I know."

"And you *do* realize the huge responsibility on a stage manager's shoulders, forget about factoring in that this position is relatively new for him; he's only been doing it for about seven months. And there are always new challenges popping up to overcome. Particularly when it comes to *your* productions."

"I do," King d.Avid said. "But this should only be for one day . . . two tops. I'm planning to send my personal plane for him. He can fly down and see me, and I'll have him back on that plane and back to New York before you can begin to miss him good."

"Oh, I doubt that it would be before I can miss him good. Look, King d.Avid, whatever it is that you want to discuss with him, can't you do it over the phone, a conference call? Hey! I know: Skype. You can even use Skype. I hear it's the next best thing to being there. It's good enough for the *Oprah* show. Come on, help me out up here," Jock said. "You know how things are when we move from one major site to another. But transporting everything from overseas and getting things set up in the states again is always tricky. We have to make sure that everything is here, and if it's not—"

"You're wasting valuable time arguing with me about this. He could have almost been here in the time you've used trying to convince me that he doesn't have time to come," King d.Avid said. "Jock, my plane is fast; really, really fast. I promise you it is."

"Fine. Ultimately, it's your concert, even if it *is* my reputation on the line. If things don't go the way you're accustomed to, I suppose that will lie with you?" Jock said. "I'll let Unzell know that you want to see him, and that you're sending your private, personal jet just for him. I'm sure he'll get a kick out of that. Who wouldn't? I know I would. And then to be able to be back home in Atlanta, too. Most likely, get to see and be with his wife after all this time of being away, if nothing more than for a few minutes, when he's there. While the rest of us can only wait, imagining that glorious day."

"Well, we only have another two more weeks after this one. Then *everybody* will be able to go to their respective homes . . . for an extended period of time, at full pay, plus a nice bonus, I might add. Two, perhaps even three, months before we possibly start this over again. I'll get Kendall to coordinate everything with you and Unzell. Thanks, Jock. I know what a professional you are. I owe you," King d.Avid said.

"Yeah. Like I don't really know who works for whom. But King d.Avid, if this is what you want, you already know it's what you're going to get. May I ask you one thing though?"

"Go ahead," King d.Avid said.

"Is Unzell Waters in trouble? Is there something going on that I should know about?"

"The answer is no, and respectfully, no."

"Okay," Jock said. "Just thought I'd ask."

King d.Avid hung up the phone and stared at it. *So far, so good.*

Chapter 26

And when Uriah was come unto him, David de-
manded of him how Joab did, and how the people
did, and how the war prospered.

—2 Samuel 11:7

U nzell was escorted into King d.Avid's activity room late in the evening. At the height of the NBA championship, the two dueling teams were headed for a seventh game. The activity room had everything real men loved. A pool table, game machines, a bar, a kitchen area all its own, and of course, a colossal high-definition television screen positioned right in front of the most comfortable leather reclining chairs on the planet.

"How are you?" King d.Avid said as he slapped Unzell lightly on his back during their initial greeting.

"Everything is wonderful," Unzell said.

"How's old Jock and the rest of the crew?" King d.Avid sat in one of the brown leather recliners and gestured for Unzell to have a seat wherever he wanted to as well.

Unzell sat down on the brown leather couch. "Jock is great," Unzell said. "In fact, all of the folks in our troop are the best. It's been a long tour for sure. But we all see the light at the end of the tunnel, and we're glad that it's not a train. We're ecstatic about all that we've accomplished over these past months, especially the overseas part. And now, what's about to happen over the next three weeks, counting the storage-packing days."

"So you feel we've done good work over these past few months," King d.Avid said.

"Absolutely. I know seeing everything come together, after we all put so much of ourselves and our hard work into it, is gratifying for every one of us. I just never knew how much was required behind the scenes to make everything else on scene appear so effortless. From the lighting to sound to what the stage looks like. Getting things onto the stage and off the stage so that the people watching don't even realize that it happened, or when it happened for that matter," Unzell said. "It sort of reminds me of those people who do magic tricks."

King d.Avid started laughing. "Yeah. Like how do magicians really make those women disappear? And where do they go so quickly?"

Unzell nodded as he smiled. "Correct. But I love it, and I've appreciated the opportunity to serve on staff, especially for your concerts these past seven months. It's been intense, that's for sure. But to see the fruits of our labor has been so gratifying, for me in particular. And I personally want to thank you for all that you do to ensure that the people who come out to your concerts get the best there is to offer. It's quite admirable."

"That's so kind of you to say. But I tell people that we're representing our Father God. There's no way any of us who are bragging about God being our Father should be out there representing Him and His name with anything less than a Spirit of excellence, quality—which is doing it right the first time, and our absolute best," King d.Avid said.

"I know. I get so tired of people who do things with a 'That'll do' attitude. And when things come to the Lord's business, it seems to run rampant. People seem to bring God anything and say, 'That'll do' while the world is bringing their A-game to the table."

"I know. Say what you will about Lady Gaga, but I hear that she puts on a full-fledged show when she performs. She doesn't hold anything back. And people are talking about her from one end of the globe to the other. Not all of it good, but she gets the bang for her bucks." King d.Avid stood up and placed his hand on Unzell's shoulder. "Well, I just want you to know how much I appreciate the job you've done and are doing. I see great things in your future."

Unzell stood up. "Thank you for that. But things are going well." He nodded. "We're just looking forward to the next two-and-a-half weeks of concerts being completed. We'll then break everything down for the last time this concert cycle, perform inventory, put things in storage, and we'll be through. We'll all likely crash for a good month. I know I'll probably not come out of my house for weeks just to get caught up on some much-needed rest."

"See, now you're making me feel bad," King d.Avid said.

"Oh, I don't mean to do that. I'm just expressing how much we've loved this adventure. Weeks of back-to-back concerts first in the states, then getting to go to London, Spain, Italy, Africa, France—places like that, I never would have imagined going to. Not in a work-related capacity anyway. I always believed I'd travel with my wife on vacation to places like that, but never for work. It's been something, that's for sure."

King d.Avid led Unzell to the bar loaded up with foods like chicken wings, shrimp, various sandwiches, potato salad, baked beans, chips, and dip. "I'm certain you must be missing your wife, too. Brianna, isn't it?"

Unzell nodded as he followed his host's lead and fixed himself a plate. He bowed his head, saying a quick grace. "Yeah, I miss my Bree-Bath-she." He grinned as they sat.

"Bree-Bath-she, huh?"

"Yeah," Unzell said, picking up a tuna salad sandwich. "That's what I call her. Her name is Brianna Bathsheba, but on occasion I call her Bree-Bath-she. Now, should you ever run into her, you can't let her know that I told you any of that." He took a bite.

King d.Avid smiled. "Okay. But I have met her before."

"Yeah. She told me," Unzell said. "I'm surprised you remember. She said she was ten years old the one and only time she got to meet you."

"Yeah, I remember. I wasn't famous at all back then. Her grandfather took a chance on me. He was my advisor. Now tell me: who could *ever* forget someone on a mission to hear the devil beat his wife?"

"She has a lot of sayings like that," Unzell said, laughing in his deep bass voice. "Old wives' tales. Some I'd heard; some I hadn't, until I married her."

"I met up with your brother-in-law this past December."

"Mack?" Unzell said. "Where did you see him? He's pulled away from the family so much, I've only seen him two times in three years, and one of those times was at our wedding."

"He came here to my house."

"Here? To your house?" Unzell had a puzzled look on his face.

"Yeah. I invited him. Actually, I invited him to bring Melvin, his adopted son."

"Oh, yeah." Unzell nodded. "Brianna briefly mentioned Mack was in the process of or already had adopted a ten-year-old named Melvin." Unzell turned up the bottle of root beer he'd chosen as his beverage. "Not that it's any of my business, but why—"

"Did I ask him to bring Melvin here to see me?"

Unzell adjusted his body better. "Yes."

"Melvin's father was at one time my best friend . . . back when we were teenagers. I owed his father a debt of gratitude for being such a good friend to me, and I wanted to repay that debt. So I asked Mack to bring Melvin here. The youngster was a bit apprehensive of me at first. But I eventually won him over. I've since ensured that Melvin will never lack for anything. If you don't mind, though, I'd like to keep that particular information confidential," King d.Avid said.

"I know Brianna said Melvin had been crippled as a young child. I think it's a wonderful thing what both you and Mack are doing to make his life better," Unzell said.

"Well, I didn't do it because it was a wonderful thing to do. I did it because it was the right thing to do." King d.Avid smiled. "And speaking of the right thing, since you're here, and I happen to know that your home is also here in Atlanta, why don't you let me do the right thing by you. Why don't you go home and see your wife." King d.Avid nodded, then smiled again. "I know she will be both thrilled and surprised to see you. You've been gone; she's not expecting you: think of the gift seeing you will be for *her*."

A smile completely overtook Unzell's entire face. "Seriously? Are you serious?"

"Yes, I'm serious. Look how much you've sacrificed for these concerts as it is—being away from your wife for months on end. And a little birdie told me that you two are still practically newlyweds. So you're here at home, be it for only a miniscule time. But we can certainly spare a few hours for you to go and put a smile on your lovely wife's face," King d.Avid said. "Don't you agree? And my driver is at your disposal."

"Well, thank you. Wow, I appreciate this so much!" Unzell said with an even bigger grin on his face as he hurried to finish eating what remained on his plate.

Chapter 27

And David said to Uriah, Go down to thy house, and
wash thy feet. And Uriah departed out of the king's
house, and there followed him a mess of meat from
the king.

—2 Samuel 11:8

King d.Avid smiled as he and Unzell walked out of the
room and headed upstairs. Unzell went to one of the
guesthouses, where some of the security guards stayed, to
freshen up, even though King d.Avid had graciously offered
him a room in the house.

King d.Avid went to the kitchen. "Chef, have you finished
that picnic basket I asked for?"

"Yes, sir," Chef said. "Everything is just as you requested."

"Including that bottle of red wine?"

"Yes, sir. An expensive one, from your private cellar. Everything as you asked."

"Great. Make sure you hurry and get that basket to Unzell
Waters. He's leaving in a few minutes. He's the man who was
here a while ago. I think he went down with the security
guards. My driver is going to take him home to visit with his
wife, and I want everything to be perfect for the two of them."

"I'm sure he's going to love this," Chef said. "Especially with
all that you've requested be included." Chef took the basket
out of the refrigerator and set it on the marble island counter.
"Two of the finest cuts of steak grilled to perfection, if I must
say so myself, merely requiring reheating. Then that special

chocolate you brought back exclusively from Europe. Exquisite." He kissed his fingers. "Can we say *aphrodisiac?*"

"Well, I want him to have a great visit with his wife. They deserve a good time. And anything that I can do to ensure that happens, I'll do it." King d.Avid pulled off a black grape sitting in the fruit bowl set out daily for him and popped it into his mouth. "These grapes are delicious!"

"Yes. Healthy, like the good part that's found in red wine. I was quite pleased with our fruit selections this time around. And yes, lots of fresh fruits are in the basket."

"Get that basket to Unzell before he leaves now." King d.Avid patted Chef on his arm, then left.

King d.Avid continued to periodically glance at his Rolex watch. Almost three hours had passed and Unzell hadn't left yet. King d.Avid wondered what the holdup was. Had this been him, and someone had given him this opportunity to be with his wife that he hadn't seen in almost three months, he would have been flying to get to her. King d.Avid called in and inquired of the driver once again.

"Why are you still here?" King d.Avid asked.

"He says that he's not ready to leave just yet."

"Not ready to leave? It's been almost three hours. He had a plane to catch tonight, which he could have easily made had he left hours ago. Now, it will be too late. He's really needed back in New York. Did he say *why* he's not ready to leave?"

"No, sir. I go to him and tell him it's time to leave for his home. He just says he will come and find me when he is ready. As yet, he has not come."

"Are you certain that he understands you're the driver and that you're going to drive him to his house? Do you think maybe he has misunderstood and he thinks you're trying to take him to the airport, and that's what he means when he says he's not ready?"

"I'm sure it's been made abundantly plain that I am to do both. My English is not that bad. I tell him you have instructed me to take him to his house to see his wife. Then I tell him, I will take him to the airport to the plane when it's time for that. He asked what time the plane is to leave going back to New York," the driver said.

"The plane is pretty much ready to go whenever he's finished here," King d.Avid said, clearly frustrated. "What am I missing here? Listen, you need to go get him and take him to his house. And that needs to happen sooner rather than later because he has to get back to New York and finish his job for this upcoming concert on Saturday. Understand?"

"Understood," the driver said, then left.

King d.Avid looked up at the ceiling. "Goodness! What's this man's problem?" He spoke to no one in particular, since he was alone in the room. "The man gets to go home and be with his wife, and what's he doing? Lollygagging around here with a bunch of hard legs. What *is* his problem?"

Chapter 28

But Uriah slept at the door of the king's house with
all the servants of his lord, and went not down to his
house.

—2 Samuel 11:9

Early the following morning, King d.Avid sent for the
driver. "Well?" he said.

"You are asking about Unzell Waters? He didn't go," the
driver said.

"He didn't go? Are you saying that he didn't go home?"

"Yes, sir. No, sir, he didn't go home."

"And you didn't tell him that this was not an option?" King
d.Avid said, a little more frantic than the situation appeared
to call for.

"Sir?"

"I'm sorry. I know this is not your fault, nor is it on you. But
here I was trying to do something good, and he just pretty
much spits it back in my face." King d.Avid paced a few times.
"So where did he stay last night?"

"From what I heard, on the couch down at the security
guards' house."

"You're kidding me," King d.Avid said. "I don't get it. Have
you checked with him this morning? Maybe he didn't want to
go last night, but he's ready this morning."

"I've checked with him. He hasn't indicated he wants to go
as yet, either."

King d.Avid nodded. "Okay. Ask him to come and see me, would you please?"

"Absolutely," the driver said, then left, obviously happy to be dismissed.

Fifteen minutes later, Unzell came in with the driver.

"Here he is, sir?" the driver said. "I'll be at my post if you need me."

King d.Avid nodded at the driver, who then left. He turned to Unzell. "I'm a bit confused. I told you it was all right for you to go see your wife, spend a little time with her. I was under the impression that's what you wanted to do as well."

"It absolutely *is* what I want. I still want. In fact, the thought of my wife and being able to hold her in my arms right now is about to drive me stone-cold crazy," Unzell said.

"Then why are you still here?"

"Well, the truth is: everybody who I've worked so hard with over these past several months, people who have sacrificed being with their family and friends, some even the parents of small children, they're still stuck in hotels away from home. They're still getting up early and staying up into the early morning hours getting things ready so that when you step out onto that stage, everything goes off without a hitch. I am no better than any of them. I've done no more than most of them," Unzell said. "Then for me to have the privilege of coming here to your home, no less, and sitting down to talk with you personally . . . that is a gift and an honor. But it's also considered to be part of my job. A job I excitedly signed up for, and a job I want to give my very best. But for me to go to *my* house, lie down with *my* wife, laugh and have a wonderful time—I'm sorry; I just can't do that at this time. It's not right, nor is it fair to my fellow associates still on post."

King d.Avid placed his left hand over his mouth and nose as he lowered himself down onto the white couch. He took his hand down. "I see."

"Don't get me wrong: I want to see Brianna so bad, I can

taste her. I struggled with going last night. I appreciate the lovely basket you had prepared. I shared the meat and other perishable items with the guys at the guards' house. The wine and other stuff that will keep, I plan on holding on to and celebrating with my wife. But that will be in the next three or so weeks. The way it's supposed to be. The same way the rest of the crew will. I pray I have not offended your kindness with my actions, as that is not my intent."

King d.Avid looked up and smiled. "No. Actually, you haven't offended me. Rather, I'm made to feel rather low right now. I've not seen anyone as dedicated to their job or cause as you are. You get this whole thing. This is ministry. This is what it is to actually serve. When we're tempted to do what our flesh cries out for, we must place our flesh under the subjection of our spirit. Even denying ourselves when it's required."

"Oh, and believe me, my flesh is *highly* upset with me today. Highly! There was a true war going on inside of me last night," Unzell said. "My flesh is mad because the spirit won out. But I did assure my flesh that when we get home and see our Brianna, he's going to find himself greatly rewarded for having stood down during this time."

King d.Avid balled his hand slightly and began to nod. He looked back up at Unzell. "You're something else, Brother Unzell. That's for sure." King d.Avid stood up. "Listen. Can I get you to join me for lunch later today before you leave going back to New York? It would be my honor to have you as my guest. Plus, we can discuss a few ideas I'd like to see implemented and incorporated into these last few performances. You know: bounce some of my ideas off of you and see what you think about them."

"I'm available whenever it's good for you. As an employee of the firm, I serve at your pleasure. But I do want to get back to the rest of the troops as soon as possible. I'm certain they could greatly use my assistance, especially right about now."

"Absolutely. And I hope you don't feel that I'm being disrespectful of your job or the rest of the crew by having you here during this crucial time."

"No. If you believe this is necessary, we're all here to do what we can to make things work and to work with a spirit of excellence."

For lunch, King d.Avid had a feast set up fit for a king, equipped with all kinds of things to eat, drink, and to be merry.

"I really don't drink, especially not when I'm on the clock," Unzell said when wine was being poured into a wineglass for him.

"Oh, please don't tell me you're going to once *again* insult my hospitality," King d.Avid said with a small laugh. "This wine is some of the best you'll find anywhere around. This one alone is a two-thousand-dollar bottle of wine."

"Whew! That's quite a price tag for a bottle of *anything*," Unzell said. "I can't say I've ever tasted wine of that great a caliber before."

"Then you must give this a try," King d.Avid said. "It will enhance the taste of the meal just as wine is intended to do. Chef works extremely hard to ensure that everything works together for the sake of our palates." King d.Avid swirled the contents inside of his wineglass, held the glass up in the air, sniffed, then took a sip.

"I definitely wouldn't want to insult anyone's efforts," Unzell said. He took a sip from his glass. "This is good," he said as he smacked. He drank some more. "*Really* good."

"Yes, it is," King d.Avid said. "Drink up, my friend. There's plenty more bottles where *that* one came from."

It quickly became obvious that Unzell wasn't a drinker. It didn't take much to get him tipsy, then drunk. King d.Avid didn't drink that much. And when he saw that Unzell was pretty close to being wasted, but not to the point of passing out yet, he sent for his driver.

"Take him to his house to see his wife. And if she becomes

upset because of his"—King d.Avid glanced over at the loud, singing Unzell—"state, please explain to her that it was *entirely* my fault that he's had a little too much to drink. But tell her that I hope she accepts my gift of her being able to see her husband again before he flies back to New York."

"Yes, sir," the driver said, stumbling as he helped Unzell to his feet. "Come on, big fellow," the driver said, almost falling with him. "He's a good solid one, that's for certain."

"Would you like for me to get you some help to get him in the car?"

"Yes, you might need to do that. This is a pretty muscular fellow right here. And right now, he's no joke; I'm talking for real," the driver said.

King d.Avid called one of the guards to come in and help with Unzell. The driver and the guard walked an overly thankful, overly grateful, Unzell, who was singing and directing an imaginary choir, out of the house.

King d.Avid went and sat back in the living room at the baby grand piano. He opened it and began to play one of his favorite melodious worship songs.

Chapter 29

And it came to pass in the morning, that David
wrote a letter to Joab, and sent it by the hand of
Uriah.

—2 Samuel 11:14

K ing d.Avid waited to hear back from the driver. He'd been
gone for two hours and hadn't come and given him a status report on how things had gone. He called for the driver.

"Well?" King d.Avid said to the driver.

"Well, sir?" the driver said with a puzzled look. "I'm sorry, I
don't follow."

"How did it go? With Unzell Waters, how did it go?"

"You mean after we left from here?" the driver asked as he
glanced around the room.

King d.Avid's patience was growing thinner by the minute.
"Yes, after you left from here."

"Oh, he's doing fine, sir. I believe he's sleeping it off, even
as we speak," the driver said with a satisfied grin.

"I certainly hope not. I hope he's having a wonderful time
with his wife. I hope, even if he's not having a wonderful time,
when he wakes up, he believes that he did." It was King
d.Avid's turn to smile now. "If anyone deserves it, that man
deserves the best God has to give. I've never met anyone like
him before. He's positively the real deal."

"I know what you mean," the driver said. "Everybody is
buzzing about him and the level of integrity he shows. He's

pushed all of us to do better in our service to you, and for sure, in our service to the Lord. He's inspirational, that's for sure."

"I agree with you there," King d.Avid said. "So tell me: what did his wife say when she saw him. How did she react?"

"His wife, sir?" the driver said.

"Yes. His wife *was* there when he got home, wasn't she? You didn't just take him and dump him in his front yard, did you? Please tell me that you didn't."

"Oh, definitely didn't take him and dump him in his front yard," the driver said, showing more nervousness the more he spoke. "I definitely didn't do that, sir."

"Ralph, am I going to have to pull every single thing out of you? Now tell me what happened when you took Unzell Waters home," King d.Avid said.

Ralph swallowed hard. "Well, King d.Avid, sir. The fact of the matter is—"

"No. I *know* you're not about to say what I think you're about to say," King d.Avid said, his voice escalating.

"I didn't take him home."

King d.Avid jumped up. "Why?" he said, blowing the word out of his mouth as though it were a musical note being pushed through a tenor saxophone.

"Because he insisted that I not do that. And all of the guards agreed. They've taken a liking to him, sir. And in his state, they knew his wife would not be at all happy to see him. It wouldn't have mattered what I told her as to how he ended up in that state. The man didn't want to go home. They agreed. So they put him up with them so he could sleep it off," Ralph said. "He's asked me to take him to the airport when he awakens so he can get back with the rest of his fellow troopers in New York. He feels they need him and that he's letting people down by being here if he's not doing anything constructive."

"Fine," King d.Avid said. "Fine. But let him know, when he awakens, I'd like to see him. I have something I'd like for him to carry back to Jock for me upon his return. Make sure you let him know that, okay?"

"Yes, sir. As soon as he's up and about, I'll do just that. And sir?"

"Yes," King d.Avid said as though his patience was past done with talking.

"I hope you don't hold this against me. To be honest, if I were to take someone someplace against their protest and their will, it *could* amount—in theory, that is—to kidnapping. And I'm trying to live right and do right—"

"It's not a problem. It's not even that big of a deal. I tried to do a good deed for someone; it was rejected. That's life. We move on from here." King d.Avid forced a smile.

"Thank you, sir. I'll make sure Mr. Waters comes to see you when he's awake."

"You may go," King d.Avid said. He looked out of the glass window and shook his head. "You know, God," he said as he looked on. "During *any* other situation, I would be trying to see if we could clone someone like Unzell. The man is a good man, that's for sure. Stubborn maybe. But a good, decent man. He has some ideas about things that I might not totally agree with, but if there were more people like him, this world would be a much better place. He's a man of integrity. But then, who am I telling? You know all of this already, don't You? Still, the question comes back: what do I do *now?*"

Unzell came into King d.Avid's living room apologizing for his recent behavior.

"I've only gotten drunk to that extent twice, back in college," Unzell said to King d.Avid. "I thought I learned my lesson then. I don't know what happened. Maybe I should stick with the cheap wine, since it looks like I can't handle the expensive stuff. Or better yet, just continue not drinking much at all. It's obvious my system can't handle it."

"No problem," King d.Avid said. "I feel partially responsible. After all, I was the one who insisted that you drink a glass when you'd clearly stated it was something you would rather not do."

"Well, I'm supposed to stand up for my own convictions. Just because you insisted didn't mean I had to succumb. Talk is cheap. It's what we do in our actions that matters. I should have stood my ground, then none of this would have ever happened. Although in truth, it is kind of hard to refuse the boss."

King d.Avid nodded. "Well, I know you're anxious to get back to New York. I'm sure everyone misses you and your expertise. If I might trouble you with one more thing: would you be so kind as to hand deliver this letter to Jock for me?"

"Sure." Unzell took the envelope and put it in his coat pocket. "I'll be happy to."

"Thanks. It's important that Jock gets it as soon as possible. What better way to ensure that he receives it, and in a timely manner, than to send it by you on my plane?"

"I won't let you down," Unzell said. "And I've enjoyed being able to sit and talk with you like we have this past day and a half. I hope I've been of *some* help to you."

"I enjoyed it as well. And I did learn a great deal about you."

"I hope most, if not all, is good," Unzell said with a quizzical look on his face.

King d.Avid gently patted him on his back as he firmly gripped and shook his hand. "Most definitely." King d.Avid nodded and smiled. "Most definitely."

Chapter 30

And he wrote in the letter, saying, Set ye Uriah in the forefront of the hottest battle, and retire ye from him, that he may be smitten, and die.

—2 Samuel 11:15

Brianna was happy to get the call from Unzell. "You're for real?" she said. "Really!"

"Yes, really," Unzell said. "I got promoted to production manager. I tell you, baby, this is huge. Huge, do you hear me? We're almost finished with this tour. I have another two weeks—one week of concerts and one week of inventory and final storage—and I'll be home for a *good* long while. And now, I've gotten promoted to boot! It doesn't get any better than this. God is faithful to His Word. He's faithful!"

"He absolutely is," Brianna said.

"So how are you feeling these days?" he asked. "Any better than last we spoke?"

"Ah, you know how it is. A lot of people have been feeling like this. Tired and listless," she said, trying to sound somewhat upbeat. "I'll be fine once you get home. I can't wait to tell Granddad the news. He's going to be so proud of you. My husband, production manager!"

"It's funny. I was there in Atlanta about a week ago, King d.Avid having sent his personal plane, just for me." He spoke the last sentence all prim and proper.

"Yeah," Brianna said. "You told me after you went back. I

still can't believe you were right here in Atlanta and you didn't even call or come by to see me . . . your *wife*."

"I know. And it wasn't because I didn't want to, believe me. King d.Avid kept insisting that I come home even if it was just for a couple of hours. Of course, I fought the temptation. It was hard, but your man stood strong in the Spirit of the Lord. I was standing, baby. Holding on for dear life, but I was standing. I didn't budge. Then the next day, I ended up getting drunk . . . almost ended up on your doorstep anyway. I can only *imagine* how *that* would have played out with you. Me, show up drunk."

"I wouldn't have been *that* bad," Brianna said. "I would have been so glad to see you, I wouldn't have cared how you came home: sauced, juiced, or toasted."

"Yeah, you say that now. But you forget that I've come home once or twice a bit out of it. I might have been somewhat impaired those few times, but I know it was *not* pretty. I mean, you hit the ceiling! That's probably why I don't care to go out much now. If I happen to mess up and come home to you, you surely don't hold back," Unzell said.

"Gosh, you make me sound like a little terror over here," Brianna said. "Am I really *that* bad?"

"Oh, you can hold your own now. No doubt about that. I'm not going to lie. But listen, I'm not calling to go there with you. Not today. I just wanted you to be the first to know that we are moving on up!"

"Yay! I'm *so* proud of you, Unzell. Really I am. Congratulations!"

"See. Now what do you think would have happened had I acquiesced, and failed what apparently was a test?"

"A test?"

"Yeah. You know. When I was there with King d.Avid. It's apparent that this was all a promotion test, to see if I was worthy of the position of production manager. They may have thought they were being slick, but God directed me on what to do. They couldn't trick me. Whatever they might have really been up to, I'd say I passed with flying colors. I've been moved up to the front line! And I'll be home in about two weeks, less if we quickly get the things into storage. Then you and I will celebrate with a bottle of King d.Avid's very own stock of expensive wine. It doesn't get any better than this!"

"No, it doesn't," Brianna said, trying to be sure she smiled when she spoke so he wouldn't hear the sadness that lingered in her heart.

"Well, I'm going to get off the phone now. You know we're super busy. I'm learning more and more about my new position. It's definitely a lot more work, but you know that your man is up for the challenge," Unzell said. "One more week of scheduled concerts, then we pack up all of this stuff for storage, and I'll be home to see my baby. And maybe then, we can work on producing our own baby?"

He hung up after sending her a kiss through the phone. Brianna sat holding the phone in her hand.

Brianna placed the phone back into its base. She lay down on the couch, face down, and began to cry.

It was good and bad happening at the same time. Good that her husband had gotten promoted. Good that he would be home in about two weeks. Good that she was carrying a sweet little innocent baby inside. Bad that she was pregnant by someone other than her husband. Bad that she would have to deal with this when Unzell came home. Bad that she just might lose him when all of this would soon become *said* and *done*.

Chapter 31

So the messenger went, and came and showed David all that Joab had sent him for.

—2 Samuel 11:22

King d.Avid finished the final concert on the leg of his long but fulfilling tour. The stage crew had always arrived prior to him, having to set everything up. With so many concerts, the schedule had been tight and grueling: the breaking down of the stage, loading up all that heavy and expensive equipment, then traveling by trucks to the next destination to set up there, usually with only four to five hours (if that) of sleep.

It was a lot on those whose job it was to do it or make sure that it got done. But King d.Avid was told that not *too* many of them had complained about it, *too* much, anyway. There are always some who'll complain no matter what. But for the most part, most of them had been happy to have a job and to be working full time. A lot of folks, including those doing what King d.Avid was doing for a living, weren't working at all. When that happens, there's a chain reaction, and it affects everyone down the line.

Say an artist doesn't get signed to another deal. First off: he or she loses. Then there's nothing new to sell or promote, so the concert crew and such are out of work. The people who work in the venues—from the ticket takers to the hot-dog man to the cleanup crew—have nothing to do because the venue sits idle, because people aren't spending money that they just don't have. Grocery stores and retailers see less business. Farmers and those producing things see declining orders since merchants need less when no one's buying. The cycle of life takes effect, or more accurately: the wheel of economics gunks up.

King d.Avid was glad to know that because of the gift God had blessed him with, he was responsible—in a positive way— for others to be gainfully employed. This tour had been jampacked with back-to-back concerts, in most instances. He'd done this to ensure he stayed relevant during this famine time. But he vowed (after these back-to-back concerts making it sometimes months on end) to never agree to something like this again. It didn't give enough time between events for *anyone* to catch their breath. And it was hard. Not as hard on him as it was for the crews that backed him. Essentially, all he had to do was show up, rehearse for a couple of hours, make suggestions or register any complaints that needed to be addressed; and ultimately, someone else took care of it. But this last round of concerts was finally over. And everyone could finally go home.

So when news came of what transpired after the final concert ended, a concert that rivaled all those that had come before it, King d.Avid was in absolute shock.

"Say *what?*" King d.Avid said to the young man that stood breathless before him.

The twenty-something, lanky guy was trying desperately to catch his breath and talk. "The moving equipment . . . they were disassembling that big heavy piece. The tow motors were holding the truss . . . yeah, the truss . . . up off the ground—"

"Tow motors . . . truss?" King d.Avid said. "What are you talking about?"

"The lamps . . . they put lamps inside the truss . . . that big massive steel thing . . . the truss," the guy said, still trying to catch his breath between words.

"Okay, don't worry about trying to explain that part. Just tell me what you're saying has happened."

"Something went wrong. The production manager was supervising everything. Then that heavy thing suddenly came crashing down. It's bad, sir. It's bad."

"So you're telling me someone was hurt?"

"Not only hurt; but someone's dead."

King d.Avid stood to his feet. "Are you sure?"

"Yes, sir," the young guy said. "One is dead and two were taken to the hospital in critical condition. Jock sent me. Told me to come and tell you before you happened to hear about it on the news or from somewhere else."

"Who died and what two were taken to the hospital? Anyone I know?"

"The production manager. The guy that just got promoted."

"What? Is he in the hospital?"

"No, sir. He's dead, sir. Unzell Waters is dead. I can't believe he's gone, but he is. I witnessed the whole thing with my own two eyes. It happened so fast. Dead. And he was so great to everybody. He looked out for us. In fact, he was the one who ran and tackled the other men out of the way. Had he not run so fast, he wouldn't have even been there to be hit. He seemed to come out of nowhere—like a bolt of lightning, yelling for them to get out of the way. Had he not reached them and pushed them, those other two men would be dead for sure, too. But they were hurt when it caught a piece of them. If Unzell hadn't run so fast, he'd still be alive. Unzell sacrificed himself to save them."

"You're telling me the production manager is dead?" King d.Avid frowned with disbelief. He sat down. "Unzell Waters is dead? And he died saving two other workers?"

"Yes, sir," the guy said. "They say he used to play football. They say he was once slated for the pros. All I can tell you is: seeing him running like he did and shoving those two big dudes out of the way like that . . . I can only imagine what he was like on the football field. He was something else all right."

"The other two . . . the two he saved, what are their names?" King d.Avid asked.

"I'm not sure, sir. But I can find out. They weren't part of our regular crew. They were temporary workers, helping us out so we could finish up and get home that much faster," the guy said. "It's been a long tour. Jock said to tell you he's certain there's going to be an investigation into this. You're going to get calls from the media. He wanted me to get word to you quick. So I got here as fast as I could. Jock tried to call you, but he said your cell phone was off, and you still have the 'Do not disturb' notifications set for your hotel room phone and your room."

King d.Avid first nodded, then shook his head. "I can't believe this." King d.Avid instantly thought about Brianna. "Has anyone called his wife? Unzell Waters's wife, has anyone called her yet?"

"Somebody's taking care of that as we speak. I think Jock said he's getting Vincent to handle a lot of these things."

King d.Avid rubbed his head, then looked up at the ceiling. "This is awful!"

"Yes, sir. It is. Unzell was really a great guy, a really good man. Really good. We're definitely going to miss him. Well, I'm going back now." The guy started for the door.

"Thank you for coming and letting me know. Oh, and what's your name again?"

"My name, sir? It's Earl Bates."

"Well, Earl, thank you for coming over here so quickly and letting me know."

"No problem, sir." Earl gave a quick nod of respect, then left.

Chapter 32

*And when the wife of Uriah heard that Uriah her
husband was dead, she mourned for her husband.*
                                        —2 Samuel 11:26

Brianna let out a curdling scream as she dropped the
phone. "No! No! No! He can't be dead!" she continued to
scream out. "He can't be! He can't!"

She fell to her knees. "Oh, God, please! Please, I beg You.
Don't let this be true! Let them be wrong! Oh, God, please, I
beg You! This has to be some kind of a mistake! They are
wrong! They're wrong! Unzell is not dead. He's not!"

Brianna was face down on the floor now as she continued
to cry. She heard the doorbell and the pounding, but she
couldn't manage to pick herself up to answer it. She felt as
though her spirit had vacated her body and only the shell remained. She then heard a voice calling her name. She heard
it, but couldn't do anything but lie there.

"Brianna, answer the door! Brianna! Brianna, I know
you're in there. I can hear you crying. Now get up and unlock
the door so I can come in," Alana said. "Brianna, open the
door! Answer the door or I'll knock it down! I promise you, I
will. You know me; I'll do it! Do you hear me? Brianna!" She
pounded some more, much harder.

Brianna finally sat up on the floor. She pulled herself up,
using the leg of a wingback recliner. She dragged her body,

which felt as though it weighed a ton now, to the front door and unlocked it.

Alana didn't wait on Brianna to turn the knob and open the door. She opened it and stood looking at her friend before grabbing her and holding her.

Brianna began to cry again, crumbling to the floor. "He's not gone," Brianna said. "He's not!" She shook her head hard. "Do you hear me?! He can't be! Unzell is not . . . gone. He's not dead, Alana. He's . . . not!"

"Come here, baby. Come on." Alana grabbed Brianna up, walking her as she would someone who was drunk. They eased down, locked together, onto the couch.

Brianna allowed Alana to hold her as she continued to cry. "Why?" Brianna said. "Why did this have to happen? Why?"

"I don't know why," Alana said. "I don't understand it either."

Brianna pulled away. "But he was a good man; he was a Godly man. Unzell didn't deserve for anything like this to happen to him. He didn't. Me, maybe. But not him. He was a good man. And he loved me. He had plans . . . we had plans. It's not fair that he's gone! It's not! It's . . . just . . . *not* . . . fair! It should have been me, not him. Me!"

Alana gathered Brianna up by her shoulders and shook her lightly. "Stop it! Okay? Stop it! Do you hear me? I want you to stop this!"

"No!" Brianna said, almost snorting the word out like a bull getting ready to charge. "I will *not* stop it! Unzell didn't deserve to die. He was supposed to be coming home. One more week, and he was going to be home. One week, Alana. One more week, and he would have been home safely with *me!*" She poked her finger into Alana's chest. "Home safely . . . with *me!* One week. One more *lousy* week." She broke down again.

Alana pulled Brianna in close to her and began to rock her as she would a crying baby. "Okay, Brianna. Whatever you need to do to get it all out, then I want you to do it and get it all out. I know this is hard. I just thank God that I was in the city when whoever that was called and told me what happened," Alana said. "It's hard, and I understand—"

Brianna jerked back from Alana's grasp. "No, you *don't* understand! You don't understand! You *don't!* You've never lost a husband. Men come and go like transfer buses with you. But you don't know what it's like to lose a husband . . . not a husband."

"Okay, Brianna. It's okay. I'm even going to let you slide on that jab you just delivered me this time." Alana looked in her purse and found a pack of tissues. Opening it, she wiped Brianna's face. "I know you're hurting. And you're right. I've had men leave my life, but none of them were like your and Unzell's relationship. Yes, I know what it is to lose a loved one. My grandmother died in my junior year of high school, remember? I loved her so much. But no, I don't know what it's like to lose a spouse."

Brianna cried more. "What am I going to do? What . . . am . . . I . . . going to do?"

"Your mother and father are on their way. It's going to take them a few hours to get here. You know they're a few hours away. But they're coming. They're coming."

Brianna pulled herself from Alana's arms and tilted her head sideways as she looked at her friend as though she were foreign to her. "Alana, he's gone. The phone is not going to ring and it be him on the other end. He's not going to come driving up late at night trying to figure out how to get in the bed without waking me. He's not coming home to me ever again. Not ever again. Nothing I say or do now is going to change that. Why would God allow something like this to happen to *him* of all people? Alana, why do bad things happen to good people? Answer me that. Can you? Can you answer that?"

Alana shook her head and unsuccessfully tried to smile. Her mouth started to tremble. "No, I can't. But I know, from having been around you, we can go to the throne of grace and pray right now. I know we can do that. What say . . . you and I pray? Right here, right now; let's pray."

Brianna began to chuckle before it became a full laugh. "*You're* suggesting that we pray? You . . . Alana Gail Norwood . . . are the one who is suggesting that *we*—me and you—pray?"

"What's so funny about *that?* I pray," Alana said, trying to stay as long as she could on a note that appeared to have calmed Brianna somewhat.

Brianna gave a quick sharp laugh. "Yeah. You pray all right."

"Well, I *do*," Alana said. "I might not be living right all the time, but I know the Lord. And we have our moments when we talk. Granted, I'm usually begging Him for something . . . mainly money or something else material that I need. Like, maybe let me not be pregnant. And generally He's telling me to stop sinning. But still, I pray. We learned how to pray when we were little girls, remember? Remember, Brianna? Our Father . . ."

"Yeah, I remember," Brianna said just barely above a whisper.

"Well, I think we should pray now. We should pray, not that Unzell makes it into Heaven, because you and I know that he had things right with the Lord."

"Yeah," Brianna said. "That's one thing he told me a long time ago. That he had gotten things straight with the Lord. That he'd given his life to Christ. And that if he died today . . ." Brianna paused as she looked at Alana. "That was exactly what he would say. 'If I die today, I know where I'll spend eternity— with the Lord.' So I know where Unzell is right now. He's with the Lord."

"And even though Unzell left us much too soon, we still know that he's in great hands. And that he's in a great place, at this very moment." Alana wiped her eyes.

"Yeah," Brianna said. "He's with the Lord. He's with Jesus." Brianna began to shake her head. "But it doesn't make it feel any better for *me*. Because he left me here. I'm still here, and it hurts like I can't put into words." She began to cry again.

"I'm just being selfish, aren't I? All I care about is *my* hurt. Unzell is with Jesus; he's with the Lord. He's face to face with our Lord and Savior, and I'm down here wallowing all over the floor because he left me to face this world all by myself without him by my side."

"No, you miss him. And it's okay to miss him. *I* miss him. Unzell was a terrific guy. He was loving and caring. And if I know nothing else for sure, I know that he loved God, and he *loved* him some Brianna Bathsheba Wright Waters," Alana said, bumping Brianna's shoulder with hers in a playful manner.

Brianna laughed, returning the bump before looking staunchly serious at Alana. "He did love me, didn't he? You know he liked to call me Bree-Bath-she."

"Yeah. I thought that was so corny the first time you told me that," Alana said. "But then again, I was probably just being envious. You know, because I didn't have a man who loved me the way you had a man to love you."

Brianna laid her head on Alana's shoulder and closed her eyes. Alana rubbed Brianna's face and wiped at her tears that continued to fall. "Pray," Brianna said, her eyes still closed. "Alana, please pray."

Alana cleared her throat. "Heavenly Father, we come to You, first of all to say, thank You. Thank You that, even during our trials and tribulations, even when our hearts are breaking, You are still with us, and we know that You care. You said You would never leave us nor forsake us. We're counting on and standing on that Word right now. Touch my friend's heart, I beg You. Heal her hurts and her wounds. And Lord, give me the right words to say. Help me to love on her the way You would have me do. Father God, Unzell is no longer here with us. He's now home with You. He no longer has to deal with the troubles of this world. And we know that to be absent from the body—"

"Is to be present with the Lord," Brianna said, interrupting Alana. "Thank You, Lord. I thank You for sending Jesus to save us. And because of what Jesus did, giving all of us an avenue back to You, my husband . . . my Unzell, though no longer here with us, is with . . . Jesus. He's . . . sleeping . . . in . . . Jesus." Brianna burst into tears again.

Alana resumed the prayer. "Father, we love You. We thank You. We worship and adore You. We magnify Your name. Comfort my friend. Comfort all those who loved Unzell dearly and will miss him equally as dearly. Help us through this most difficult time. These and other blessings we ask in Jesus' name. Amen."

"Amen," Brianna said. "Amen." Brianna got up and kneeled in front of the couch. "Alana?" she said.

"Yeah?"

"It still hurts." She burst into tears again as she laid her head on the couch. "It *still* hurts!"

Alana scrambled and quickly kneeled beside Brianna, putting her arm around her. "I know," she said as she cried with her. "I know."

Chapter 33

Cast thy bread upon the waters: for thou shalt find it after many days.

—Ecclesiastes 11:1

The homegoing service for Unzell Michael Waters was a true celebration of his life. King d.Avid ensured that no expense was spared. He'd called and spoken briefly with Brianna immediately following the tragic incident, then gone to her home when he returned home to Atlanta. Brianna's parents were there, doing what they could to comfort her. But for Brianna, there wasn't much comfort to be had.

King d.Avid had been sincere about his feelings of having lost Unzell. And because Unzell was so loved by so many—those from college, those from his football days, and the concert crews he'd worked with—and so many wanted to attend the funeral, King d.Avid insisted that Brianna let him pay for the use of a church that could accommodate the number of people that were expected to be in attendance.

And one other thing King d.Avid had insisted upon: he wanted to sing at the service. After all, it was the least he could do for one who had given so much of his own self and service to what King d.Avid was doing, especially these seven, almost eight months Unzell had been a part of his concert tour crew.

Sure, Unzell had been paid for his work. But King d.Avid aptly pointed out to Brianna how much Unzell always went above and beyond any monetary amount he received in compensation. How he'd exemplified what Jesus spoke in Matthew 5:41, "And whosoever shall compel thee to go a mile, go with him twain."

Brianna had agreed. Unzell would have certainly been humbled knowing that the largest gospel recording artist around would be leading the celebration of his life as he, a humble saint, went marching home. It was definitely going to be a spiritual revival for those in attendance. But what convinced Brianna to agree was her knowing that, even with the grief of their loss, this would be one more opportunity to worship and praise God at the level God so richly deserved. One more time to offer a lost soul Jesus.

Brianna prayed that during the service, someone's life would be touched. Not because that person was overcome with emotion or grief. But because they would hear the Word of the Lord go forth and come running to the altar asking what they needed to do—just as Unzell had once done—to be saved . . . to know Jesus.

King d.Avid sang a song he'd recorded based on the words found in Psalm 8. "O Lord our Lord, how excellent is thy name in all the earth! who hast set thy glory above the heavens." But when he sang the verse from Psalm 8:4, "What is man, that thou art mindful of him? and the son of man, that thou visitest him?" people all over the church began to shout and cry out like a roaring forest fire gets out of hand having originated from one tiny spark.

At the end of the song, as King d.Avid sang his final round of, "O Lord our Lord, how excellent is thy name in all the earth," he kneeled down and raised his hands to the Lord. The minister brought the Word, and the floodgates seemed to open as people came pouring into the aisles, down to the altar, to give their lives to this "excellent God" who loved, with an everlasting love, and was most certainly deserving of all the praise.

At the gravesite, Brianna picked up a handful of red dirt and tossed it onto the copper-tinted coffin. King d.Avid rushed

over when she broke down. He held her up . . . and she, too
exhausted to think about anything at this point, allowed him.

"He's gone," Brianna whispered. "What am I going to do?"

King d.Avid held her even tighter.

"What am I going to do without him?" she said as she stum-
bled away, King d.Avid continuing to hold her. Suddenly, and
without warning, she collapsed in his arms.

Brianna came to on the back seat of a limousine. She
looked around. "What happened?" she asked. "Where am I?"

King d.Avid rubbed her hand that he held. "You fainted,"
he said. "You're in my limo right now. I brought you here after
you passed out."

She struggled to sit up. "I fainted?"

King d.Avid gently pushed her back down. "Just lie still a
few more minutes," he said. "Brianna, I know you're grieving.
I know you are. But have you been eating like you should? Are
you taking care of yourself the way you ought to be doing?"

Brianna began to cry. She knew that he was concerned
about her, but she also knew he was thinking about the baby
she carried, the baby that was *not* her husband's. Once again,
she struggled to sit up.

King d.Avid helped her, then hugged her. "It's going to be
all right," he said, stroking the back of her hair. "But Brianna,
you're going to have to take care of yourself. You know this. I
realize you're hurting. I know you are. And I know right now
it's hard to think of anything else except your pain and the
loss you feel. But you *must* take care of yourself. You understand?" He scrunched down, fixing his eyes with hers. "Brianna? Do you understand?"

She looked down at her open palms. Tears began to fall
into them, drip by drip, quickly forming a pool of water. She
nodded. *Yes, I understand.*

"Because if you don't. . . ."

"I know," Brianna said softly. She fully recognized that she
was pregnant, and that her actions no longer affected only
her life. There was another life to consider now. An innocent

life she carried inside of her. A life that was depending on her for its very health and survival, whether she was grieving or not.

"Now, I've expressed to you," King d.Avid said gingerly, still crouching down, "that if you need *anything*, anything at all, at any time, I'm here. And I'm going to *be* here. I'm not going anywhere. But you have to help me. You have to do your part. You have to meet me halfway. You have to. No ifs, ands, or buts. No matter how hard all of this might be right now, you must—"

"I know," Brianna said. "I got it. You don't have to keep repeating yourself." She then quietly positioned herself back down on the seat, drew her body into a ball, closed her eyes, and allowed the tears to continue to fall. It was then that she felt King d.Avid's coat to his black Armani suit gently cover her.

Chapter 34

I sink in deep mire, where there is no standing: I am come into deep waters, where the floods overflow me.

—Psalm 69:2

"Baby, why won't you just come on home with us?" Brianna's mother, Diane, said as they sat next to each other on the bed in Brianna's bedroom.

"I can't. Not now," Brianna said.

"Why? There's no reason for you to stay here."

"I just don't want to leave. Not now. Maybe later, but not now. And I really don't feel like thinking about it at this juncture."

"Sweetheart, you don't need to be here all by yourself. Not at this time." Diane reached over and took Brianna's right hand. "Come home with me and your father. Come stay with us a few weeks or as long as you need. Get your strength back. Let us take care of you."

"Mother, I love you. And I appreciate what you're trying to do. But I just want . . . I *need* to be alone for a while."

Diane slowly shook her head as she frowned. "That's not good. Now is not a time for you to be alone. We're here to help you get through this. That's what families do."

Brianna's eyes were weak. But she used her eyes, as best she could, to help plead her case. "I just don't want to leave here yet. I need some time to think. So much has happened, so quickly, I haven't had time to even think." Brianna balled up her left hand.

"Well . . . then, I'll just stay here with you," Diane said, folding her hands into each other.

"You really don't need to do that."

"I know," Diane said. She reached over, put her arm around Brianna, and pulled her to her. "So, it's settled then. I'll tell your father to go on back to Montgomery without me, and I'll be home later."

"Mother, I really don't know what I'm to do at this point. I feel so lost."

"That's natural. You're still in shock. Your mind needs time to process all that's happened," Diane said. "I understand you wanting to stay here for now. I promise I'm not going to get in the way of whatever you feel you need to do to heal or, at least, get to a place where you can cope with everything." She pulled her daughter even closer.

"But I don't want you to have to stay here while I'm doing whatever it is I'm doing," Brianna said.

Alana rapped on the doorjamb and walked into the bedroom. "Hi," she said, and sat down at the foot of the bed. "Can I get you anything?" Alana asked Brianna.

Brianna moved out of her mother's arm and shook her head.

"I was just telling Brianna she should come home with me and her father," Diane said, directing her gaze at Alana.

"I think that's a great idea!" Alana said.

"Well, she won't listen to me," Diane said, obviously happy for reinforcement.

"Why won't you, Brianna?" Alana said.

Brianna sat up straighter. "I want to stay here. This is my home, at least at this time. I want to be in my own home right now."

"Well, since she won't come home with us, then I'm planning to stay here with her," Diane said.

"And I told her I don't want her to do that," Brianna countered. "She needs to go home with Dad. He hasn't been feeling all that well. I'm a little worried about him. I'll be all right here by myself." Brianna sat Indian-style, leaned forward slightly, and rocked before stilling herself.

"I don't want her here alone. Not now. I know that's what she *says* she wants." Diane shook her head. "I don't think that's a good idea. Not right now, anyway."

"You know . . . I could stay with her," Alana said.

"Oh, no"—Diane began to shake her head slowly—"I couldn't impose on you like that, Alana. I'm her mother. I should be the one to stay. I don't mind."

"And I'm like her sister," Alana said. "And I don't mind. I already live here in Atlanta. Actually, you know: I could move in with her for as long as she needs me to."

Diane shook her head again, this time faster. "That's admirable of you, Alana. But you shouldn't have to disrupt your own life when it's not a real problem for me to stay."

"But you'll be disrupting your life . . . and Dad's," Brianna said. "And you'd be doing that, even though I'm telling you that I'll be fine and that I really don't need you to do it. I love you, Mother, and I appreciate you *so* much. But why don't I let Alana come and stay with me." Brianna looked at Alana. "It's like she said: she already lives here in Atlanta. And if I need anything, she'll make sure that I'm okay."

"Is this *really* what you want?" Diane asked Brianna.

Brianna nodded. "Yes. This way I'll have the space I need, but someone will be around . . . just like you want."

Diane looked at Alana. "Are you sure about this? Because it's not a problem for me to stay."

"I'm positive," Alana said.

Diane turned to Brianna. "Now, you know if you need me, all you have to do is pick up the phone and say the word. I'll be here as quick as the freeway will let me."

Brianna forced a smile. She was developing a slight headache. "Thanks, Mother."

Diane hugged Brianna as she rocked her. "My baby. My sweet little baby. I just don't understand why things happen, but I know that God is able to keep you. Let the Lord minister to you, Brianna. There *is* a balm in Gilead. I found that to be true when I lost my mother; then two years later, my father. The pain can be intense at first, even when you know the one you love is with the Lord. I still miss my parents, but God is able. And it really has gotten better over time. You just have to force yourself to keep going. You can't stop living just because they're gone."

Brianna started to cry as her mother spoke and kept her wrapped up in her arms.

"Oh, baby. I didn't mean to make you cry. I just want you to know how much I love you and how much God loves you. I may not be able to always be with you, but God is always there. No matter where you are, no matter where you go, God is there. Through it all, God is there. He's there during the good times and the bad. And I know God is going to bring some good back into your life real soon. I know He is. And I know right now it doesn't feel like He is or that it's possible, but I know that God will."

"Can you leave me with Alana?" Brianna said to her mother, wiping her eyes.

Diane stood up, then leaned down and, with a tissue, wiped some of the tears from Brianna's face. "Sure." She kissed her daughter on the forehead, then left.

Alana got up and went to sit beside Brianna.

"I told her I wanted to be by myself right now," Brianna said, almost mumbling the words.

"Well, I think it will be good for you to have someone around, at least at this juncture," Alana said.

"Alana, you know me. You know there are times when I need to be alone. Then again, I know you." Brianna looked sternly into Alana's eyes. "Alana, I'm going to ask you this one time, and I want you to tell me the truth."

Alana scrunched her mouth. "Okay," she said, almost sounding like she was surrendering before the question even came.

"Do you have a place to stay right now?"

"You mean *today?*"

"Alana, I'm not in the mood to play games. You know *exactly* what I mean. My last time asking you: do you . . . have anywhere to stay . . . right now?"

Alana diverted her eyes from Brianna's unrelenting stare. "No. I don't have anywhere to stay right now." She looked at Brianna. "After Vincent came back home and politely thanked me, and helped me carry my things to my car, I went back to Dre's. That's why I was so close and got here so fast when they called and told me Unzell had been killed. I've been crashing at his place for the past week while all of this has been going on with you. But I can't stay there." Alana began to shake her head. "I have to get out of that place! Dre is crazy. And after those two months of experiencing peace and serenity, I just can't do crazy again. I can't!"

"All right," Brianna said. "Then you're more than welcome to stay here with me. My folks are leaving tomorrow because my daddy has to get back. You know my mother was insisting on staying, but I need time to myself, and I truly don't feel like having people hovering all over me." Brianna quickly wiped her face with her hands, then locked eyes with Alana again. "And that includes *you* as well."

"You don't want hovering? Done! I can oblige," Alana said with a smirk.

"Okay. So pack your things, and tomorrow you can move in here."

Alana hugged Brianna. "Thank you, thank you, thank you! I know it looks to your mother like I'm doing you the favor, but you and I know that you're actually the one blessing me by doing this. Thank you." She let go.

"Alana, you're really going to have to get your life together. You've played around long enough. You either need to enroll in college or get a job. Or both. Something."

"Now you're starting to sound like you think you're my mother," Alana said.

"I don't mean to. But I love you. And the way you're living right now is going nowhere. You can't bounce from one man to the next looking for someone to take care of you. You say you want a good man? Then you need to be what you desire for your *own* life. This way you'll attract a good man while also bringing something to the table." Brianna stretched her legs back out. She closed her eyes and laid her head back. She wasn't feeling well at all.

"Are you okay?" Alana asked, springing to her feet. "Do you need something?"

"I just need to eat something," Brianna said. "I haven't had an appetite much. But I need to eat." Brianna sat up straight. "Would you mind fixing me a little something to eat and bringing it in here? Not a lot; just something to keep my strength up."

"Sure. There's a lot of food in there. People have been dropping things by since we came back from the cemetery. You and Unzell are definitely loved. There were so many people at the funeral today. I couldn't believe the number of people that were there. And then to have King d.Avid, of all people, to think and care enough about Unzell that he would sing at his funeral." Alana stood there shaking her head. "It was absolutely wonderful. And then to see Vincent Powers there. And to learn that he actually works for King d.Avid, oh, my goodness . . . that he's King d.Avid's actual manager, no less—"

"The food," Brianna said. "My food."

"Yeah"—Alana clapped her hands once—"right." She pointed at Brianna and made a quick clicking sound. "Your food."

"Not a lot now," Brianna said. "I'm really not that hungry. But I know I have to eat."

Alana had a quizzical look on her face, but she didn't say anything. She left to get Brianna's food.

Brianna positioned her hand on her stomach and gently cradled it. She then put her other hand on the bed, on Unzell's side where he usually slept. She rubbed her hand over his pillow sham a few times, then burst into tears once more. Lying on his pillow, she pressed her face into it, effectively muffling her cry.

Chapter 35

King d.Avid called Brianna and told her he was sending the car for her. She told him she appreciated him caring so much, but she still didn't feel like going anywhere just yet. Unzell had died a little over a month ago, and she was nowhere near pulling herself together. But King d.Avid insisted; told her this time he wouldn't take no for an answer.

The Escalade drove up. Chad came to the door and escorted her to the vehicle. Having secured a job a week after she moved in with Brianna, Alana was at work. Brianna had planned to attend college in the fall, but knowing that she was pregnant (something only she, her doctor and his office, and King d.Avid presently had knowledge of) had caused her to reevaluate those plans.

It wasn't that pregnant women couldn't attend college; she knew *that* old-fashioned way of thinking had long ago lost its life of usefulness. But having buried her husband *and* being pregnant . . . she didn't know if her mind would be on the lessons as would be needed.

King d.Avid didn't mince his words. He absolutely didn't want her worried about doing anything right now. All he wanted was for her to concentrate on her heart healing and to make sure that she took care of herself and the baby she was carrying. That's it.

King d.Avid had been great. He had checked on her every single day, sometimes two to three times. Brianna didn't have to worry for money; the insurance policy Unzell had on him was more than enough to take care of her for years to come. Still, King d.Avid wanted to do for her.

At first, she thought the reason was because he'd felt guilty that Unzell had been killed while working on the set for his concert tour. She quickly learned that the investigation of the accident had cited an error that could be partially attributed to a decision Unzell may have made. Something a production manager with more experience might have known; something all new production managers generally have pointed out and emphasized to them in the beginning of new appointments. But without Unzell there to answer, no one would ever know for sure whether or not he'd been told at all or whether he'd been told but still ended up possibly miscalculating.

King d.Avid met Brianna at the door. He hugged her. And even though she felt bad that she was lingering so long in his arms, for some reason she just couldn't manage to find the strength or the mind to pull away.

King d.Avid walked her over to the living room like she was one of those large walking dolls from years ago. They sat down, still linked together, on the couch. He didn't utter a word, just looked at her as though she was the most beautiful thing he had ever seen.

"How are you?" he finally said.

She nodded, afraid that even one sound would open up the floodgates of her crying again. As long as she didn't think too long, too deep, or too much, she was okay.

He kept one arm around her and just held her. "Have you eaten?" he asked.

She nodded her yes answer.

"How long ago?"

"I don't know. About three . . . four hours ago, maybe," she said in a small whisper. "I had a little something for breakfast."

"Well, I had Chef make a fruit tray and some other healthy things. It's here on the table. I want you to at least eat some fruit. They say fruit is good for you."

Brianna nodded. She knew he was meaning "good for the baby."

King d.Avid picked up the tray and held it before her. She shook her head. "No, thanks," she said. "I'm not really hungry right now."

He put the tray back down on the table. Picking up a large, perfectly red strawberry, he held it up to her mouth. She shook her head again. He smiled and put the berry up to her lips just the same. She looked into his eyes. He smiled again. She bit the strawberry. After she finished that one, he picked up yet another piece of fruit and repeated the process . . . chunks of cantaloupes, honeydew melons, pineapples, mangos, peaches, and grapes, plucked from a bunch.

After she told him she was truly full, then, without thinking, placed her hand on her stomach, tears began to mist his eyes. He held up his hand as asking permission to touch her stomach as well. Brianna looked down, then slowly took his hand and gently placed it on her abdomen. He instantly laughed. After a few minutes, he took both of his arms, wrapped them around her, and just began to hug and rock her.

He hugged and refused to let go. "Marry me," he said, after what felt like fifteen minutes of nothing but him holding her without a word being exchanged between them.

Brianna instantly pulled back from his embrace. "What?"

He smiled, then dropped down onto one knee, took both her hands, and said, "Brianna, I would like for you to be my wife. Marry me."

Chapter 36

O God, thou knowest my foolishness; and my sins are not hid from thee.

—Psalm 69:5

Brianna frowned at King d.Avid. "But you don't know me," she said. "And you definitely don't love me. How are you going to ask me to marry you?"

"I know enough, and right now I love you and our baby enough for it to do nothing but grow into more than either of us can imagine," King d.Avid said. "You're the right woman for me. I feel this so much in my spirit. I can't explain it. But I feel this is what you and I are supposed to do."

Brianna shook her head. "My husband just died. How can you be asking me to marry you like this, knowing everything that you know? This is wrong on so many levels," she said.

"No. It's right on so many levels. Other things we may have done in the past could be considered wrong or just the wrong time. But to meet someone that you believe God has—"

She vigorously began to shake her head. "Don't you *dare* bring God into this. You and I both know the truth. We know what we did. And what we did was wrong. And now, my husband is gone, and you're down there on your knees asking me to marry you as though this is normal . . . that it's what we're naturally supposed to be doing."

King d.Avid smiled. "I know you might not agree with me

on that. But Brianna, somehow I believe you and I were meant to meet someday and be together. I believe it was ordained."

"What? You're really crazy, aren't you?" She tried to pull her hands out of his, but his grip was firm.

"Hear me out. This is not as crazy as you might think. Do you remember the first time we met?"

"Of course I do. I was ten and you were much, much older than me. And if you had looked at me in any way other than as a ten-year-old child, you'd be considered a pedophile."

"I didn't see you then as anything other than a ten-year-old child. But what I was going to say is that, on that day, you told me something . . . something that a woman at church had spoken over you and your future. Do you remember? Because I certainly do."

Brianna dropped her head. "I remember. She said I was going to be great or produce something great one day. She saw me as royalty, ruling in the office of a queen."

"Well, I can recall your *exact* words," King d.Avid said. "They were, 'I plan on being the queen of something myself. Just not exactly sure what I intend to rule over. But I'm going to be somebody great, or at least produce something great one day, just like you. I promise you that.' You said a woman at church had spoken a 'Word' over you. Well, I believe in that Word that was spoken. It was prophetic. Maybe somehow you and I got in God's way of how He planned on bringing things about between us. But I believe we were destined to be together and to do something great for the Kingdom of God."

Brianna struggled again to pull her hands out of his.

"I'm not going to let you go until you agree to be my wife."

"This is crazy, David. You don't fix one mistake by compounding it with another. You and I did something we shouldn't have. That's a fact. Otherwise, you wouldn't be down on your knee right now."

"And a little FYI here: I'm not as young as I used to be. So if you could show a bit of mercy and say yes pretty quickly, then me and my knee—both knees, in fact—will greatly thank you."

Brianna shook her head without cracking a smile. "You can't *joke* this away!"

"Who's joking? I want to marry you," King d.Avid said. "That's a fact."

"How many times have you already messed up by marrying the wrong person or maybe not the wrong person, but it was too soon . . . or at the wrong time?" Brianna asked.

"Four times married and divorced, two times officially engaged, and this last lady who claims we were engaged is absolutely off her rocker. There's no way I *ever* planned or intended to marry someone like her, I don't care what she's claiming in the tabloids."

"See, that's seven women. Six you felt were the one God had called you to, a few of them you have children with. I'm sorry, but your track record is nothing to write home about. And I don't plan on being number eight." Brianna shook her head. "So you need to get up off the floor and save your knees and let's talk about something else."

King d.Avid got up and sat next to her, reaching once more and taking her left hand in his. "Brianna, let's just say you *would* be number eight. Eight is the number of new beginnings. When I saw you at the beach, do you know what I heard in my spirit?"

Brianna looked at him and drew her head back away from him. "You saw me at the beach? When?"

"Back in early May when you were there with your friend Alana."

"You saw me? I didn't know you were there." She cocked her head to one side. "Wait a minute. Chad. Of course! He came to the beach house where we were staying."

"Yes. He came upon my instructions."

"That was *your* beach house Chad came from that evening?"

King d.Avid nodded. "Yes. Mine."

"So when did you see me? I don't recall seeing you at all.

The beach was pretty much deserted the two days I was there."
Brianna looked at him with a locked gaze.

"That evening. When you went into the outside shower and
came out of it wearing nothing but a cute little purple robe."

Brianna widened her eyes. "You saw that?"

"Yes. And I've since informed Vincent that he needs to put
a roof on that shower."

"Then you also saw me when I went into the ocean waters?"

"Yes."

"What else?" Brianna asked, tilting her head down as she
stared even harder into his eyes, almost willing him to speak
the truth. "And I want you to look directly in my eyes so I can
tell if you're lying to me or not."

"I'm not going to lie to you, Brianna. Not now; not ever. Do
you hear me? I'm making a promise to you right here and
now: if you ever ask me anything, I don't care how difficult it
might be to answer it, if it's at all within my powers to give you
the answer, I'm going to," King d.Avid said.

"Okay. So tell me what you saw." Brianna folded her arms.

"I saw you walk into the ocean. You wore the robe until you
were sure your body was hidden by the ocean's waters. You
then slipped off the robe and submerged your entire body, including your head, into the water. Which, I'm going to admit,
I thought a bit strange." He chuckled. "You even had me worried there for a minute or two. I almost ran from the roof
where I was standing at the time, thinking I might need to
save you."

"Save me? Save me from what?"

King d.Avid grinned. "I didn't know what you were doing.
When you went into the waters like that, your hair not protected to keep it from getting wet, and then you immersed
completely in the waters in some kind of a ritualistic way. I
didn't know if you were trying to drown yourself or what."

Brianna laughed. "Drown myself?" She laughed some more,
a hearty laugh this time where she was almost forced to hold

her stomach. "Please. Oh, my goodness! There's no way I would *ever* try and commit suicide. Not *ev-er.*"

"I eventually figured that out. But what *were* you doing?"

Brianna closed one of her eyes as she contorted her face a little. She looked back over at him. "I was doing my domesticated, improvised version of mikvah."

"Oh," he sang the word. "Mikvah, huh?"

"Yeah. So, you're not going to ask me what mikvah is?"

"Nope. I happen to know what a mikvah is, thank you very much."

"You do?" Brianna said, allowing her surprise to shine through.

"Yes." He grinned, then leaned in closer to her face. "A mikvah is a place of pooled water used for a process of purification, repentance, restoration, and if you happen to not be of the Jewish faith and convert, it denotes the completed status of conversion."

"I must say, I'm impressed," Brianna said.

"You're impressed? Well, I happen to know a Jewish guy at the recording studio. So *now* will you marry me?"

Brianna laughed. "*What?*"

"Don't you see? It's our destiny. We were meant to be together. We both know mikvah."

"No, we're not," she said adamantly.

"Yes," King d.Avid said, grabbing her hand and caressing it softly. "We *are.* So you might as well quit wasting time and just go on and consent. You know you can't outrun the calling or the will of God. And for whatever reason, at least I believe it to be true: we're supposed to be together."

"You really are serious, aren't you?"

"I promise you, I feel so strongly in my spirit about this; I can't explain it."

"Well, I believe you need to go and dip yourself in a mikvah or do something for purification. But truthfully, you need to ask God to forgive you. Because what you're saying right now is going to get you in a lot of trouble with God, a *whole* lot."

"I'm just speaking what's in my heart and in my spirit," King d.Avid said. "I truly believe you and I were already destined to be together at some point in our lives. But even if I'm wrong about that, one fact *does* remain. And that is that you and I have a baby on the way." King d.Avid promptly got back down on one knee again.

"Don't *do* that!" Brianna said, trying, without success to pull him back up.

He grabbed her left hand. "Brianna Bathsheba Wright Waters, I don't want this baby of ours to come into this world without a father. I know you don't believe me, but I truly do love you. I do. And for the record: I'm not asking you to be my wife just because of the baby—"

"Okay, stop it," Brianna said, effectively snatching her hand out of his. "This is wrong. Everything about this is wrong. I sinned against God and against my husband when you and I laid down together. I got pregnant, and *this* baby is *not* his." Brianna shook her head as she rolled her tongue around inside of her mouth. "Just saying all of this leaves a sour taste in my mouth."

"Brianna, in a perfect world we would all do the right thing." He grabbed her hand back. "But we don't live in a perfect world. The fact remains that you and I *did* sleep together. The fact remains it *was* a sin. The fact remains we asked God to forgive us. I believe that He has. Granted, you did get pregnant from that one night that I still don't regret spending with you. I hate I sinned. I hate it. But I don't regret being with you. Your husband was tragically killed. I know all of this hurts, but they are all facts."

Brianna began to cry, but King d.Avid would not let go of her hand, nor did he stop. "The fact remains, my dearest Brianna, you are carrying my child. That's *my* baby you cradle in your womb, no matter who you were married to when the baby was conceived. And I would love more than anything right now to be a husband to you and a father—a *present,* in my child's life, father—to him or her. So"—he caressed her hand, and reaching up, he brushed her tears away—"please do me the honor of being my wife. Please give me the opportunity to prove to you just how much I really can love you."

"What will people think if you and I get married? Huh? Answer that. Especially so soon after my husband's death? It's only been a little over a month. Not even six whole weeks."

King d.Avid stood up and pulled Brianna to her feet. "A month is longer than some folks in the Bible waited. But tell me: what will people think and say when you start showing? What will you say when people start asking you about the baby that you're carrying? You've already said you're not going to lie. Everybody will assume the baby is Unzell's. You're going to have to deal with a lot more than you want if you're by yourself as you go through this. But"—he softly brushed a strand of hair from her face, then lovingly tucked it behind her ear— "if you marry me, then no one will say anything to you about the baby. I'll help make sure of that."

Brianna leaned her head back. Her tears began to roll toward her ears now.

"I'm sorry. I don't mean to make you cry. That's not what I'm trying to do here," King d.Avid said, pulling her forward and wiping her tears with his thumbs. "I want to make your life easier. I can do that for you. I can. If you don't want to marry me because you don't love me right now, then fine. Marry me so that I can make things easier for you. I owe you that much. It's something I want to do for you . . . and for me."

"So you would marry me knowing that I'm not in love with you?"

"Yes."

"And you're telling me *that* would be okay with you?"

"Absolutely," King d.Avid said. "We can date while we're married. Get to know each other better. I'll gladly give you all the time and space you need. I promise you, there will be no pressure coming from me. We don't even have to consummate the marriage until you decide you're ready. In fact, when you're ready, I have a special place I want to take you. And I think you'll really love it. All you need to do, when you're ready, is to tell me: 'Take me to that special place.'"

"What if I'm never ready? Then I'll just be the eighth woman you were wrong about."

"There won't be another. I promise you that. You're the one God has sent to me. I found you, which is *absolutely* a *good* thing. I won't lose you. We'll work through whatever problems come our way. I'll be a good husband to you and a good father to our baby."

"And what are we supposed to tell people about this baby?" Brianna said, quickly glancing down, then back up.

"Whatever you decide you want us to. If you want people to think the baby is Unzell's, I'll not take that from you publicly. But in every sense of the word and in every aspect financially speaking, this child will be mine and will lack for nothing. Nothing." He cocked his head one way, then the other. "But if you want people to believe this baby is mine, conceived on our wedding night, we can do that as well. However, if you want to go the route of this baby being mine, we don't have a moment to waste getting to the altar. Because as it already is, anyone who can count will be able to count from the time the baby is born to when we were married and figure out something is a little off."

Brianna flopped down on the couch and placed her head inside of her hands. She shook her head. "I don't know what to do!"

King d.Avid sat beside her, lifted up her head, essentially pulling her hands from her face. He took both her hands into his. "Let's start by you agreeing to marry me. Let's start there. Then, we'll get married. After that, I'll be right there by your side. And together, we'll decide what to do . . . as one. Together. All right?"

Brianna looked unwaveringly into his eyes. "All right," she said. "I'll marry you."

Chapter 37

Who can understand his errors? Cleanse thou me from secret faults.

—Psalm 19:12

"What do you mean, you're married?" Alana said, standing near the door of the house that belonged to Brianna. "You're kidding, right? I know you're kidding. Tell me you're kidding."

"I'm not kidding, Alana. I got married."

Alana grabbed Brianna and pulled her into the den where they sat down. "Okay, if you're trying to be funny, this is *not* funny. And if you're serious, then we need to get you to a hospital as soon as possible because you're obviously suffering from a nervous breakdown."

Brianna held up the back of her left hand to show Alana her wedding band. "I'm married. And I'm fine." Brianna put her hand down as quickly as she'd thrown it up. "This band is temporary until I can pick out the rings I want."

"Okay, Brianna. You just sit right here. I'm going to call your mother. Okay?"

"Alana, you'll not be calling my mother. I plan on calling and telling her myself. I'm not crazy . . . I'm not having a nervous breakdown. I'm married. That's all. That's it."

"So exactly whom did you marry?" Alana said it as though she had to speak softly and slowly in order not to set Brianna off, possibly pushing her all the way over the edge. "You know Unzell is gone, right? You *were* married, but he's gone now. He died a month and a half ago."

"I know this, Alana. I told you, I'm fine. I know Unzell is dead. He's dead, okay? He died, and I know it because the pain still hurts like all get out."

"I know, baby," Alana said. "And you've been having a hard time coping with his death. But we're going to call a doctor after we call your mother—"

"I married David."

"David?" Alana said with an edge. "David who?"

"David Shepherd . . . King d.Avid."

"All right." Alana said it softly and without emotion as though she didn't really believe Brianna. "So you're telling me that you and King d.Avid got married? The guy you had a crush on when you were a teenager. You and he are married now. And you have the ring—albeit a very plain and modest little thing—to prove it?"

"Stop it, Alana. Stop talking to me like I've lost it or like I'm on the verge of losing it. I'm fine. I'm married. I married David R. Shepherd, aka King d.Avid, the gospel recording artist, psalmist, worship leader, and minister. We married this evening. I came home to let you know, as well as my parents, and to pack some things."

"You're telling the truth," Alana said, standing up. "You really *are* married. But why? How? How could you get married so fast? And without any of us being there. I'm your best friend, and you didn't ask me to come and stand with you . . . to come to the wedding? And you didn't tell your family . . . your mother or father? This makes no sense."

"It makes plenty of sense," Brianna said, also standing. "It was no big deal. David and I talked. We agreed this was something we wanted to do. I didn't bother telling you or my folks because I knew that exactly what's happening now is what I would have encountered had I told anyone before I did it. So we went and got a marriage license, David called his minister,

Nate Jones, and we married at David's house this evening. That's it. All there is to say on the matter. End of story." Brianna sat back down.

Alana eased herself down next to Brianna. "Okay. So I won't say anything about how much older he is than you—fifteen, close to sixteen years, is it? I suppose this also means that congratulations are in order. Congratulations, Brianna. Shepherd is it? Mrs. Brianna Shepherd."

"Thank you," Brianna said with a quick nod. "Now as for where you're going to live now."

"Oh, yeah," Alana said, her body slumping slightly.

"As I indicated already, I'm moving in with David. He and I both agreed that I can decide what I'd like to do with this house. Therefore, I've decided to rent it out."

"Oh," Alana said. "So how long do I have before I have to be out of here?"

"I suppose that's up to you. But I was thinking I could rent it out to you, possibly even with the option to buy. We could figure out some kind of lease payment that works for both of us."

Alana perked up, pulling her shoulders back. "Are you serious?"

"Yes," Brianna said with a primped smile. "That's if you're interested."

Alana cocked her head to the side. "I have nowhere to go. My credit score is in critical condition, on life support, expecting any day for the plug to be pulled. I couldn't get a place to live using my credit if I tried. Yes, I'm interested! But you don't have to do the option to buy. Just let me pay rent and that will be a blessing."

"Fine," Brianna said. "Then it's all settled."

Alana grabbed Brianna by her shoulders. "But are you sure about this marriage? Are you *sure*? Because you know I'm here for you. If you need me to help with something, I'm here for you. I'm your girl."

Brianna smiled. "It's all good." She hugged Alana. "But I

appreciate you. You know that I do." She let go. "Now, I need to call my folks and break my *glorious* news to them."

"If I could give you *one* piece of advice before you tell your folks or anyone else, for that matter."

"What's that?" Brianna said.

"Try to sound a *little* more like you're happy about it. Because honest and truly, you positively *sucked* when you told me."

Brianna chuckled. "Okay. I'll be sure and keep that in mind when I tell them."

Brianna went to her bedroom and called her mother. She concluded she must not have succeeded in sounding *too* happy when she told her, since her mother had pretty much the same reaction as Alana to her *blissful* news.

Still, she was married to King d.Avid now. And *that* was *that!*

Chapter 38

And the Lord sent Nathan unto David. And he came unto him, and said unto him, There were two men in one city; the one rich, and the other poor.

—2 Samuel 12:1

It was February and Brianna had just given birth on the fourteenth to a beautiful baby boy. King d.Avid was so excited, he could hardly contain his joy. Three days later, mother and son were home and doing well.

Minister Nate Jones took off his black Stetson hat and set it on the coffee table as he sat down on the couch in the living room.

"Congratulations," Minister Nate said.

King d.Avid grinned big. "Thank you."

"Yes," Minister Nate said. "A son."

"Yep. A healthy baby boy."

"Well, I was just thinking when I got the word a week ago that the baby had come," Minister Nate said, seeming to measure his words. "How can this be your biological son? You married in August. That means you and Brianna have only been married for six months. Not the nine months required to produce a full-term baby. And at five pounds, twelve ounces, I believe that's what you told me the baby weighed, he's definitely not a preemie."

"Does it matter?" King d.Avid said. "In every sense of the word and in every sense that matters, I'm that baby's father."

"Please don't misunderstand. Let's just say that if you stepped in to be sure the baby had a father after his father died, that wouldn't be a bad thing at all, now would it? One might even applaud such an act."

"Well, I'm just happy the baby is healthy, and here, and doing well. Brianna has been through a lot these past several months," King d.Avid said. "Too much."

"Yes, yes," Minister Nate said. "You know, I was just thinking of a story I heard the other day. There were these two men: one was rich; the other was poor. The rich man created a small investment stock fund practically out of nothing more than his sheer talent alone. His business soon became mega. The fund was said to be making money hand over fist, while other investments were losing or merely remaining stagnant."

"Why does this have a smell of a setup about to happen?" King d.Avid said.

"Anyway, the poor man, like any good man as stated in the scripture who wants to leave an inheritance for their children's children, didn't have the kind of money to invest like the now megarich man. He had scrimped and saved his whole life just trying to make it . . . trying to get by. And he'd managed, through sacrifice and dedication, to put a little something away. He'd been putting back a little here and a little there into a savings account for years, trying to store up something for his family to have later down the road. Believe me: this man sacrificed for the little he'd acquired. But what he'd acquired was solid, built on love, and it was his very own."

King d.Avid began to shake his head. "Oh, I can *definitely* see where *this* is going. I'm starting to get a bit upset already just from hearing the little I've heard so far."

"The rich guy made folks believe the investment fund was exclusive, that not everyone was privileged to invest money in it unless they were recommended to be approved, by someone who was already a member of the fund. The rich man convinced the poor man—along with other poor, unsuspecting folks—to take their money and invest it in this fund upon *his* recommendation." Minister Nate readjusted his body. "The rich man took every dime of those folks' money before it finally came to light that his fund was nothing more than a Ponzi scheme. The rich guy, on the verge of being found out, first tried to cover up what he'd done, doing things to hide it. And when everything did finally come out, he simply said, 'That's life. A lesson learned. Deal with it.'"

King d.Avid frowned and began shaking his head profusely. "You know . . . that *really* makes me mad. That is just as *wrong* as *wrong* can be! That rich man should go to jail and be locked up for the rest of his sorry excuse for a life. Just like that Bernie Madoff guy who made off with all those folks' money. They should also give this guy 805 years and put him *under* the jail. That's pitiful! Doing that poor man like that. I hope they take everything the rich guy has and then some, and give it to the guy and others he stole from. That rich man should have to pay the poor man fourfold. It's a shame and a disgrace that people who do things like that are allowed to walk around this earth free!"

Minister Nate looked sternly and directly into King d.Avid's eyes. "God spoke to me, King d.Avid. God said *you* are *that* man. God anointed you to do great things through your gift of music. He delivered you from the hands of your enemies. He gave you this mansion." Minister Nate made a show of slowly looking around the room. "The Lord said for me to tell you that if what you already had wasn't enough, He would have gladly given you more. But for some reason, you chose to do evil in His sight. Now, the Lord didn't tell me *exactly* what took place. But *you* know. So that's between *you* and God. But I do know, by His Spirit, that something is not right. And then, you so quickly took Unzell's wife to be your own." He shook his head.

King d.Avid put his hands up to his face and covered it. "Oh, God. Oh, God." He shook his head as he cried out. "Lord, oh, Lord! Oh, my Father God!" He cried.

"The Lord said that what you did, you did in secret. But what He does will be done in daylight. They say sunshine is a great bleach and the best disinfectant."

King d.Avid fell to his knees and began to cry even more. "Minister Nate, I have sinned against the Lord. And when I asked Him for forgiveness, I really wasn't sincere. I wasn't. I was merely being religious, simply going through the motions of what I knew was right to do. I was wrong, so wrong. But I'm asking God to forgive me now. I am . . ."

King d.Avid continued to cry as he bowed before the Lord. "From my heart, O Lord. Please, forgive me. Please forgive me. Please!"

After King d.Avid settled down, Minister Nate helped him to his feet. "David, the Lord has forgiven you of your sin. But because of it, and the way you tried to hide it, you have unwittingly opened the door for Satan to have entrance and access."

"Then what do I do to fix it?" King d.Avid said. "Please tell me: what do I need to do to make things right again?"

Minister Nate picked up his hat off the table. He placed his hand on King d.Avid's shoulder. "On this one, and at this point, I believe it's out of all of our hands. I will keep you and your family in my prayers." He patted King d.Avid's shoulder twice.

King d.Avid escorted Minister Nate to the door. After he left, King d.Avid went to his study, closed the door, got down on his knees, and began to fervently pray.

Chapter 39

*Have mercy upon me, O God, according to thy loving-
kindness: according unto the multitude of thy tender mercies blot out my transgressions.*

—Psalm 51:1

Brianna burst into King d.Avid's study with the baby in her
arms, having searched throughout the house for King
d.Avid. "David, the baby is sick! We have to get him to the hospital."

King d.Avid got up off of his knees. "What's wrong with
him?"

"He has a fever. And he's not breathing right . . . his breathing is labored."

"Let's go," King d.Avid said, hurrying with his wife out of
the door.

They got to the hospital and the baby was immediately admitted to intensive care.

Brianna and King d.Avid waited for hours before finally
seeing the doctor and receiving word that the baby had
neonatal sepsis.

"It's an infection infants can get during the first twenty-
eight days of life. It's also known as sepsis neonatorum. It at-
tacks the lungs," the doctor said. "Look, I'm not going to
sugarcoat or hide anything from you on this. This is life
threatening. The baby's white blood count is abnormal, another indication of what we're dealing with. It's like blood
poisoning. Adults get this in the form of MRSA sepsis."

"So what are you going to do to make him well?" Brianna asked as King d.Avid held his arm tightly around her, essentially holding her up at this point.

"Of course, he'll have to remain in the hospital. We've already begun administering antibiotics intravenously," the doctor said. "But this infection can all too quickly cause organ damage, so we're in for a fight here. We're in for a fight."

"What can we do?" King d.Avid said, alternating his glance from the doctor to Brianna. "I have plenty of money. We need to get the best in here. Whatever our baby needs, I want it done. Money is no object. We just want our baby to get well."

The doctor looked at King d.Avid. "I assure you, we're going to do everything within our power to make him well. Money is not the issue. But let me say this to both of you: if you know how to pray, then I would suggest you do it. I'm not going to lie to you: this is going to be an uphill battle. And even though I'm a doctor who deals in science and medicine, as a Christian I also know the power of what God can do. And at this point, in addition to our efforts, we can use all the help down here we can get."

Brianna broke down and began to cry. King d.Avid fought to keep his tears at bay.

"I'll leave you two, but if you need me . . ."

King d.Avid nodded without saying anything more. The doctor left them alone.

"Oh, God, please help my baby," Brianna said. "David, I can't believe this is happening. He's such a tiny little thing. God *has* to hear our prayers. He *has* to!"

"I know. And our baby is going to be all right," King d.Avid said. "I know God is going to heal him and bring him through. I know it. We just have to have faith in God."

They stayed at the hospital through the night. King d.Avid was able to get Brianna to go home a little after noon, if nothing else but to shower and change. Brianna's mother had also arrived at Alana's house. Diane and Alana came with Brianna when she returned to the hospital with her overnight bag in hand, determined she wasn't leaving again until her baby was completely out of danger.

"I'm going to stay here with him. I'm not going to leave him," Brianna said first to King d.Avid and then to her mother and best friend. "I'm not."

King d.Avid went home that night. He hadn't eaten anything since learning that little Jason was sick. Fasting now, King d.Avid was determined he would do whatever it took to ensure his son was healed from this sickness he'd been informed could very well take his life. He prayed, lying on the floor at times, as he stayed before the Lord in prayer.

The next morning, he was still on the floor praying. He stayed in his room all day and night, into the following morning. Vincent came into his bedroom, without knocking, and found him face down on the floor.

"King, now I know you're hurting. But you have to pull yourself together. You need to get up from here," Vincent said. "Everybody's worried about you now. They say you won't eat. They say it's been at *least* two days since you've eaten anything at all. Brianna's asking for you and about you. She's already frantic about the baby. Now she has to worry about you. Her mother is also inquiring as to what's the deal with you."

"Is there any change in the baby's health?" King d.Avid asked as he sat up and stared into nothingness.

Vincent shook his head. "No. They're saying, so far, he isn't getting any better."

"I'll call Brianna in a little while. You can leave now," King d.Avid said, kneeling down again.

"But you need to eat *something*," Vincent said. "If you like, I'll have Chef bring something up here to you. You don't even have to go downstairs—"

"I said you may go."

"But King, this is not rational. I know you're upset. I know you're worried. But what good are you to Brianna *or* the baby, if you get sick yourself?"

"I'm going to stay before the Lord until He heals my son. I

will fast and I will pray for as long as it takes. I know God can heal him, and I'm going to stay on my face and before the Lord, and do whatever is necessary until God raises that baby up from his sickbed and brings him back home to us again," King d.Avid said. "Do you hear me?"

Vincent nodded. "Well, I'm praying for all of you." He placed his hand on King d.Avid's shoulder. "But will you at least shower and shave, then go over to the hospital and see them? Brianna's mother is wondering why you've not been there in the last two days. And Brianna doesn't need to be worried about you along with Jason, she doesn't."

"I'll talk to Brianna. But right now, all I know is that I have to get God to hear my plea. God can heal Jason; I know He can. Then everybody and everything will be okay."

"Yeah," Vincent said, sounding empathetic but not convinced. "Well, if you need anything, you know how to reach me." Vincent left, closing the bedroom door behind him.

King d.Avid got back on his face and began praying again. He prayed for another two hours, then called Brianna and explained his need to fast and pray during this crucial and critical time. If God didn't hear their cry, all was, essentially, lost.

Chapter 40

Against thee, thee only, have I sinned, and done this evil in thy sight: that thou mightest be justified when thou speakest, and be clear when thou judgest.

—Psalm 51:4

Seven days had passed since Jason had been admitted to the hospital. King d.Avid wasn't at the hospital but at home in his bedroom—on his knees, at times lying face down on the floor—sending up fervent prayers to the Lord. He hadn't eaten in all those seven days, drinking only water to remain hydrated.

King d.Avid heard them when they came into his bedroom as he lay face down. He heard the whispering. Unsure of his mental state and how he might react at this point, no one in the house wanted to be the one to tell him. He heard them. "Brianna needs him at the hospital." He could tell Chad and Vincent were in there, along with two of his housekeepers. He even heard Chef's voice. "Someone has to tell him."

"Is he dead?" King d.Avid asked without looking up or getting up.

Vincent cleared his throat. King d.Avid heard one housekeeper begin to whimper.

"*Is* the baby dead?" King d.Avid asked again, still on his face.

Vincent walked closer to him. "Yes," he said. "The baby died a few minutes ago. But King, you have to be strong. You're going to get through this. I know you are. And we're all here for you, every one of us."

King d.Avid got up without saying another word. He picked up an apple from the fruit bowl on the coffee table and bit it. Finishing it, he went into the master bathroom, showered, shaved, rubbed oil on his hair, dressed, then got in one of his cars and left.

It was midday when he pulled up to the church and went inside, thankful that it was open that time of the day. The church he attended was always open during midday for the convenience of those who wanted to come by and pray in the middle of the day. King d.Avid walked in, headed straight to the altar, kneeled down, and began to worship the Lord, all by himself.

When he finished, he got up and headed back out. Minister Nate came up behind him just as he was about to push open the sanctuary's tall wooden door.

"The baby died, didn't he?" Minister Nate said.

King d.Avid stopped without turning around. "Yes, a little while ago." He then turned and faced Minister Nate. "Just as you implied might happen."

"That wasn't my doing," Minister Nate said. "I was only repeating what I heard from the Lord in the office of a prophet when I spoke that Word from God to you."

"I prayed . . . I asked God to save the baby, to heal him. But he died just the same."

"Just like it happened with King David in the Bible, recorded in Second Samuel, chapter twelve."

King d.Avid pressed his index finger against his lips and nose as though he were gesturing for someone to be quiet, then took it down. "King David in the Bible," he said.

"I'm sure you've heard the story of David and Bathsheba," Minister Nate said. "David had done something awful that he thought he'd covered up pretty well. Of course now, in the biblical account, David was *actually* responsible for a man, Uriah the Hittite, being killed just so he could cover up the truth of his wrongdoings." Minister Nate wriggled his nose a couple of times.

"The truth that he'd slept with Uriah's wife and gotten her pregnant while the man was away fighting gallantly on the battlefield in David's army," Minister Nate continued. "At first, good old King David sent for Uriah, made it where he was able to come home early just so he could send him to *be* with his wife. A noble gesture, huh? Not really. He wanted Uriah to think—without question—that the baby was his when he would learn that his wife was pregnant. King David was attempting to pull one over on Uriah. You'll find the entire account in Second Samuel, the eleventh and twelfth chapters. You should read it, if you haven't already. It's *fascinating* reading," Minister Nate said.

King d.Avid looked at him with a blank stare. "Yeah. I'll be sure and do that."

"To make a long story short: Uriah wouldn't betray his fellow troops who were still sleeping outside in tents and having to be away from their families. Even when David got Uriah drunk, he held true. David's plan failed. So he wrote a note to Joab, the person over the troops, and got Uriah to personally deliver it. Now, had Uriah been like some of us, he just might have read the note before handing it over. And *had* he read it, he would have found that it was instructing Joab to put him on the front line to be killed." Minister Nate shook his head. "That's some rough stuff, huh?"

"So Uriah was killed?" King d.Avid said, not really posing it as a question.

"Yes. Uriah was killed. And surprise, surprise: King David ups and marries Uriah's poor, unsuspecting widow who—as you'll recall—was pregnant with *his* child."

"And soon after the baby is born he dies," King d.Avid said, somberly . . . defeated.

"Yes," Minister Nate said. "He became deathly ill and died seven days later."

"And of course, King David couldn't be upset with God because he'd been the one to sin and to essentially open the door for Satan to come in and do what he does best: steal, kill, and destroy. And even though it looks like the baby seemingly was the one to pay the price for a sin he didn't commit, the baby was actually in the bosom of Abraham, later with the Lord—a place many of us pray we'll be one of these days . . . with the Lord."

Minister Nate placed his hand on King d.Avid's shoulder. "You got it. The Bible says, 'Man that is born of a woman is but a few days and those days are full of trouble.' "

King d.Avid nodded. "Well, I don't profess to know what all God is doing, nor do I know His ultimate plans. But I'll tell you what I *do* know. After all of this, I do know that God is God and that God is sovereign. God reigns."

"Yes. God reigns. We may not understand everything that happens or is happening, but God is a forgiving God. And in spite of us and all of the things we do to mess up, God loves us with an everlasting love. So much so, He sent us His Son Jesus."

"So where did King David go after all of that happened to him . . . to them?"

Minister Nate smiled. "He pulled himself together. And even though his life was full of trouble following that, God also blessed him tremendously. You see, even though David messed up, he was still a man after God's own heart. And that's what you're going to have to do, King d.Avid. Despite what has happened, you and Brianna must seek the Lord, find out what His will is for you from this point on, then boldly walk in that will. It's not about us; it's still about the Kingdom of God. There's too much work to be done. And God is ultimately left to use imperfect people who sometimes mess up. For all have sinned and fallen short of the glory of God. But that's no reason to stop going or doing."

"And all of this was the reason David wrote Psalm 51," King d.Avid said.

"Yes," Minister Nate said. "It was after a prophet, ironically named Nathan, similar to my own name, had gone to David and confronted him about what he'd done wrong. In Psalm

51, David was praying for cleansing. He acknowledged that he'd sinned against God and God only. He confessed his sin nature, that he was shapened or brought forth in iniquity. That in sin his mother had conceived him. This was merely referring to the sin nature of humanity and not anything his mother had necessarily *personally* done."

"Psalm 51 is also where David wrote, 'Purge me with hyssop, and I shall be clean: wash me, and I shall be whiter than snow.' " King d.Avid nodded as he reflected.

"Yes, that's the seventh verse. But it's the tenth verse that so many of us know and love to quote. In fact, people have used it in their songs," Minister Nate said.

" 'Create in me a clean heart, O God; and renew a right spirit within me.' Yes. I love those words. And I better understand and appreciate them so much more today than I ever have in my entire time of existence on this earth," King d.Avid said.

"But David didn't stop at that verse. He went on to say, 'Cast me not away from thy presence; and take not thy Holy Spirit from me.' " Minister Nate beamed. "Oh, yes."

"This is some good teaching right here," King d.Avid said. "A powerful Word. I can feel the presence of the Lord, right here where we stand. God is ministering to my spirit right now, Minister Nate. 'Restore unto me the joy of thy salvation; and uphold me with thy free spirit,' " King d.Avid said, quoting verse twelve. "Man! God is good! He's *so* good! Yes! Yes, Lord! Restore unto me the *joy* of *Your* salvation! And renew a right spirit within me! Thank You, Lord. I thank You. Thank You. Oh, Lord, I love You!"

"Thank You, Lord," Minister Nate said as he placed his hand on King d.Avid's heart. "Thank You, Lord." He then began to pray, as King d.Avid continued to praise.

Chapter 41

*The sacrifices of God are a broken spirit: a broken
and a contrite heart, O God, thou wilt not despise.*
—Psalm 51:17

Two weeks had passed since the baby's funeral. Brianna
and King d.Avid were alone. People were *really* gossiping.
Mostly because King d.Avid was famous, and that gave people
permission, in their opinion, to talk about what they felt was
the truth. Folks were being speculative, claiming that the baby
that had died couldn't possibly have been King d.Avid's because the woman he'd recently married had been married to
someone else a mere month before marrying him. They concluded she had to have been pregnant by the husband killed
in that tragic accident, and that King d.Avid had married her
merely to keep her from suing him for every penny she could
because of the death.

The debate was further fueled by the fact that some said he
had rarely been seen visiting the hospital when the baby was
so deathly ill. So that proved the baby wasn't really his own.
Had the baby been his, he would have been there around the
clock just like the mother had been or at least visited every
day. Some were so cruel as to contend that he'd secretly
wanted . . . prayed for the baby to die so he wouldn't have to
raise another man's child. Pure cruelness.

It was crazy, and King d.Avid had to teach Brianna to do as
he'd learned to do a long time ago: to either not read or listen

to stuff written and reported, or to simply ignore it. "People are going to talk, and people are going to lie," he said to her. "People love to build you up just so they can tear you down. It's part of the world we live in."

Minister Nate had come by the house to check on them. He prayed with them and spoke with them about keeping their eyes on the ultimate goal. There were still people out there who needed to hear about Jesus. There were people who—somehow, some way—still needed to be touched. In many cases, their very souls depended on King d.Avid and Brianna doing what God had called them to do so that they might hear the Gospel.

After King d.Avid excused himself from the room for a few minutes, Minister Nate quickly turned to Brianna.

"Daughter," he said, even though he was only thirty-one; not old enough to be her father, but he considered her a daughter in the Lord. "I have a Word for you from the Lord."

Brianna looked at him. She neither smiled nor frowned. She didn't do anything. Her heart was hurting so, she almost didn't feel much of any real emotion anymore.

Minister Nate took her hand and patted it. "God knows you're hurting. He knows you're broken right now. God knows everything, Brianna. But you *must* keep going."

"Why? Why, Minister Nate. Why should I? Why?"

"Because this is not about us," Minister Nate said. "It's not about you. It's not about King d.Avid. It's not about me. It's about the Kingdom of God and the Kingdom of Heaven. It's about Jesus."

Brianna shrugged. "Jason was just an innocent baby. He hadn't done anything to anybody. He was a good baby. He rarely ever even cried, unless he was hungry or wet. Our baby didn't get a chance. *We* didn't get a chance to—" She stopped and waved it off. "Oh, well, it's over now. And there's nothing we can do to change anything or to bring him back. I prayed, David prayed, our family and friends prayed, people we didn't even know were praying. And still . . . my baby is missing from these arms that ache to hold him more than I can ever express to you."

"Brianna, right now you have a broken spirit. I understand that. But think back over everything that you know, being completely honest with all that you know, then tell me: do you think God is unfair? Do you really believe He is unjust?"

"No, of course not. I don't mean to say or imply anything like that. God is God . . . period. I merely wanted our baby to live, and I didn't happen to get what I . . . what we prayed for . . . what we believed God for. Not that I'm saying God is there to do our bidding. I'm not saying that at all, because He's not. And honestly, as much as I'm hurting right now, I know God loves me. I know our son is with the Lord, and that he's in a better place than even we are. We're down here with sometimes mean and cruel people who have nothing better to do than to heap lies and hate on us during our time of hurt and grief. This is the world our son would have grown up in. Still . . ." She shook her head. "So, even though I would have *preferred* our son be here with us now, I know in my heart that it doesn't get any better than to get to spend eternity with our Lord."

"I can see that you do get it," Minister Nate said. "You're a strong woman. I can sense your heart. And God said for me to tell you that what He spoke to you some years ago, He means for that to come to pass. He said for you to stop beating yourself up about your past transgressions, and to get yourself back on the field to accomplish the will and the path He has set before you. God is saying right now that there is a greatness to come from you and King d.Avid, but you *must* get back on the battlefield. And God is saying to me that you know *exactly* what I'm talking about. You know. You know."

Brianna started crying. Then she laughed. "I hate when God does that!" she said.

"Does what?"

She laughed again. "Tells my business."

"Oh, now, I don't have a clue what all I just told you actually means. It's just what God was telling me to relay to you."

264   *Vanessa Davis Griggs*

"Well, I know exactly what He's talking about. God does not desire sacrifice in the way we think of sacrifices. Right now, I have a broken spirit. Right now, I have a broken and repentant heart," Brianna said.

"And God will not despise," Minister Nate said, completing the scripture she was referring to. "Whatever it takes, you need to pick yourself up, dust yourself off, and be about our Father's business."

"I know," Brianna said.

"You know what?" King d.Avid said as he casually strolled back into the living room. "What have you two been talking about while I was gone?"

Brianna wiped her eyes. "We were just about to discuss when Minister Nate might be available for a wedding-type ceremony, a renewal of our vows, if you will, ceremony." Brianna looked at King d.Avid as he slowly eased down next to her. "Me and you, where, this time around, we invite some of our family and friends."

"Are you sure?" King d.Avid said, knowing full well what she was saying now.

"Yes," she said, nodding and gazing lovingly into his warm, brown eyes. She took his hand. "David, I want you to take me to that special place."

King d.Avid dropped his head slightly, practically blushing now. "Are you sure about this? Are you *sure?*"

She squeezed his hand, made him look deep into her eyes, and nodded as she also smiled. "I'm sure. God needs us on the battlefield together . . . as one. Whatever has happened in the past is the past now. Nothing we do in the way of sacrifice will change what has been. But we can affect our now. We can make a difference now. I know God has something more for us to do for His kingdom. No more sacrifices of tears and pain. I merely want to be in a place to bring God a sacrifice of praise. So we need to put aside what *has* been and embrace what *is* and is before us now. I want to do the will of Him who sent me. And I can't do that living in a past that's in my rearview mirror now."

"If you're sure," King d.Avid said with a grin so wide, you could see most of his teeth. He turned to Minister Nate. "If you'll check your schedule and agree, we'd love for you to perform another ceremony for us."

"Oh, I'm sure that can be arranged," Minister Nate said. "I don't understand why another ceremony is necessary. But that's between you two and God."

"And Minister Nate, block out about two to three days. The ceremony won't be here in the city."

"Of course not." Minister Nate stood up to leave. "That would be too easy. Well, call my office, and we'll work out all the details. Somehow, I have a feeling this is going to be a blessing for me as well as the two of you." He pointed his index finger at them.

King d.Avid nodded. "Trust me: it's going to be good. But it's what God placed on my heart, so that makes it Godly, which is *better* than good." King d.Avid accompanied Minister Nate to the door.

When he returned, Brianna smiled. "Okay, so we're not having the ceremony here or at the church?"

"No. I told you that I have a special place I want to take you. So, we're going to go there for this ceremony. In fact, we can have a total of twenty-eight people to stay overnight. Wait a minute: make that twenty-six since you and I must be included in the count. And I plan to take care of all the expenses for everybody, so all that is needed from the attendees will be for them to have about two days available to be there. Oh! And to pack a bathing suit, just in case."

"So where is this place?"

"You'll see. Now, let's pick a date. I'll check to see if the place is available then. And we'll go from there."

"Okay," Brianna said. "But I'm not sure that I like surprises."

He hugged her. "Trust me: I think you're going to like this one." He looked into her eyes, leaned down, and gingerly kissed her. She kissed him back.

It was the first time they'd actually kissed since their nuptials, which, incidentally, only garnered a quick, one-second peck on the lips.

Chapter 42

But let judgment run down as waters, and right-
eousness as a mighty stream.

—Amos 5:24

"**I** want to know what's *really* going on," Alana said when she walked into the all-white living room. This was only her third time in Brianna's new home since she'd moved.

"I don't know what you're talking about," Brianna said.

"You call me and tell me that I'm invited to a wedding ceremony. Are you trying to say that you and King d.Avid were never actually married?"

Brianna frowned. "Of course we were married. What do you think? I've been living here and not married to the man I'm living with? I'm not you." She laughed.

"Ooh, that was a low blow," Alana said. "No, I'm not saying you may have been living here in sin. But it's highly possible you and King d.Avid made this whole marriage thing up. That's what I've read in the tabloids, anyway. They say your marriage is a sham. That you and King d.Avid don't even sleep in the same bedroom. Now, something like that *had* to come from someone in this house who would know."

"You never said anything to me about hearing anything like that," Brianna said.

"Truthfully: it really wasn't any of my business. If you and King d.Avid want to pretend to be married and sleep in separate beds, that's on you two."

"And why on earth would you believe we'd do something like that?" Brianna asked. "I'm talking about the pretending to be married part."

"I don't know. To protect you maybe," Alana said. "But don't think I didn't notice how you just completely ignored the part about you two sleeping in separate bedrooms."

"So you're telling me that you, my best friend—someone who knows me better than anyone—truly believes something like I'm not actually married?" Brianna said.

"Did you invite me to witness this *so-called* wedding?" Alana cocked her head to the side, as she primped her lips and nodded.

"No. But I also told you that we decided, and then we just did it. But I have my marriage certificate, proving that we were married. If you'd like to see it—"

"Uh-huh. I bet you do," Alana said. "King d.Avid has enough money to make anything appear like it's the real thing. But I *was* your best friend. I was right here in the city already, living in *your* house, as a matter of fact, with *you* at the time. All you had to do was tell me, and I would have been there, Johnny-on-the-spot. But is that what happened?"

"Hold up. What do you mean: I *was* your best friend?"

"These past months, I don't truly know you anymore. You've been keeping things from me. You think I don't know it," Alana said. "But I know when you go out of your way to keep me from knowing something. We hardly ever see each other. This is only my third time stepping foot in your house over here in the 'Beverly Hills' of Atlanta. You and I hardly ever talk. And when I look back, it seems to all have started a little after we were at that beach house. That's when you got all secretive and hush-hush on me."

Brianna shook her head. "Maybe you were just looking for something to make you feel better about the things you were doing."

Alana held her right hand up like a stop signal. "Oh, don't even go there. *You* shut down. And I'm going to tell you. I know you well enough to know that when you're afraid you're going to tell the truth about something, you always pull back from people. It's like you don't trust yourself to be able to lie, so you just avoid folks altogether. Even your mother said you've pulled away from them. It's like King d.Avid is your best friend now."

Brianna nodded. "Oh, so you and my mother have been talking about me? And *shouldn't* my husband be my best friend? Isn't that the way it ought to be? Married folks being each other's best friends?"

"The reason your mother and I have been talking is because we're trying to figure out what's going on with you," Alana said, looking Brianna squarely in her eyes and refusing to back down. "You've not been rational, especially since Unzell died. Six weeks! You ended up marrying some famous guy a little over *one month* after Unzell died. Come on, Brianna! What do you really think all of that looked like to everybody?"

Brianna stood up and began to pace behind the sofa where Alana remained seated. "I don't know what it looked like."

Alana turned around to see Brianna better. "So what made you do it? Why won't you tell me what was going on then? They say confession is good for the soul. Free your soul: tell me what the deal was or is? Confess! Did King d.Avid threaten you? Does he have something he's holding over your head, even now?" Alana stood and walked over to Brianna. "Did he have something on Unzell that you didn't want to get out? *What?*"

Brianna laughed. "You really have *some* imagination. Is everything a conspiracy in your eyes? My husband died, Alana. I married another man. Granted, there was not much time between those two events. But you're really out there, don't you think?"

"Okay, so help me to understand," Alana said, grabbing Brianna by her hand and leading her back to the couch where they both sat down together. "Make me understand how all of this made perfect sense to you in your mind."

"Like I really have to explain myself to you."

"You're right. You don't owe me anything. But if it made sense to you at the time, why can't you make it make sense to me now." Alana folded her arms. "I'd like to see you make it make sense. Unless you see how crazy it was back then, and you can't."

Brianna leaned forward and looked down at her hands as she spoke. "It was a bit complicated," Brianna said.

"Oh, you mean because you were pregnant?" Alana leaned forward as well.

Brianna looked over at her as their eyes locked, both seeming to dare the other one to be the first to look away.

"Yeah, of course I figured that much out." Alana sat back up straight. "You know my wheels are always turning. I thought I saw a baby bump when I was in the house with you. But you moped around so much, wearing all of those oversized clothes. So I dismissed the thought. Then your baby was born in February, so that meant you had to have gotten pregnant some time around May or June, not the middle of August, when you remarried."

Brianna sat up and back against the couch. She leaned her head back, and briefly closed her eyes. She sat back up straight. "Okay. So what's your point, Alana?"

Alana scooted back a little, then looked over at Brianna. "My point is: Unzell was out of town during that time. At least, he wasn't anywhere around you."

"And you mean that to say what?" Brianna stared at Alana without any emotion.

"I'm just stating facts," Alana said. "That's all. Just stating the obvious facts."

"Well, did you know that Unzell got to come back to Atlanta for a few days when they came back to the states and they were setting up for the New York concert? Did you know *that* fact?"

Alana squared her body with Brianna's. "He did?"

"Yes, he did. He was summoned to Atlanta for a private,

special meeting with King d.Avid. It was right before he was promoted to production manager."

"Oh," Alana said with a quick shrug. "I didn't know about that."

"Of course you didn't. Because I never told you. And you're right," Brianna said. "I *have* kept some things to myself. Sometimes, it's best to keep things to yourself."

"So you *were* pregnant when Unzell died," Alana said. "And you didn't tell me." Alana sounded resigned. "But I still don't understand why you would marry King d.Avid like that. You know we were here for you. Me and your folks would have stepped in and helped you with the baby. You didn't have to marry anybody else to be sure you'd be all right." Alana shook her head. "That part I still don't get. You've never been one that struck me, at least, as someone who needed a man to take care of you. Now me, on the other hand, I could see me doing something like that. But not you."

Brianna chuckled as she shook her head. "You sure don't pull any punches, do you? Even when it comes to knocking your own self out. Pow! Right in the kisser!"

"So why did you marry King d.Avid at the time that you did?"

"Let's just say I had my reasons. And at the time, it worked for me. I didn't have to deal with people asking me all kinds of questions or hovering all over me, driving me crazy. People trying to gauge whether or not I was all right," Brianna said. "My mother didn't even want me to stay at my own house by myself. If I hadn't told her you were going to be there, she was going to move in whether I wanted her to or not. There are times when you just need time to think . . . to heal . . . to sort things out. And you don't feel like hearing people yak at you or ask you twenty thousand questions about how you're doing."

"So you married him to get away from all of us?" Alana said, obviously hurt.

"Let's just say marrying King d.Avid at that time worked for me, and we'll leave it at that. But now, I'm in a different place. I lost my husband. I lost my baby." Brianna pressed her lips tightly, relaxed, then continued to speak. "I can either stay stuck in my grief, or I can move forward and walk in the vocation I know God is calling me to, beginning with those close to me." Brianna took Alana's hand. "For starters, I need to get it through your thick head that you have *got* to make a change in your life. You can't keep selling yourself short. One day you're with this man; the next day with another. Alana, I don't want to sound like a song, but you're looking for love in all the wrong places." Brianna shook her head. "You're better than this, much better than this."

"I know," Alana said, her head first dropping, then coming back up. "But thanks to some of your tough love, I've already begun improving in *some* areas. I'm working now at a call center. Eight whole months, it's been. And I'm taking care of myself for a change."

"But you're still giving yourself to men who aren't your husband," Brianna said. "That's a sin." Brianna lowered her head because for that *one* second, she felt convicted by her having done the same thing once herself. But she recalled the scripture, Romans 8:1, that declared there was now no condemnation. She was forgiven. She lifted her head high. "Look, I'm not judging you, Alana. Please don't get that from what I'm saying. I've made my own mistakes, believe me. But I've repented for my sins. I want you to do the same. Repent, then go in another direction . . . the right direction. I love you. You're my friend."

Alana began to wipe her eyes. "You're making me cry." Alana looked at her like a hurt child who had been given a motherly hug. "You really do love me, don't you?"

Brianna hugged Alana. "Absolutely. I love you enough to want the best that God has for you. But you have to want that for yourself. No one can do it for you."

"That's why you want to have another wedding ceremony with King d.Avid," Alana said. "You want to allow us to see the good in your being with him."

"Truthfully, I want to make some things right myself. Not just with my husband, David, but right in the sight of God. There's some redeeming that has and *is* taking place in my life. And you're right. There are things I've kept from you. Some things, I'll likely not ever share with you, or anyone else, for that matter. But I *will* tell you this much: King d.Avid told me when I was ready to truly give myself to him, for me to let him know. Well, I'm at that place now. Having this *big* ceremony is all his idea. But honestly, I like it. I think it's a great way for he and I to begin again. So, what do you say? Are you coming to our ceremony or not? We're only allowed to invite twenty-six people. I need to know for sure one way or the other."

"Only twenty-six? Oh, well, I guess that's better than your first ceremony to him. So"—Alana began to grin—"has he told you where you're going?"

"No. He just told me the dates. And that our guests should plan to stay for two days, being sure to pack a bathing suit, of all things, for this end-of-March event," Brianna said. "He's taking care of everything. And of course, the place is a secret, and will remain one, until we get there."

"Famous people sure do go to a lot of trouble just to be able to do private things in their personal lives," Alana said.

"Absolutely. So no one, including me, will know where we're going to be until we get there."

"That sounds like a bumper sticker. YOU NEVER KNOW WHERE YOU'RE GOING TO BE UNTIL YOU GET THERE. I know I never would have believed I would be going to an exclusive wedding ceremony . . . renewing of vows . . . whatever this is going to be, all expenses paid, with my best friend, who's married to a super-mega star. But here we are . . . here we *be*."

"So I can put you down as a yes?" Brianna said, smiling.

"Oh, you'd better!" Alana said. "Because if anybody will be there; I will. And I'll be there with bells on. Ring, ring. *Hel-lo!*" She popped her fingers and swerved her head like a dance.

Brianna leaned over and hugged Alana. "Thank you," she said. "Thank you." She wasn't merely thanking her for agreeing to come. She was also thanking her for caring so much, and for being a constant, steadfast, and true friend.

Chapter 43

Let the redeemed of the Lord say so, whom he hath
redeemed from the hand of the enemy.

—Psalm 107:2

The twenty-six invited guests were all gathered at the lavishly posh hotel per King d.Avid's instructions. Brianna realized how difficult it really had been for them to keep the number of guests down to that amount. She didn't understand why only twenty-eight people were allowed to be at the ceremony (she and King d.Avid made it twenty-eight), although the truth was: it would be a lot more than had attended their initial ceremony.

When they were married before, Vincent and Chad were in attendance. This time, only Chad would be present. Brianna had noticed, especially right after Jason died, that King d.Avid had pulled away from Vincent. King d.Avid later told her that Vincent was doing too many things to advance his own agenda, and the vision King d.Avid was pushing for was being sabotaged in the process.

He was also tired of "secret" things being leaked to the media. He had become suspicious that it was coming from Vincent, no matter how much Vincent denied he was the "anonymous source." King d.Avid now had undeniable proof that Vincent was the one putting his personal business out there. Things like King d.Avid's marriage to Brianna were nothing but a sham to keep her from suing for her husband's death; that the two of them didn't even sleep in the same bed-room—these all came from Vincent.

There was also some discrepancy when it came to the money. King d.Avid had called in his own auditors to audit the books, and the initial findings were not looking good when it came to Vincent. King d.Avid admitted he should have taken Oprah's and Bill Cosby's advice to heart and signed *all* of his own checks. Better late than not at all.

Mack and Melvin came for the ceremony. Brianna was so happy to see her big brother and new nephew. Mack still kept to himself when it came to her and the rest of the family. Then again, her folks were probably saying the same about her. But he seemed to be a really great father to Melvin, who, from all indications, was positively thriving in his environ-ment. His legs were on the mend and getting stronger every day.

King d.Avid's mother and father were there. That was a good thing since they, as well as his sister and brother, had been estranged for at least the past five years. In fact, this was Brianna's first time getting to meet any of King d.Avid's side of the family. Unzell hadn't been close to his family, either. King d.Avid told her, when she'd asked about his family, that a lot of it had to do with money and what his sister, especially, felt he should be doing for them financially. A lot of it could be attributed to Vincent and some of his antics in keeping King d.Avid separated from anyone Vincent felt might be a threat to his position as manipulator in chief. That was what had happened with anyone Vincent thought could impose on his influence in King d.Avid's life.

Of course, King d.Avid admitted to his share of the blame. He had allowed Vincent to do things, very rarely ever keeping him in check. There were things King d.Avid should have done himself that he abdicated and allowed Vincent to han-dle. Big mistake. And Vincent absolutely took full advantage of his power and position, sealing his place in King d.Avid's world forever. Or so he had thought.

But King d.Avid had been locked in deep prayer with the Lord. He'd fasted during the time he had prayed so mightily for God to heal his son. And it was during that time when God began to speak to him on a whole *host* of issues he'd been too busy to hear God on in the past. God gained access back into King d.Avid's life. And God opened d.Avid's eyes, essentially telling him to get his house in order, which also included his business house.

So King d.Avid had begun to work toward that end. He had called his family and talked with his mother and father, then his sister and brother. It had been hard, but they had all expressed how they'd felt. King d.Avid heard them speak about how he hadn't done much for the family financially when he had made so much money. King d.Avid expressed to them that, number one: he hadn't owed them any money, and anything he might do was not something anyone was due just because they were family. That was number one. And number two: it would be nice to feel like his family cared about *him* and not what he had or what he could do for them. That was number two.

"No one wants to feel like they're being used," King d.Avid had said. "I want people to love me for *me,* not for what I have or what they think they can get out of me."

In the end, it had been a taxing process. But each had heard the other's heart, and they had come to the place that: they were still family. And family was important.

So King d.Avid's sister was there with her husband and three children from ages three to sixteen; and his brother was there with his wife and two sons, ages eight and ten.

The others in attendance (besides Brianna's entire immediate family, including her grandfather, Pearson, and Alana) were Minister Nate, his wife Jo Ann, Helena the wedding coordinator, and a few other close friends of King d.Avid's.

Of course, the paparazzi were there. They'd been effectively tipped off about the hotel where the wedding would be taking place. King d.Avid was certain now who'd leaked the information, since there was really only one person he'd told about the hotel plans: his trusted assistant, Kendall McNair. He had informed Kendall that he was personally taking care of all the ceremony arrangements, including the venue. He knew the hotel hadn't been the one to leak the information, even though when he confronted Kendall, that was *exactly* whom she tried to blame.

"Kendall, don't worry about reporting to work," King d.Avid said. "Your things will be cleared out and waiting for you at the guard's station."

"But I don't understand," Kendall said. "I'm telling you, I wasn't the one who leaked this. It wasn't me! I'm telling you: it was most likely someone here at the hotel or one of your guests."

"No, Kendall. You see, none of my *guests* knew we were coming to this hotel. I sent a car to pick each of them up, along with their luggage, and bring them here. They didn't know where they were coming until the car they were riding in pulled up at the entrance here."

"Well, it had to be someone on staff here at this hotel then. I don't care how much you told them to keep it hushed or how much you paid extra for them to keep it quiet. I'm telling you that it wasn't *me!* So it had to be someone who works here." Kendall was on the verge of tears now. "It had to be."

"Kendall, believe me: I know it was you. You know it was you. I appreciate your years of service, but I can no longer have people employed in my organization whom I can't trust. That's why I terminated Vincent as my manager."

"But you can trust me, King d.Avid. I'm telling you, I can be trusted. Just please don't let me go. Listen, you're right. Vincent had me doing some things, but he's gone now. And now I can be totally loyal to you. Vincent was holding the threat of me losing my job if I didn't do what he asked. I needed this job. I still need it. I have two children to clothe and feed. I desperately need this job. Please don't let me go." She was really crying now. "Please, I'm begging you."

King d.Avid looked at her, then at the gathering of people waiting on him in the lobby. "I'll tell you what: I have a ceremony to attend. I will pray about what to do when it comes to you. But as for now, I don't want you anywhere near my office. And just so you'll know: locks, access, passwords, and codes are being changed, even as we speak."

"Yes, sir. I just pray God leads you to give me another chance. We've all messed up at some point in our lives. I just hope you consider that as you pray about me. And I hope you'll be merciful to me, the way we desire God to be merciful when we mess up and ask *Him*. Let the redeemed of the Lord say so. I've been redeemed. I really have."

King d.Avid looked at her, then nodded before he walked away.

"What was all that about?" Brianna whispered when King d.Avid came over.

"Just some business I needed to take care of," King d.Avid said.

"Well, it looks like everybody is here," Brianna said. "Including everybody and his brother with a camera. This is *definitely* not what I was thinking about when I agreed to a ceremony. How are you planning on keeping all of these cameras out? This is a circus!"

King d.Avid gave a nod to Chad. Chad motioned to all of the plainclothes security guards planted throughout the area. They began to usher the people who were in attendance for the wedding to a back area, effectively keeping the paparazzi away for the moment.

"Where are we going?" Brianna asked as she walked alongside King d.Avid.

King d.Avid smiled as they walked outside through a back door and stepped up into a seven-passenger van. There were six such vans out there. The rest of the attendees filled up those vans, along with the security personnel and everyone's luggage.

King d.Avid didn't say anything as they rode. He merely smiled occasionally at Brianna as he held her hand.

They arrived at the airport and were quickly directed to King d.Avid's private plane. Some of the paparazzi had followed, but they were effectively stopped at the gate.

When everyone, including their luggage, was loaded onto the luxury plane, they took off.

Sitting with King d.Avid in an area to themselves, Brianna looked sheepishly at King d.Avid. "*Now* will you tell me where we're going?"

He grinned, then made a show of buttoning his lips prior to turning away to stare out of the window.

Brianna reached over with her hand, gently touched his chin, and turned his face back toward her. She leaned her forehead forward, effectively placing it against his chin.

He stroked her hair. "Patience, my lovely," he said. "Patience. You'll find out soon enough." He kissed her on the top of her head.

Chapter 44

*As cold waters to a thirsty soul, so is good news
from a far country.*

—Proverbs 25:25

Brianna, King d.Avid, and their guests landed at Tortola
(Beef Island), one of the British Virgin Islands close to
their destination. They transferred to a helicopter and were
flown into their final destination of Necker Island, Sir
Richard Branson's private, seventy-four-acre paradise in the
British Virgin Islands.

Brianna gasped as they flew over the prettiest turquoise waters she'd ever witnessed, a sparkling white sandy beach, with
several Balinese houses including the house she and King
d.Avid were to stay in, called The Great House. King d.Avid
told her that The Great House was known as the heart of the
island. There was the Bali Beach house, a mere two steps away
from the plunge pool; a three-tiered house called Bali Hi
where the top floor gave magnificent views of Turtle Beach.
Bali Cliff was just as its name implied, perched off the mountain, exuding nothing but romance as it faced the turquoise
ocean, with its open-air bathroom that amplified the view and
the sounds of the ocean. In the middle of the island, more
private and in seclusion, were Bali Lo, Bali Buah, and Bali
Kukila. A small stream ran between Bali Lo and Bali Buah.

"Do you know what Bali Buah takes its name from?" King

d.Avid said to Brianna as they walked around, taking in and admiring the beauty of the island as he schooled her.

"What?"

"It's the Indonesian name for fruit."

"Wow, that's interesting."

"And Bali Kukila takes its name from the Indonesian word for bird."

Brianna and King d.Avid came upon Mack and Melvin. Melvin was beaming. "Auntie Brianna! King d.Avid! This place is awesome! I can't believe I'm actually on a private island. And it's all ours for a whole two days."

King d.Avid walked up to Melvin. "Oh, so you like it here?"

"Like it? I love it! I love the palm trees everywhere. I love being able to sit here and look out over everything. I can sit in this lounge chair and just feel the breeze. It's beautiful here. I don't think I ever want to leave," Melvin said.

"Well, we're going to have to leave after two days," Mack said.

"Maybe we can come back again," Melvin said, looking at Mack when he said it.

"I don't know about that. I'm sure it cost a pretty penny to come to a place like this." Mack looked at King d.Avid and gave him a quick smile.

"How much does something like this cost?" Melvin said to King d.Avid.

"Melvin, it's not nice to ask people things like that," Mack said. "We're guests here and that's all we need to know for now."

"I bet bringing all these folks here cost a lot," Melvin said. "Doesn't it, King d.Avid?"

King d.Avid leaned down and hugged Melvin. "Well, don't you worry your head about what it cost me. You just enjoy yourself. And make sure you get Mack to take you down to the Necker Nymph."

"Necker Nymph," Melvin said, laughing. "What's a Necker Nymph?"

"It's a three-person aero submarine that goes down about 30 meters."

Melvin laughed again. "I bet you think I don't know how much that is in feet."

King d.Avid pulled back. "You're telling me that you do? You're saying that you can convert meters into feet, just like that? No pen or paper? No electronic gadget?"

"Yep," Melvin said, looking up into the sky. "That's a little over 98 feet."

"Whoa, I'm impressed." King d.Avid said, having quoted it as meters because that was the only way the information had been conveyed to him.

"Oh, he's really good when it comes to math and science, especially," Mack said. "He's a little genius. Actually, he was being modest with you." Mack turned to Melvin. "Tell him the entire number."

Melvin grinned. "The total number would be 98.42519685 feet to be exact."

King d.Avid turned to Brianna. She stood with a smile on her face, then shrugged. "Don't look at me," Brianna said. "I would still be trying to figure out that 30 meters equals 98 feet, if it was left up to me."

"Well, little Mister Genius," King d.Avid said. "You make sure you check out the coral reefs. I hear the colors are poppin'. And there are a few ancient shipwrecks down there, as well as exotic marine life swimming around." King d.Avid rubbed his head. "And if you don't get to do everything you want this time around, I wouldn't doubt that Mack will bring you back here again in the future, if you'd like to come back, that is. They have what's called the Family Fun Celebration Week that allows people to come here without having to rent the whole island the way I did. In fact, I'm almost certain Mack is going to bring you back again." King d.Avid looked over at Mack and winked.

Mack nodded, picking up on the unspoken words that King d.Avid would make *sure* they did. That had been one of the promises he'd made to Mack when they met that day in December. Melvin would not ever have to do without. Whatever was needed to make his life good and exciting, King d.Avid had promised to ensure that it happened. And so far, he had been *more than* true to his word. And no one was the wiser.

"Since Melvin brought it up," Brianna said after they walked on. "You always say if a person wants to know, they should ask. So, how much *does* something like this cost?"

"I'd rather *you* not ask that. This is my gift to you. And I was always told that it was impolite to ask someone how much a gift cost."

"Yeah . . . well, just so you know: it's going to bother me not knowing," Brianna said with a twinkle in both her voice and her eyes.

"Seriously?" King d.Avid said, tilting his head slightly. "You would do me like that? Because you know I promised to not ever deny you the truth, should you ask."

"That *is* wrong of me, isn't it?" Brianna said. "To make you tell me on this one."

"It is." He grabbed her and hugged her. "Let's just say there is no amount of money that can ever be placed on your happiness." He tapped her on her nose.

"And I *am* happy right now. This was such a great surprise. And to have our family and friends here to share it with us, that's priceless." Brianna gave him a quick peck on his lips. "Thank you. Thank you for being so patient with me. Thank you for loving me enough to wait. And thank you for just being you."

Brianna and King d.Avid walked into The Great House with its slanted roof and chandeliers looking like hanging mangos. She loved the dark, shiny floors made from Brazilian hardwood. Of course, there were mosquito nets, which were necessary, since everything was so open to the outside. There was bamboo wallpaper and bamboo furniture, sitting areas with purple and pink pillows, and loungers everywhere. The dining tables were long, one made out of solid teak and in the shape of a crocodile.

"I still can't believe that this is the surprise place you had in mind for me," Brianna said, having completed their tour of the entire island. "Well, this certainly exceeds anything I could have ever imagined."

"That's how our God is," King d.Avid said. "He will do exceedingly, abundantly, above all that we can ever ask or think. We just need to line up with His Word, then watch Him wow us with His wowness and pow us with His unlimited power."

"Amen to that," Brianna said.

"Because I must confess: when I told you I would take you to a special place, I didn't originally have all of this in mind," King d.Avid said.

"You hadn't intended to bring me here?"

"Oh, I had fully intended to bring you here. But I was planning on it just being me and you. Then God placed it on my heart to go farther . . . bigger. This is a new beginning for you and me. And I wanted us to do it the right way this time," King d.Avid said. "And what better way to begin than to renew our vows to each other in a place of forgiveness and newness, a place of God's redemption. I guess you can call this my own attempt of redeeming Waters. You—whose last name was Waters—in every sense and respect becoming a Shepherd, with our family and closest friends sharing the moment."

"Well, you certainly will get no complaints from me," Brianna said. "So, since you're the one coordinating everything, and I'm merely left to be a spectator, or at best, to follow your lead: what's the plan from here on out?"

"We will all be here today enjoying the island. And tomorrow, you and I will repeat . . . renew our vows to each other."

"Except this time, we'll really mean it from our hearts," Brianna said.

King d.Avid smiled. "I meant it from my heart when I said it the first time. So does that mean that you love me now?"

She became serious. "Yeah," she said, gazing into his eyes. "I . . . *love* you. You've become my best friend. You've been positively wonderful these months. I've seen and gotten to know who you really are. And I've seen how much you truly love the Lord."

Brianna and King d.Avid reaffirmed their vows before the Lord with family and friends in attendance. The ceremony was simple, yet extravagant at the same time.

Brianna had originally purchased a cute but unpretentious little dress. King d.Avid had commissioned Helena, the woman he'd hired to handle the things for the ceremony, to purchase a special dress for his wife. Helena chose a stunning Vera Wang, ivory, Victoria wedding gown from the Luxe Collection, also called the Ribbon dress, priced at $15,000. King d.Avid didn't care how much it cost; he merely wanted his wife to have the best. The A-line gown consisted of individual Duchesse silk ribbons, hand sewn, with every third ribbon having a herringbone pattern. Originally not intended for sale and merely for display only, it was the Princess of Kuwait's insistence on having one for her own wedding that caused the gown to be placed into production.

Wearing a light yellow tea-length dress, Brianna had chosen Alana to stand with her. Surprisingly, King d.Avid asked Brianna's grandfather, Pearson, to stand with him. And Pearson had been both touched and honored by the request.

Brianna and King d.Avid recommitted themselves to each other outside on the sandy white beach, at the height of a beautiful sunny day, the last Saturday in March. Yet another piece of information Brianna learned about Necker Island: the lows averaged between 67 and 73 degrees (depending on the time of the year), and the highs averaged from 79 in January to a high of 87 degrees during July and August. Their end-of-March, 82-degree-weather timing couldn't have been more perfect—not too hot; not too cold. Absolutely perfect!

Brianna's mother cried, happy she was able to witness this.

Almost everyone cried when King d.Avid sang his song from the Twenty-third Psalm, "The Lord, My Shepherd."

Minister Nate prayed a special blessing over them. "I declare and decree, in the mighty name of Jesus, that your latter days will be greater than your former. What God has ordained, nothing and no one can or will stop it. I pronounce that you *are* redeemed by the blood of the Lamb and by the word of your testimony with all of the benefits afforded the children of the Most High God." Minister Nate smiled.

"So, by the powers invested in me as a minister of the Gospel of Jesus, I now pronounce you even *greater, closer,* and more *loving* husband and wife. Now you, David Rondell Shepherd, may salute your bride . . . your wife. And you, Brianna Bathsheba Waters Shepherd, may receive the salute from your husband . . . the priest of your house."

King d.Avid looked at Brianna with such love and adoration. He slowly leaned down and gave her the most touching, most loving, the tenderest kiss she'd ever received. He kissed her again. Then again. And she couldn't keep herself from giggling with joy after he delivered the final kiss and she saw him smiling with such love.

Chapter 45

*Let thy fountain be blessed: and rejoice with the
wife of thy youth.*

—Proverbs 5:18

Everyone had been flown off the island and back home.
Everyone except King d.Avid and Brianna. They now had
the entire island to themselves (with the exception of the un-
obtrusive, year-round staff that took care of things on the island).

It had been a wonderful ceremony, followed by a joyous
and fun time with family and friends. The island had a minimum stay of five nights, which worked out perfectly for King
d.Avid and Brianna. They had arrived, spent two full days on
the island with their family and friends, then were left with
three days and nights alone . . . together.

Looking over the deep blue lapping waves from their open
bedroom, the two had yet to consummate their marriage in
all of these months. Brianna was ready now. But there was
something special, different, that she wanted the two of them
to do first.

"If I ask you to do something, would you do it?" Brianna
asked.

"Ooh, that's a potentially loaded and dangerous question.
If I say yes, what might I be agreeing to before I even know it?
If I say no, then how can I deny my lovely bride who has cap-
tured my heart in every sense of the word." His eyes slowly

roamed her face . . . her forehead, her eyes, her nose, her lips, her chin, then back to her eyes again.

"Do you believe I would ever do anything to hurt you?"

"Not on purpose," King d.Avid said. "But I've not run into too many people who set out to hurt me, at least in the beginning. It happens though."

"Yeah. I know. I feel like I've hurt people, and they don't even know I was responsible for it," Brianna said. "I absolutely hurt Unzell."

"I know you're still hurting over Unzell, but—"

She touched his arm. "You don't have to worry; I'm not going to talk about Unzell. Not here, not during this time. I was just mentioning him because I'm sure I hurt him. And not just with what we did that he never found out about. Just during the course of life and our marriage. I've hurt my parents. I've hurt Alana with some of my comments that she felt were judging her, instead of showing her the love of God."

"Well"—he wrapped his arms securely around her and leaned back, drinking her in with his eyes—"sometimes love hurts. There's tough love that's for our own good. Then there's love that just hurts without any rhyme or reason for it to hurt."

"And . . . I've hurt you," Brianna said, finishing up her verbal list.

He stepped back and shook his head. "No. No. I'm the one who has been wrong in so many areas that I was ashamed when I was confronted with them." He moved back to her. "Early on, I had people who gave their lives and heart to what I was doing. And when I reached the place we'd all worked so hard for, what did I do? I sat back passively and allowed others to take over when I should have been a real man and stepped up."

"That wasn't all your fault though," Brianna said. "In your position, you can't do everything. You can't know everything. You rely on others to do their jobs. Maybe you did make a few bad judgments in who some of those people should have been. But God still has a way to use the bad for our good . . . for His ultimate purpose. However, the fact remains: we can't go back and change any of our past or our past decisions. You can't; I can't. We just have to start where we are and make better decisions now."

King d.Avid wrapped his arms around her again. He then stooped down a little so his eyes would be comfortable with hers. "So, my beautiful, wonderful, and amazing wife: what would you like for us to do?"

Brianna released a mischievous grin. "Well, you may think it's crazy. And I know it's not required. But it's really on my heart. It's something I feel like we should do . . . together, as husband and wife—you being my husband and the priest of our house."

"Oh, so you caught what Minister Nate said about the word 'husband' meaning 'priest' and that meant you had a priest in the house," King d.Avid said.

"Sure. I always listen to Minister Nate. As our spiritual covering, he loves us. But more important: he loves and listens to the Lord. I believe God has given Minister Nate messages to, not necessarily give *to* us, but to confirm what God has already spoken or is speaking to us."

King d.Avid nodded in agreement. "That's a good way of putting it. Because you're right. God confirms His Word. I know some believe that God will tell someone else things about them before telling them. But I believe God tells us, then confirms it by bringing that same Word through a party who was not in on our original conversation with God. And God confirms it through actual manifestation of what was told."

"Yeah. Like I know that you and I have much work to do for the Kingdom. And although I can't say exactly what it is or when it is to take place, I know there's something big God has called into our lives, called into this union. I now know this in my heart. I do."

"Okay, quit stalling. What do you want to do?" King d.Avid

said. "You have me all hyped up now. I can feel a few words and beats to a new song coming on." King d.Avid started popping and moving to a silent beat obviously playing only in his head.

Brianna moved up closer to him in a flirty way. "So, what you're saying is that I inspire you. Is that what you're saying, Mister Shepherd?"

He stopped moving and gazed lovingly at her. "Oh, you *definitely* inspire me."

"All right. This is what I'd like for us to do. We have this island all to ourselves. Sort of like our own Garden of Eden. There are natural waters flowing at every turn. Do you remember that time you said you saw me in the waters at the beach."

"Oh, yeah." King d.Avid blushed, then his eyes widened. "Oh-h-h, I see where you're going. Oh, yeah! We're going to have a *good* time; I see that already."

She playfully hit at him. "Stop that. I'm being serious now. And this is a spiritual thing on my heart. I want us to start anew. I want us to begin our relationship with a clean slate. I know in the real world that's impossible. But from a spiritual standpoint, and with God, all things are possible. I would like for you and I to really give ourselves to the Lord, in a truly dedicational way, as one. I would like for us to go to a mikvah, a pool of nonstagnant water, where we outwardly consecrate, purify, dedicate, and show that new life is emerging forth, just as it has inwardly been done through Jesus Christ. Like a baby emerging from the mother's womb, I would love for me and you to do this together . . . as one. And I can't think of a better place than here, God's natural mikvah in its primal form, and right now, as we embark upon a *true* committed journey as man and wife."

He kissed her. "Oh, I love that! I have chills going all through me right now. My spirit *absolutely* agrees with this. Yes! Let's do it!"

"And then, to keep with the tradition of what happens *after* going to a mikvah, we can come back here—"

"Or any one of these houses. Pick whichever one you want. I rented the whole island, so every house here is at our disposal, Mrs. Shepherd," King d.Avid said, smiling and playfully raising his eyebrows rapidly and in succession.

"Oooh, it looks like when we're done with mikvah, we're going to have our work cut out for us. There are like six houses on this island."

"Yeah. Absolutely. And I want to be a good steward of God's money that He has entrusted in my hands. We're paying a pretty penny for this place, so I think we definitely should get our money's worth."

"Oh, absolutely. And as your wife, I plan on doing my part. Waste not, want not."

"Okay. So let's do this," King d.Avid said. "Quickly."

Keeping with the mikvah tradition, they showered first. They then wrapped in their robes and went down to the waters with the large rocks and the waterfall below it.

They prayed sincerely and laid everything on the altar before the Lord, all of the dead stuff in their lives. They prayed some more, then immersed seven times, praising God each time they broke the water's surface. Then once more, synchronized this time, number eight—the number of new beginnings—they went down and came up together. Putting on now-wet robes, they got out of the water, giving God praises for resurrecting, restoring, refreshing, reviving, refining, renewing, replenishing, and redeeming them as well as their marriage, and for where He'd brought them from and was leading them to.

After that, they went to Bali Cliff, the Balinese house perched off the mountain, and finally sealed their vow—finally, truly they became one.

Chapter 46

Draw me not away with the wicked, and with the workers of iniquity, which speak peace to their neighbors, but mischief is in their hearts.

—Psalm 28:3

Vincent Powers was not going down without a fight. He was convinced that it was he who had made King d.Avid, and he was not going to be denied.

"How dare he tell me my services are no longer needed?" Vincent said as he paced back and forth in his living room.

"Well, there's nothing any of us can do," Kendall said. "We've talked with lawyers, to no avail. We're *all* out now. And yeah, I could get another job, but who's going to pay me anywhere *close* to what I was making when I worked for him?"

"Yeah, well, I hope you know your salary was all my doing. You definitely wouldn't have been raking in that kind of money if I hadn't been the one there guaranteeing and manipulating it. In fact, you wouldn't have even gotten your foot in the door had it not been for me," Vincent said.

"I know that, Vincent. But you got your money's worth, and then some," Kendall said, snarling as she looked him up and down.

"Yeah, okay. So you and I had a little thing on the side. I hope you know what was between us in the bedroom didn't mean anything. It was merely fringe benefits on the side, for both of us."

"Yes, Vincent. I'm well aware that what we had together didn't mean *jack* to you. I know about all the other women you paraded in and out of your bed. Many of them actually believed you might do something to promote their pathetic little music careers, be that as it may." Kendall crossed her legs and began swinging the top leg in a rhythm.

Vincent stopped pacing. "It's not my fault most of those women didn't really have any talent to speak of. Because you know me: if I believed I could have made a buck off of any one of them when it came to some *real* talent, I would have had their names on the bottom line of a binding contract quicker than they had time to let a lawyer review it."

"Yeah, we know, Vincent. You got it like that." Kendall uncrossed her legs and looked up at Vincent. "The question now is: what are we going to do? You're no longer King d.Avid's manager, and I'm no longer his able-bodied assistant. We're both out."

"I'm working on it. I'm working on it." Vincent eased down in the wingback chair across from Kendall. He crossed his leg.

"You're the genius. It's been three months now. So what have you come up with so far?"

"I was thinking that we might be able to make King see the error of his ways with a little bit of info that I'm pretty sure we can use to *persuade* him to see things more our way. I mean, it's not like *any* of our hands are completely clean. He fired me because he thought I'd been doing underhanded things, maybe steering money to certain places he didn't authorize or approve, including into my bank account," Vincent said.

"What little information are you referring to?"

"Well, for starters, that crippled child. What was his name?" Vincent snapped his fingers as though that would help him to recall.

"You mean Melvin Samuelson, now Melvin Samuelson-Wright?" Kendall said.

"Yeah. Why would King care anything about that child? And why is it that Mack Wright took such an interest in a child that was no relation to him? What's the real story behind all of that?"

"There's nothing there," Chad said, closing the door with fanfare behind him.

Vincent looked up. "I didn't hear you come in. And how did you happen to get in here, anyway?" Vincent said, quickly rising to his feet.

"Still have keys," Chad said, holding up his ring of keys to Vincent's house.

"Yeah, well, I need those back," Vincent said. Chad threw the keys to him. Vincent caught them, although barely. "So why do you say there's nothing there with Mack and that little Samuelson kid?"

"Because I checked them out thoroughly myself." Chad gestured toward the couch, requesting permission to sit. Vincent nodded his okay. Chad sat down next to Kendall, who quickly scooted closer to him. "Believe it or not, Mack and Jonathan Samuelson became friends when King d.Avid was signed with Mack's grandfather, Pearson Wright, as his manager."

"*Another* loser," Vincent said, dismissing Pearson's name with the wave of his hand. "Pearson was going nowhere fast with the hottest talent out there. If I hadn't stepped in and taken over when I did, people would still be saying, 'King *who?*' instead of 'King d.Avid.' See, that's the difference in a manager and an *effective* manager.

"I still don't get what would cause a single man, who is no kin at all, to step up and take on the responsibility of a child that's number one: not his own; and number two: has major health issues," Vincent said. "Was Mack gay and he and Jonathan had some kind of relationship we don't know about? Could that be why Mack stepped in like he did? Or is Mack a pedophile with his eye on children? What better mark than a child no one apparently wants, who can barely get around? A child with no power to tell. And if he did tell, who would he tell, who would believe him, and what might he lose in the process?"

Chad shook his head. "No, man. Don't even go there."

"Well, no one said it had to be true to spread it. And you know what they say about a lie making its rounds around the world before the truth can even put its boots on good, or something like that," Vincent said.

Chad shook his head again slowly but deliberately. "Drop that, Vincent. I'm serious now. Drop it."

"I wasn't planning on actually *putting* it out there. But if I told King that I was, the way he feels about his dead friend Jonathan, I'm sure he wouldn't want something like that out there, possibly tarnishing his friend's memory. Then there's the son, who's still here. King wouldn't want that little boy to have to suffer through anything like that."

"I'm telling you," Chad said. "Squash that noise. You're not going to do that to either of them. You're not even going to *threaten* to do it."

"Excuse me," Vincent said, drawing his body back. "But *who* exactly invited you, first off, into my house; and second, to this private discussion?"

Chad leaned forward. "Look, man, I'm just telling you not to go there."

"Okay, since you want to play the role of advisor today. What about this? Unzell Waters was married to Brianna Waters when he's *mysteriously* killed in some freak accident that, by all accounts, should never have happened. The question is: was it really an accident or did King d.Avid order the death of an innocent man just so he could take the man's wife, who happens to be a gorgeous little lamb?"

"Ooh," Kendall said. "Now that's scandalous for real. And you know: it *positively* has legs. I was thinking about that one myself. I mean, did you see how fast King d.Avid swooped in after her husband died? The man wasn't in the grave six weeks good before they were running off and getting married."

"And then the baby was born not six months after the wedding," Vincent said. "I'll tell you what I'd like to know. And that is: whose baby is it? Really?"

"Wow. I hadn't thought of that. Do you think it was possibly King d.Avid's?" Kendall asked as she arched her curvy body to show off her assets better. "Scandalous."

"Who knows and who cares?" Vincent said. "The thing is to get that out there. For that matter, put it out there about him and Jonathan's questionable, close friendship. Let people debate what may have been between *them* as well. Or more to the point: tell King d.Avid that's what we'll put out there. We'll see if that's something he wants to have to battle down, especially now that he has his little wife on his sweet little arm. They made that big old show, having that *rededication* ceremony a few months back."

"Do you think they were really even married?" Kendall asked.

"Oh, yes, they were married," Vincent said. "Chad and I were there to witness that sham. They didn't even *really* kiss. It was one of those old folks' wimpy lip pecks. And Brianna seemed so out of it, I had to wonder what he'd done to force her into marrying him. She was definitely not a blushing bride. Maybe I should try again to hook up with Alana, Brianna's little friend; see what she knows and can tell me. Although she blew me off the last time I tried. But there's too much not adding up. She might talk."

"Yeah, right. Good luck with Alana, now that she sees you're really not about anything. But I know they say the happy couple didn't even sleep in the same room," Kendall said. "So you're right. There was something going on that just didn't add up."

"Well," Chad said, standing to his feet, "I would be careful when it comes to talk of blackmail and extortion. Last I checked: that was a crime—punishable by jail time."

"Yeah, like I'm worried about King d.Avid standing up to something like this," Vincent said. "The man cares too much about his brand and about not disappointing his fellow Christian zealots. Christians have enough scandals to deal with as it is, especially lately. I'm sure he doesn't want to be the cause of one more, specifically one that could tarnish his good name in the process."

Chad walked toward the door. "I'm out of here. Y'all be good now, you hear?" Chad said it like the show *The Beverly Hillbillies* where, at the end, Elly Mae Clampett would wave and tell folks to come back. Chad then left.

"Why did you let him hear what you were planning on doing?" Kendall said after Chad was gone. "What if he runs back and blabs it to King d.Avid?"

Vincent smirked and ticked his head two times. "That's my plan. If Chad tells him, then King will know that we're absolutely serious. If Chad doesn't, then that lets me know maybe we can pull him over to our side, and we'd have someone on the inside again. Either way, we win." Vincent nodded with satisfaction. "Either way, my dear Kendall . . . we win."

Chapter 47

The Lord said unto my Lord, Sit thou at my right hand, until I make thine enemies thy footstool.

—Psalm 110:1

King d.Avid opened the door for Vincent.

"Thank you for agreeing to meet with me," Vincent said. "I think this is something you and I can work out in an amicable way. I don't want to hurt you or your family. Oh, and congratulations on your recent announcement. So, when is your baby due?"

"What do you want?" King d.Avid said.

"I just want what is due me," Vincent said. "That's all Kendall and I both want."

"So you don't believe I have the right to sever my dealings with you when I don't believe it's any longer a workable relationship for me, nor in my best interest?" King d.Avid said.

"Of course you do." Vincent shifted his weight. He made a show of looking toward the living room as though he were questioning why they were still standing in the foyer, instead of sitting in their usual meeting place. "But I don't believe you've thought this whole thing through. I don't believe you've weighed all of the pros and cons in letting someone, such as myself or Kendall, for that matter, go. We know more about you, your dealings, and your operation than I'm sure you'd care for the world to hear about."

"What's that supposed to be? Some kind of threat?"

Vincent chuckled, as he looked down at his brown leather Prada shoes. "Now how long have we known each other again?" The question was completely rhetorical since he continued without waiting for an answer. "You know me. I make promises; that's all. Not threats . . . promises. I promised I would take you to the top and beyond. I delivered on that promise. I promised that your name would be known from one end of the world to the other. Did that. I promised that you'd never have to lack for anything when it came to having more than enough money." Vincent made a big show of scanning the area where they stood. "Check. I'd say, merely by glancing around this place alone, that I *more* than delivered on that promise. That's why you're able to afford this fourteen-million-dollar house and all of its costly upkeep. That's why you were able to take your lovely wife, along with a host of family and friends, to a place like Necker Island at a little over $54,000 per night, for your little group of twenty-eight, for five whole days."

King d.Avid nodded. "I see, as usual, you've been snooping around in my business again. How else would you know about Necker Island and how much it cost me? And for the record: the other twenty-six were there for only two days. Brianna and I had the whole island to ourselves the rest of the other three days and nights."

"Yes, I know all of that. I know, because as I've said: if nothing, I'm thorough. I told you *that* when you hired me. I see my mark, and I get things done. And I've given you many years of dedicated service, along with my blood and sweat," Vincent said.

"And you were well compensated for your service, too," King d.Avid said.

"I don't disagree. But now, I'm further along in age. It's not as easy for me to start over. Had I seen my termination coming, I might have put back enough to tide me over until I get back to where I desire to be. Same thing with Kendall. Neither of us saw our separation from the organization even *nearing* the horizon, let alone about to totally be pushed off the cliff. We were loyal—"

King d.Avid chuckled in a sarcastic way. "Oh, yeah. You two were loyal, all right. Loyal to your own pockets. Listen, I'm not going to stand here and put the entire blame on you. I should have signed my own checks, *all* the time, every time, and not allowed you to have so much power. That's on me. I should have watched a bit more. But as they say: when you know better, then you do better. I know better now. So . . ."

"Okay. Let me get right to it then," Vincent said. "I worked hard to keep gossip out of the media when it came to you. Take your first wife, Michaela, the one where the marriage was annulled. She tried to sink you before you got going. That woman was madly, I'm talking crazy in love with you. And she didn't take kindly to you constantly remarrying, going on without her. Well, I squashed that. Then there was Michaela and Jonathan's father who *really* hated you and definitely had it in for you. The man was out for blood. I took care of *that*. And we won't even *begin* to address your other wives and women in your life with their scandals and scorn, coupled with their desire for revenge."

"Would you please just say what you came to say so you can vacate my premises," King d.Avid said, on occasion sneaking glances toward the second floor of his house.

"King, you and I both know there are some things that *could*—note that I said *could*—start making their rounds on the media circuit and make your life a living—"

"Watch your mouth in my house," King d.Avid said.

Vincent nodded. "Okay. I'll respect your home. But let's be real: there are things about your life and people you know that could be raised and seriously cause you a lot of headaches, heartache, and difficulty."

"Like?" Brianna said.

Vincent watched as Brianna made her way down the stairs like a queen descending from her throne, holding the intricate, ornate, spiraling wrought-iron banister.

"Hi, Brianna," Vincent said, leaning over and giving her a hug when she reached the floor where he and King d.Avid stood. "I didn't see you up there."

"I wasn't exactly *up* there. I heard voices and decided to come down," Brianna said to Vincent, then turned to her husband and gave him a quick peck on his lips. "I hope you don't mind me barging in like this, dear," she said to King d.Avid.

"No," King d.Avid said. "And I don't expect Vincent to be too much longer."

Vincent shook his head slowly as he grinned. "Maybe you and I should finish this conversation at another time."

"No. Why don't you just finish what you have to say now?" King d.Avid said. "I have nothing to hide from my lovely wife. This way, you'll save me the breath of having to repeat to her what you and I talked about. So please . . . continue."

"I don't think that's a good idea, if you know what I mean," Vincent said. "I don't care to say or do anything that might hurt or upset Brianna." He turned to Brianna. "I heard that you're pregnant." He glanced down at Brianna's baby bump. "Three months, is it? Congratulations."

Brianna nodded. "Thank you."

"Yeah"—he nodded—"I was there when you lost the last baby. I certainly don't desire anything I may say or do to be the cause of any stress that might negatively affect *this* baby you're carrying." Vincent deliberately looked at King d.Avid when he finished.

"Okay," King d.Avid said harshly. "We're done!" He started for the door.

"No," Brianna said to King d.Avid. "Let Vincent have his say. That way, there will be no reason for you and him to have this conversation later. Whatever he has to say won't bother me. I'm carrying a strong, healthy baby, who will be just fine."

"Well, as I was saying to King here," Vincent said. "I have worked hard to protect his good name and stellar reputation. But there is a grave possibility some things may begin circulating regarding him and those he deeply cares about."

"Gossip," King d.Avid leaned over and said to Brianna. "He's referring to friendly—according to how you want to look at it—gossip, right now."

Vincent continued. "Well, from my experiences, when people hear things, they don't know whether it's true or not. And if you don't know how to shoot it down before it grows legs and starts traveling, things can *really* get away from you. You understand."

"Like?" Brianna said.

Vincent looked at King d.Avid. It was obvious he was uncomfortable saying these things in front of Brianna.

"My wife asked you a question," King d.Avid said. "If you have something to say, then say it. If not—"

"Okay," Vincent said. "Like what's the real deal behind your brother Mack adopting that child named Melvin?" Vincent said to Brianna. "That's one."

"I believe it's called compassion and love for your fellow man," Brianna said.

"I know," Vincent said. "It's not something *I* think is a problem. But if something like that got started—a grown man, a helpless, crippled, young boy. Folks asking: What's the real deal there? Something like that could get nasty and morph into a life of its own."

"That Mack values what it is to feel unwanted?" Brianna asked. "So, what else?"

"Well, in regard to you: there could be some question about your late husband's untimely death. Like: was it really an accident? And with all due respect to you"—Vincent nodded at Brianna—"why was it you married King d.Avid so quickly following his death? Was there something going on between you and King d.Avid prior to his death?"

King d.Avid folded his arms and began to sway slightly. Brianna reached over and placed her hand on one of his arms. He became still.

"Anything else?" Brianna asked, taking her hand down from King d.Avid's arm.

"Well, besides some of the charities that King d.Avid has been a spokesperson for and a supporter of, and what is the *real* deal with some of them, there is the sensitive matter of . . . please forgive me . . . but the baby that died." Vincent looked at Brianna when he said the word *baby*. "I'm not trying to upset you. Believe me. I'm not."

"Oh, please." Brianna waved him off. "Save the commentary and finish already."

"Well, there is some question about the true paternity of that baby. I'm not saying that *I* personally have questions, but there is buzz building about it," Vincent said. "In fact"—he chuckled—"there are those who actually believe the baby was King d.Avid's. And that he had your husband killed just to keep your infidelity a secret and be able to marry you afterward. Which of course, he *did* end up doing—marrying you, that is."

"Okay," King d.Avid said. "We've heard just about enough." King d.Avid went and opened the front door.

"Listen, all I want to do is to *keep* doing at least some of what I was doing before," Vincent said. "I would like to keep your good name in good standing with the people who are being blessed by your music and ministry. I want to protect you from those who are looking . . . hoping . . . *praying*, actually, for you to trip, just so they can make fun of yet another Christian who has fallen. King, you've often said this was not about you, but it's about Jesus and about spreading the Gospel throughout the world."

"Well, I know you didn't come here for my little opinion on any of this," Brianna said to Vincent. "But it sounds to *me* like you're trying to blackmail my husband."

"No, that's not what I'm doing at all," Vincent said. "All I want is my job back."

"Well, that's what it sounds like to me," Brianna said. She turned to her husband. "What about you? Does it sound like blackmail to you? If you don't do what Vincent wants, give him back his job, then things are going to mysteriously start coming out about you . . . things are going to get rough for you. The truth? Irrelevant. Who cares?"

"Yeah. It sounds like blackmail to me, too," King d.Avid said, closing the door.

"Well, I told you. It's not," Vincent said. "I just want my job back and Kendall's job restored, and you won't have to worry about *any* of these horrific things hitting the airwaves or print world. I get my job; you get assurance that nothing ends up getting out."

Brianna pulled out her cell phone and pressed a button. "Chad, could you come to the foyer, please?" She pressed the END button and returned her phone back to her pocket.

"What are you doing?" Vincent asked.

"Oh, I just called for Chad," Brianna said. "You remember Chad, don't you? He's head of our security."

"I know who Chad is. I was the one who hired him," Vincent said, agitated.

King d.Avid cleared his throat and cupped his ear. "Excuse me? What was that again?"

Vincent looked at King d.Avid. "Okay. I hired him after you okayed it."

King d.Avid smiled and nodded.

Chad came in. "Yes, ma'am?"

"Chad, we're having a slight, fundamental debate here," Brianna said. "I figured since you're into laws and such, and you have friends who are into the law, you might be able to settle this debate for us, or at least point us in the right direction."

"Okay," Vincent said. "I see where this is going. I suppose it's time for me to go."

"Oh, please," Brianna said. "Don't leave just yet. I think we need to put this question to bed once and for all. Right here, right now." She pointed at the floor.

"How may I assist you?" Chad asked.

Brianna pulled out a minirecorder from her pocket. She rewound it, then pressed PLAY.

Vincent's eyes widened when he heard his own voice talking on what he wanted in return for doing what. "Turn that thing off!" Vincent said. "You can't do that!" He turned to Chad. "Is it legal for her to tape me without my permission?"

"Well, I would say there's an even *bigger* question looming," Chad said. "And that is: what is the penalty for blackmail . . . extortion?" Chad shook his head. "Jail time . . . pretty bad, especially for someone soft and cute like you," he said to Vincent. "I'm not exactly sure how you'd fare in jail with a Jimbo or a Sonny."

"What are you talking about, jail?" Vincent said. "All of you are blowing everything completely out of proportion." Vincent took a step toward the door. King d.Avid again opened it for him. "Why don't we just pretend none of this ever happened?"

"I don't know," Brianna said. "I mean: if what I did by having my tape recorder on in my own house, having given my consent to record me, in a one-party permission state, while you were also talking, is wrong, then I by no means want to be doing anything that may be illegal or breaking the law and could possibly come back and bite me later."

"No," Vincent said. "You're right. This is your home. I was a guest here. And I hope that what I was proposing here is not being misconstrued."

"Then I take it our business here is done?" King d.Avid said as he furrowed his forehead. "For good?"

"Absolutely," Vincent said. "For good. You'll have no more problems from me."

"And we agree that I don't owe you anything more than what you've already been paid, along with my gratitude for services rendered?" King d.Avid said.

"Yes," Vincent said, scratching his brow.

King d.Avid gently slapped Vincent on the back. "Well, it's been real," King d.Avid said, nodding, then escorting him through the open door.

Vincent strolled out and hurried to his car as King d.Avid continued to look on.

Brianna walked over to Chad, touched him on his arm, nodded, then smiled. Her way of thanking him for the early warning and the heads-up he'd so graciously given her on what was about to come, as well as the valuable information on Georgia's taping laws.

Chapter 48

When a man hath taken a new wife, he shall not go out to war, neither shall he be charged with any business: but he shall be free at home one year, and shall cheer up his wife which he hath taken.

—Deuteronomy 24:5

K ing d.Avid had decided not to do any concerts or to go back into the studio for a while. He wanted to take some time off from a schedule that had been pretty much nonstop since he first hit the music scene as King d.Avid, more than thirteen years ago.

He had definitely made changes in his life, from the top to the bottom. He'd cleaned house when it came to his manager and personal assistant. He'd hired another assistant, a hard-working, single mother of three who was a member of the church where he and Brianna attended. Marissa Cade had worked extremely hard to get her associate's degree while holding down a full-time job, hoping to better her life and her children's lives.

"So what are you going to do with yourself?" the president of the record company asked when King d.Avid informed him that he was taking off for a while.

"I'm going to spend time with my new wife. I believe I have more than enough money to tide us over for at least a year," King d.Avid said with a mischievous grin.

"Oh, you *think*," the president said sarcastically and with a chuckle. "I'm pretty sure you won't go hungry for a few decades, if you choose not to record, which you'd better not choose. We love making money. Seriously, though, your songs are hotter than ever. And we appreciate you, to say the least. But I don't get why it has to be for a whole year. One month, I can see; maybe even two to six. But a *whole, entire* year?"

"Oh, you see, there's this scripture in Deuteronomy that pretty much said I should take a year off to 'cheer up' my wife," King d.Avid said. "So I'm going to take that Godly advice, and see if I can't put, and *keep*, a smile on my beautiful wife's face. You know, Proverbs 5:15 encourages us to 'drink waters out of our own cistern, and running waters out of our own well.' Then Proverbs 5:18 says, 'Let thy fountain be blessed: and rejoice with the wife of thy youth.' So that's my assignment, beginning right now. After getting them started, I plan to keep the home fires burning for the rest of our born days."

"Brianna is a lucky woman," the president said.

"No. First of all, I don't believe in luck. People like me call the good that comes our way being blessed by the Lord. That's first. And as for the one who is blessed in all of this: I'd definitely have to say that I got the better end of the deal. Brianna is an amazingly wonderful woman of God. She's strong. And I'm just glad I found her."

"Oh, *you* found *her,* huh?" the president said with a laugh. "I know women now."

"Yeah," King d.Avid said, "I found her. Have you not heard or read in the Bible where it speaks of a man who finds a wife finds a good thing? Well, I found a *good* thing. And my *good* thing's name is Bri . . . an . . . na." He sang Brianna's name. "See ya!"

At the end of December, on the twenty-ninth, nine months to the time from when Brianna and King d.Avid went to Necker Island, renewed their vows, and truly (in every sense and aspect of the word) became one, Brianna gave birth to their seven-pound son.

"Look, I'm telling you, this boy is brilliant already," King d.Avid said, his chest stuck out like a proud red rooster. "Look how alert he is. He's looking around, just taking in everything."

Minister Nate looked on as King d.Avid held his son in his arms. "I already see the wisdom of this child. He is definitely going to be brilliant, all right."

"You two need to stop," Brianna said. "He's only a day old."

"Yeah, but have you seen the other day-old babies?" King d.Avid said. "I watched the others while they were in the nursery. And I'm not trying to brag or anything, but this little champ here, this little blessing of the Lord, I see an anointing on him like the world has never witnessed before."

"Well, you'd better be careful then," Minister Nate said. "He just may supersede you when he fully hits the scene."

"Oh, I'm counting on it." King d.Avid walked around, gently bouncing him. "You talk about a proud papa; this daddy here can only pray that his child does better than him." King d.Avid smiled and continued to look at his son.

"Okay, so what are we going to name this little anointed genius?" Brianna said as she watched her husband march around the hospital room gawking at the baby, refusing to take his eyes off of him for even one second.

"I say we go with the obvious," King d.Avid said. "I mean, what are the chances that my name would be David and I would actually marry a woman named Bathsheba?"

"My name is not Bathsheba," Brianna said.

"Your middle name is," King d.Avid said.

"I know, but no one knows me by my middle name," Brianna said.

"Okay. So the obvious name for this little, wise warrior in the Word is Solomon," King d.Avid said.

"Solomon?" Brianna said. "Are you serious or are you just messing with me?"

"I mean that Solomon is a nice name. You know: I'm David. He would be Solomon. Most of his battles would already be won."

"How about the name Rondell?" Brianna said.

"You mean after my middle name?" King d.Avid said.

"Yeah."

"You want to name our son Rondell?"

"Yeah. That way you two would share a name," Brianna said. She looked at Minister Nate. "What do you think?"

Minister Nate held up both hands. "Oh, I'm not in this. This is something the two of you need to decide."

"Oh, come on," King d.Avid said. "Tell us what you think." King d.Avid walked over to Minister Nate. "Here, hold him."

"He's too little for me to hold," Minister Nate said as King d.Avid, despite his protest, gently placed the baby in his arm as though he were made of crystal.

"Okay," King d.Avid said to Minister Nate. "So what name are you hearing?"

"It doesn't work like that," Minister Nate said, looking down at the baby.

"Yeah, but I'm sure you're getting something. Fix your eyes on that little face and tell us what God is saying to you," King d.Avid said.

Minister Nate looked at the baby and bounced him a little the way King d.Avid had done before transferring him into his care. "Hi there, little fellow," Minister Nate said in baby talk. Minister Nate glanced over at King d.Avid, then down at Brianna. "Second Samuel—"

"Oh, no," King d.Avid said. "We're not going with Samuel. Please tell me you're not hearing the name Samuel."

"What's wrong with Samuel?" Brianna teased.

"I'd rather name him David Junior than Samuel," King d.Avid said.

"May I please finish?" Minister Nate said with a slight laugh in his voice.

"Sorry," King d.Avid said. "Please. Finish."

"Second Samuel, chapter twelve, verses twenty-four and twenty-five, says, 'And David comforted Bathsheba his wife, and went in unto her, and lay with her: and she bare a son, and he called his name Solomon: and the Lord loved him. And he sent by the hand of Nathan the prophet; and he called his name Jedidiah, because of the Lord.' The name Jedidiah means 'Beloved of the Lord,' " Minister Nate said, carefully placing the baby in Brianna's loving arms.

"Jedidiah," Brianna said, gazing down at her son. She raised him close to her face. "That might be a hard name to saddle on a child." She looked up at Minister Nate and King d.Avid. "And you just *know* that people will ultimately end up calling him Jed or possibly even Jedi, for short."

"I hadn't thought of that," Minister Nate said. "Jedi, huh? A *Star Wars* throwback. Hmmm. You're really quick with your thoughts there, Mrs. Shepherd."

"That she is," King d.Avid said. "You should have seen her dealing with my old manager, Vincent, about six months ago. Priceless! I'm telling you, it was *price*-less! My baby, Brianna, doesn't play."

"So what do we call you, little prince?" Brianna lifted the baby up to her ear. "What's that?" She started smiling. "Well, okay then," she said. "If you're sure now."

"What did he say?" King d.Avid asked, moving in closer.

Brianna tilted her head to one side, grinned, then shook her head at her husband.

"I'm just kidding," King d.Avid said. "I know he can't talk yet. Can he?" He grinned. "Okay, Mama. So what's our little prince's name?"

"Solomon Rondell Jedidiah Shepherd," Brianna said.

King d.Avid stood as tears began to fill his eyes. He bent down and kissed Brianna, then stroked his son's little tiny fingers. "Solomon Rondell Jedidiah Shepherd."

Minister Nate was keying something into his cell phone. He smiled, looked up, and said, "Okay. Solomon is Hebrew, meaning 'peaceful'; Rondell is French, and it means 'short poem'; Jedidiah is Hebrew, it means 'Beloved of the Lord'; and Shepherd is English, and ironically it means 'shepherd'—'one who tends and oversees.' "

Minister Nate placed his hand on the baby's heart as Brianna held him. King d.Avid held his son's hand. "I call you a child of the Most High King," Minister Nate proclaimed. "I call you wise. I call you blessed. I call you a blessing. I call you peaceful, who pens short poems, and is the beloved of the Lord, who will care for and guide a group of people as you teach and, with wisdom, minister the Word of God to those who are in need. I declare you Solomon Rondell Jedidiah Shepherd." Finished, Minister Nate gave a nod, removed his hand, and raised both his hands to Heaven. "Amen!" he said.

"Amen," Brianna said, as tears began to roll down her face.

"Amen," King d.Avid said. He then bent down and kissed his little Jedi, then kissed the woman who had blessed his life in more ways than words could ever express. "Amen."

Discussion Questions

1. In the prologue, Brianna and her friend Alana are outside because Brianna's father believed children should have balance in their playtime. What are your thoughts? Had you ever heard what Alana revealed was taking place when it rains and the sun is shining prior to this? What are your thoughts . . . experiences?

2. Brianna's husband was headed toward making millions of dollars. Discuss your feelings about men making that kind of money playing professional sports. What are your thoughts, if any, when it comes to college players not being paid and possibly ending up the way Unzell did?

3. What did you think of Brianna and Alana's friendship as adults? Discuss.

4. In Brianna's religious studies, she visited a mikvah. Address your thoughts when it comes to this, even down to a desire to learn of other religious practices.

5. Discuss the things that took place at the beach house, including Brianna's actions and the fact that King d.Avid was watching her from the roof.

6. Did King d.Avid do the right thing in sending Chad to see who was staying at the beach house? Discuss this as well as Chad's visit with the women. Should King d.Avid have gone to see them while he was there?

7. Was Brianna wrong to have accepted King d.Avid's dinner invitation? Discuss.

8. What do you think about Brianna's time spent with King d.Avid and her staying overnight? What do you believe was the real reason that she "fell"?

9. Do you think Brianna went overboard in her reaction when she realized what she'd done? Did King d.Avid take it too lightly?

10. Upon learning she was pregnant, did Brianna handle things correctly? What did she do that you would have advised her to do differently? What do you agree with?

11. Did you agree with King d.Avid's cover-up plans? Why or why not? If you disagree, then what should he have done?

12. Should Brianna have talked with someone about what was going on? If so, whom?

13. Did Brianna do the right thing remarrying when she did? Was it too soon? Should she have let people believe the baby was her late husband's? What would you have done?

14. Discuss the baby (Jason) and everything surrounding him, including his parents' varied reactions. What do you feel about the end result?

15. Discuss Brianna's decision to renew their wedding vows and the way it was ultimately carried out, together with King d.Avid's secrets and surprises.

16. What did you think of Mack and Melvin?

17. Discuss Vincent Powers and all his antics, including his final push to get his and Kendall's jobs back. Do you be-

lieve there was any merit to some of the things Vincent talked about that people might be discussing when it came to King d.Avid and Brianna, along with the people they loved? Do you believe King d.Avid had anything to do with Unzell's death? Was Brianna right to step into the private conversation that her husband was having with Vincent as she did?

18. Discuss your thoughts on Brianna and King d.Avid's eventual blessing of Solomon.

Sister Betty returns in time for Christmas in
Pat G'Orge-Walker's
No Ordinary Noel

Coming in October 2011 from Dafina Books

Turn the page for an excerpt from *No Ordinary Noel*...

It was well past midnight when the reverend's phone rang. He'd hardly slept a wink, but when he saw the number on the caller ID, he immediately woke up.

The reverend yawned and answered, "Hello, Sister Betty."

"I'm sorry to call this late, pastor," she apologized. "This storm has made everything a mess. My bus ran late from Belton, and when I got home to Pelzer, I was too pooped to do anything. I saw that red light flashing on my phone, but didn't bother to check it right away because nothing good ever comes out of me doing so."

By the time Sister Betty finished with her long apology and her aversion to checking her messages, the reverend was fully awake. He'd barely explained to her about the mess caused at the church by Mother Pray Onn accusing him of mishandling her one-hundred-forty-dollar-and-twenty-six-cent tithes and his reaction to it, when Sister Betty started to whip him with the Word. She gave him scriptural uppercuts from the Old Testament. "Psalm One Hundred and Forty-four says, "Blessed be the Lord my strength which teacheth my hands to war, and my fingers to fight!" She then TKO'd him with scriptures from the New. When she finished, he'd apologized more to her than he had to God.

"How God gonna give you a vision about leading folk to The Promised Land and then not give you the provision?" Sister Betty hissed, "Now I don't mean no further disrespect, but you acting like you forgot that God gave me that same vision and it was about the same time He trusted you to bring it about." She waited for the reverend to dispute what she said, but he didn't. He couldn't.

"Reverend Tom, now tell me we didn't shout about it in your study when God showed us back then that there wasn't gonna be a need for a mortgage? You can't. And didn't the good Lord say to name it the Promised Land? Now I already told you that I'm tired from this long trip. I had to go see about a dear ole friend that's getting up in age and pray with her. Now my body is sore. I ain't got time to feed you Bible Similac like you a new babe in Christ. You're the head of the church, and if the head don't believe, then why would the body?"

Sister Betty went on to say a lot more as he held the receiver away from his ear. His shoulders slumped and a numbing pain began from the back of his head to the front. He held his hands to his ears to avoid the truth of her words.

Headache or not, he respected her words. So he brought the receiver back to his ear and discovered she hadn't finished rebuking him. He heard Sister Betty's warning, "If your faith ain't increased by tomorrow when I go down to that bank, then don't you come with me. I may have a ton of money in that bank, but I can't blackmail them with haters and faith blockers in my way."

The next morning, Reverend Tom was exhausted. Sister Betty's telephone rebuke had pushed sleep aside and given him a lot to ponder.

However, despite her rebuke last night, that Monday morning he couldn't help but to remember his history with Sister Betty. As he started to read the morning paper, the thought of her brought a surprised smile to his face.

Sister Betty was one of his most senior members and had been a blessing to him ever since he took over as Pastor. Her quirkiness was well known to some and a puzzle to most. As far as he was concerned, she was a woman who had God's ear. He had also adopted her as his spiritual mother, especially since both of his parents passed away long before he had finished college, and she was always telling him what to do anyhow.

She also watched his back and stood between him and the desires of several unmarried females at the church who were looking to add the title of First Lady to their letterhead and bank account. Sadly, there were also a few married women who would have made an exception to their marriage vows had he given them a reason.

Through the good and the bad, Sister Betty had never left his side. She made certain that he knew that God had not left either.

Before he knew it, it was around noon and time to pick up Sister Betty. He rechecked the weather and learned the forecasters had upgraded their report to an almost certainty that an early winter storm would cause havoc on the roads.

As he pulled out of his driveway, Reverend Tom whispered an affirmation, "God in heaven, forgive me for my unbelief and my unmerited pride in what you've placed in my hands. But Lord, all days are your days too. Now if Moses didn't let the Red Sea stop him from helping his people, I'm not about to let the threat of a snow storm, lack of finances, or a congregation of unbelievers stop me from helping mine."

After a short drive, Reverend Tom slowly pulled into the winding driveway of Sister Betty's luxurious home. Before he could step from the car, she stepped outside to meet him.

Sister Betty was dressed in her traditional all white everything. At that moment, her everything was a heavy wool overcoat, gloves, boots, and hat. On this particular day, she'd bundled up so tight she looked like a white box with a large bible attached to its side. She stayed ready for any storm—natural or spiritual.

Sister Betty's small feet hopscotched through the slush until she made her way inside the car. Without ceremony or waiting for him to open the door, she said, "Praise the Lord, Pastor."

"Sister Betty," the reverend replied. He chose to leave it at that.

Sister Betty chuckled as she fastened her seatbelt and gave him the once over. "You look like you still holding on to about a quart of faith, so I sure hope you're ready to roll for the Lord this glorious day."

Judging by the way she acted at that moment, it was hard to believe she'd just chewed him out the night before. Nevertheless, the joy only lasted long enough for him to put the car in drive. Before they'd gotten off the block, she'd become more like a Mama Betty than the Sister Betty he'd needed.

Sister Betty adjusted the scarf around her neck and pointed to the car's heater. "It's so cold in here I can see my breath. Now turn that thing up. I told you I don't have hot flashes no more and I need a lot of heat."

Reverend Tom did as she requested. He then waited a moment until she adjusted to the blast of heat from the heater before he added, "Okay, my short but powerful Ride or Die gal. Let's go and reclaim the Promised Land."

"I don't know how many times I need to remind you that I really don't like the word *die* used in the same sentence as my name," Sister Betty murmured.

"Don't worry about that," the reverend laughed as he finally pulled out of the slow-moving traffic. "You are not going anywhere anytime soon. Heaven doesn't need you up there as much as I do down here."

"From your lips to God's ears and His will." Sister Betty sat back. Her head leaned to the side as she thought *I want to thank you, Lord, for Your grace and for Your mercy too.* A smile crept across her face as she praised her God.

The reverend looked over and smiled, too. "I see you're smiling," he said softly. "Are you and God collaborating again?" He let out a laugh when he saw the surprised look upon her face.

"Why yes, Reverend Tom, we are constantly in cahoots."

"Mind sharing what God has revealed?"

"It's not so much what He's revealed to me as much as me discussing with Him where we're going to end up."

"Oh, I see. You mean the Promised Land."

Sister Betty shifted her bible and winked. "That's right, me and the Lord; we are chatting about the Promised Land. So now you quit interruptin' before I have to start speaking in tongues to keep you out of my heavenly business."

The reverend returned her wink with a smile and turned up the heat just a little more in the car. "Well, Sister Betty, I'll get us to the bank and see about the Promised Land in about ten minutes instead of forty years."